A Love To Remember

FRIENDS TO LOVERS REGENCY ROMANCE

DISGRACED LORDS

BRONWEN EVANS

A Love To Remember Blurb

A Love to Remember
A Disgraced Lords Novel
Bronwen Evans

A fiercely independent duchess and a brooding, reclusive earl are tested by the demands of desire in this unforgettable romance from the *USA Today* bestselling author of *A Kiss of Lies* and *A Night of Forever*.

For Rose Deverill, one husband was enough. As the wealthy widow of the Duke of Roxborough, she has cultivated an unsavory reputation meant to discourage wife hunters. Thanks to a string of steamy affairs, Rose is perfectly content to be known by polite society as the "Wicked Widow"—until she's reunited with the man she fell in love with at age fifteen. Their bedroom encounters are scorching, but it breaks Rose's heart to wonder whether her reckless behavior ruined her for Philip Flagstaff.

The second son of the Earl of Cumberland, Philip never wanted the title. But after Philip's older brother, Robert, follows him into the Battle of Waterloo, his worst fears come to pass. Now Robert lies in a soldier's grave, and Philip is determined never to pass on the inheritance to children of his own. Then Rose appears, soothing the pain with her delightful curves and passionate kisses. The notorious Duchess seems to want nothing from him—and yet Philip has never ached to give a woman more.

A Love to Remember is a work of fiction. Names, places, and incidents either are products of the author's imagination or are used fictitiously. Any resemblance to actual events, locales, or persons, living or dead, is entirely coincidental.

Copyright © 2017 by Bronwen Evans

Copyright © 2023 re-issue edition Bronwen Evans

Excerpt from *A Dream of Redemption* by Bronwen Evans copyright © 2017 by Bronwen Evans

All rights reserved.

This book contains an excerpt from the forthcoming book *A Dream of Redemption* by Bronwen Evans. This excerpt has been set for this edition only and may not reflect the final content of the forthcoming edition.

Cover design: **Cover Art by Forever After Romance Designs**

Prologue

Devon, England, July 1815

I'll wear your memory proudly
My honorable brother . . . my true friend
May my love for you reach heaven above
Until we meet again

Philip Flagstaff, the new Earl of Cumberland, barely heard the words as he stood beside his elder brother's open grave. All he felt was the chill of Robert's absence, and the burning stares that came at him from every side.

Whether friend, foe, or family, Philip knew each one thought the same: *Why are you alive, you selfish bastard? Why are you alive when your brother lies dead?*

He'd asked himself the same question every moment since Waterloo.

Their father's firstborn and favorite, Robert was destined to be the earl. Yet he'd never lorded it over his siblings. He had loved them, taken care of them, and stood up for them. As a brother, he was perfect.

When their father died, Robert turned the estate and family fortune around and proudly—earnestly—took his seat in the

House of Lords, determined to play his part in making England great.

Everyone loved him.

Everyone wanted to be him.

And everyone gathered at his grave today in the pouring rain knew why they had lost him.

Because of Philip.

Philip, who had been trouble since the day he was born.

Philip, who had almost burned the house to the ground lighting a campfire in the nursery. Philip, who had cost his father a champion horse when the animal had failed to jump the river, broken its leg, and had to be shot. Philip, who had pretended to lose their sister Portia in the forest just before a storm, only to *truly* do so, and find her hours later, ill with fever and at death's door. Philip, who only the previous year had invested in a "sure thing" only to lose more than a year's allowance.

Philip, who—against Robert's advice—had taken a commission, and dragged his brother onto the battlefield with him because there was no way Robert would let a genuine walking, talking, breathing disaster go to war alone.

If anyone should have died on the battlefield of Waterloo it should've been Philip. Instead, he had watched as if in a macabre dream as Robert, selfless to the last, shoved between his brother and a French bayonet and took the mortal blow.

He hadn't believed it. Had seen his own shock and disbelief mirrored on their friend Grayson Devlin's face as he fought his way to them. And then nothing else mattered. He'd dropped to his knees beside Robert's body, pressed his ear against the blood-soaked jacket, and caught his brother's final words. "Look after the family. You'll make a fine earl."

Moments later, Robert had died in his arms.

And nothing would ever be the same again.

Philip's stiff shoulders almost buckled under his guilt. It should have been his body, not Robert's, in the grave at his feet.

His life over and done. Instead, he stood in the churchyard, alive—and the new Earl of Cumberland.

You don't deserve the title. Everyone at the graveside knew it. Was thinking it. *It's your fault he's dead.*

And they were right. He should have tried harder to make Robert stay home, to acknowledge that, as an eldest son, his duty was to his family. But he had not tried harder. He'd loved having Robert with him. Somehow it made him feel safer to have his perfect, indestructible brother riding by his side.

Perfect? Yes.

Indestructible? No.

Look after the family. You'll make a fine earl.

Philip stared blankly down at the elaborate coffin in the gaping hole in the earth and vowed he would be a man his brother could be proud of. He would look after his family. He would become a fine earl. But he would not continue his family line or profit from his selfishness. He had that much honor. Better that he never marry. Never produce a legitimate heir. Then the title would pass to Thomas, his younger brother, a younger replica of Robert, and one far more worthy of the line of succession than Philip would ever be.

He barely noticed as the others left the graveside. He didn't know how to face his three younger brothers. Maxwell had tried to draw him away but he'd brushed his brother's hand from his arm. Douglas had barely looked at him. Thank God Thomas was in India.

If only he could go back to Waterloo. Shove Robert away. Take the killing blow himself as he should have. He'd be in that grave, his guilt and pain finally over—and Robert would be here, alive, with a future bright before him.

He had no idea how long he stood in the downpour before a small, warm hand slipped into his chilled one.

He glanced down.

Rose Deverill, the Duchess of Roxborough, stood beside him. She was his sister Portia's best friend. When they were younger she had adored him, following at his heels like an obedient puppy wanting attention. God knew why. She'd been one of the few people to ever see good in him. In the past few years she'd grown into the most beautiful woman, and since her elderly husband's death— Well, he'd heard her nickname. The Wicked Widow.

"The grave diggers need to finish their work before the grave floods," she said gently. "Come home, Philip. Your mother and siblings need you."

The compassion in her eyes almost undid him. For an insane moment he wished Rose would be the Wicked Widow with him, that she'd take him in her arms and make the pain go away. Make him forget—

No. A shudder ran through him. Nothing would take the pain away. Nothing would make him forget his guilt.

Nothing.

"Philip." She tugged his hand. "Your mother needs you. Come. *Please.*"

For the brief moment that he looked into her eyes it wasn't only compassion he saw. It was also tenderness. It was—

He jerked his gaze away and straightened to his full height. There was no room in his life now for more than duty to his family. That was what he would live for. He would ensure the Cumberland seat was the most profitable in all England when he handed it to Thomas or Thomas's children on his death. God willing, that death would be sooner rather than later.

Silently, Philip squeezed Rose's hand and let her lead him back through the waterlogged garden, toward the house.

To a life, title, and estate that should not be his.

Chapter One

Scotland, early August 1817—two years later

Rose Deverill, Duchess of Roxborough, had not always enjoyed sex. Sexual congress with her elderly husband—the man to whom her family had literally sold her—had been something to endure. Then, as a young widow of one-and-twenty, she'd taken her first lover.

Imagine her surprise. Her older brother's friend, Viscount Tremain, had been a marvelous teacher who had introduced her to a world of desire and pleasure, and she was forever grateful.

But on that same day she'd made a decision. She would never marry again.

Marriage held few advantages for a woman. As a widow, no one told her how to behave, what to wear, what to eat, what to drink, or where she could go. It was a glorious freedom. She had her son, money, and a title. She did not want for anything.

The *ton* of course did not understand her resolve, or why she would turn down so many eligible proposals. She was still young and beautiful. She needed a man to make her life complete.

But Rose *had* men—a different man whenever she wanted, in fact. She just didn't have a husband. Which meant she did not have to put up with a man's tantrums, his boring displays of jealousy, or worry that she might be left financially ruined by his profligate spending. When a man bored her, she simply sent him on his way. After all, none of them really mattered to her.

The reputation she had crafted and built over the five years of her widowhood—and the double standards of their society—ensured most men would never again look at her as a potential wife. Although she could not guarantee it. Having a title and money forgave many sins.

Now six-and-twenty, Rose could say that she still enjoyed pleasure, the giving and receiving of it—especially the receiving. Who wouldn't? But she'd learned from her experience of many paramours that not every man was as considerate, or as skilled a lover, as her viscount.

To her consternation, she'd also come to realize that making *love* was far more fulfilling than simply experiencing pleasure. Lovemaking was the most sensual and exquisite experience a woman could have. It was like touching heaven, and Rose had only ever felt that touch at the hands of one man. And she knew she'd only ever feel that with one man.

Philip Flagstaff, the Earl of Cumberland.

The man who'd become her lover on that wet, stormy day they had buried his older brother. The one man who could perhaps get her to change her mind and marry—if he asked.

The man currently naked and buried to the hilt inside her.

"Oh, God, Philip!" Rose fought to keep hold of the headboard as he thrust forcefully into her from behind. "Yes, that's it, I'm going to—"

And she did, her words lost in a scream of pleasure as her world exploded in a vision of color. Only his strong arms about her waist prevented her from slumping to the bed as his thrusts became more frantic. Suddenly, and with a roar, he pulled out of her body and spilled his seed onto the sheets.

Panting from his exertions, Philip tumbled sideways onto his huge bed, pulling her with him so that she landed curled into his side. Rose struggled to get her own breathing under control. She knew she should be grateful that he was so scrupulous about not getting her with child. But lately she hoped for a sign that he wanted to take their relationship further. A sign that he might want more from her. He'd invited her to Scotland, after all. He hadn't done so last year. She'd thought, perhaps, he was thinking of marriage. His actions just now, ensuring his seed did not take root in her womb, indicated that if he was thinking about marriage, it probably wasn't with her.

The thought should have made her happy. It didn't.

She glanced out the large windows and saw the sun low in the sky. "What is the time?" she asked, pushing at Philip's arm, still pinning her to his side.

"We have time."

"Time for what?" She giggled as he tightened his hold. "You can't possibly have that much stamina."

They'd been in his bed since her arrival at lunchtime. Philip hadn't even let her recover from her journey. He'd wanted her with a ferocity that excited and warmed her. After their third bout of lovemaking, her body was numbly sated and she needed a bath.

He lifted her hair and pressed a kiss to her neck. "I have missed you, darling. It's been eight weeks since I saw you. Eight long weeks."

Very long weeks. "I missed you, too. But Lord Kirkwood didn't need my reputation shoved in his face while he was in London visiting Drake."

Drake was her five-year-old son. The Duke of Roxborough. The only person she loved more than Philip.

Philip snorted inelegantly. "Kirkwood knows we are lovers. Hell, the whole *ton* knows."

The Marquess of Kirkwood had been Rose's husband's *and* her father's best friend. Luckily for her, the late Duke of Roxborough had named him guardian of Drake.

Luckily for her because he was a kind man. He had always thought it wrong that she had been married off at such a young age to a man old enough to be her grandfather, so he tended to be lenient when it came to her behavior. But while he indulged her need to be free, Lord Kirkwood controlled every aspect of Drake's life. Kirkwood had a son of his own, Francis, and he was a bit on the wild side. It was as if Kirkwood wanted to ensure he did not make the same mistakes with Drake.

Of course, he consulted with her. But ultimately, he was the one making decisions both as trustee of the Roxborough estate and as Drake's guardian.

Yes, Kirkwood knew about her relationship with Philip, and he, like the rest of the *ton*, wondered why Philip had not yet proposed.

"There's a difference between suspicion and incontrovertible proof," Rose said. "He can deny the rumors if he doesn't witness any scandalous behavior."

One day, she knew, Kirkwood would order her to settle down. Probably apply gentle pressure to force her to select another husband. She'd fight that battle when it came.

Perhaps marriage would be bearable if Philip was that man. They had been lovers for two years and he didn't seem to be tiring of her. She had certainly not tired of *him*.

Surely the fact that she had not ended their affair, as she normally did after a few months with a paramour, must have told Philip what was in her heart. Or did he believe the tale she'd spun to the *ton* that she never intended to remarry? Worse, did he not see her as worthy of marriage? If she'd ever imagined she had a chance of winning Philip's heart, she would never have cultivated such a wicked reputation.

Her reputation, while no worse than his—*definitely* no worse than his—counted against her. Men tended to want their wives chaste, virginal, and young. She was none of those things. How she hated that damnable double standard.

She told her heart not to expect more from Philip. The only reason they'd become lovers in the first place was because of his grief. Never in her wildest dreams had she imagined that, two years later, he would still need her. Still want her. As far as she was aware, he had no other mistress or lover.

But a man never married his mistress. An earl certainly did not.

She rolled over to face him. Simply looking at him still took her breath away. Bright blue eyes framed in a face of artistic angles and aristocratic lines, lips full and inviting, and deep auburn hair glinting copper in the sunlight. He could make her wet with a simple smile.

"Sebastian and Beatrice arrive tonight with Drake," she said, trying to sound practical instead of needy. "We should get ready to greet them. Christian and Serena, Marisa and Maitland and their children will arrive tomorrow."

Sebastian Hawkestone, the Marquis of Coldhurst; Maitland Spencer, the Duke of Lyttleton; and Christian Trent, the Earl of Markham, were three of Philip's closest friends, and Rose was grateful that her reputation had not kept them from staying with Philip and bringing their wives and children with them.

Philip pressed more kisses over her bare shoulder. "Damn your bloody carriage losing a wheel. I wanted you to myself for a few days. Instead, all I get is an afternoon."

"I'm as disappointed as you, darling. But we still have three weeks together with our friends. You'll likely be keen to wave me goodbye by then."

She made her tone both light and teasing, hoping he'd deny the possibility. He didn't, and she felt absurdly hurt.

She should have been pleased that he wanted to spend time with her—and she was—but it almost sounded as if he resented her son's imminent arrival.

That was just too bad. She would not let her affair with Philip distance her from Drake. Her son came first. The only reason he was traveling with Sebastian and Beatrice was because Drake and Henry, Sebastian's ward, were about the same age, firm friends, and wanted to make the journey together.

It had been Beatrice's suggestion that Rose leave three days ahead of them. It was rare for Rose to spend uninterrupted time with Philip, especially once the Season ended. He'd leave London to attend to his estate in Devon. She was expected to spend time at the Roxborough seat in Cornwall, and although Cornwall was not far from Devon, she could not openly call on him unless Portia was in residence.

Sadly, since Portia's marriage to Grayson Devlin, Viscount Blackwood, she did not return to her family home nearly enough, in Rose's opinion. Now a brand-new mother, Portia would travel even more infrequently and Rose's excursions to Flagstaff Castle would be rare.

"I thought I'd take Drake and Henry fishing tomorrow," Philip said, breaking into her thoughts.

She wanted to hug him. Only a moment ago she'd wondered if he resented her son. "They would love that. Thank you."

"You are never too young to learn how to catch salmon." He narrowed his eyes and his mouth curved in a smile. "Just watching them jumping out of the water . . . I still remember my first fishing trip with Father and Robert—" His smile dimmed and he rolled away and onto his back.

Rose had a sudden desire to seize him by the shoulders and shake some sense into him. Two years, and Philip still refused to come to terms with his brother's death. She used to try and talk to him about it, but he first refused to discuss the subject and then got angry with her for bringing it up. She understood his feelings of guilt that he had survived Waterloo when his brother had not. But Robert had been a grown man who had made his own decisions, and the choice to fight for his country had been one of them.

She reached out, took Philip's large hand in hers, and squeezed. He didn't squeeze back. Rose wished she knew where he went inside his head when these moods came upon him.

The silence lengthened, their intimate moment destroyed by Robert's ghost. A far too frequent occurrence of late.

Finally, Philip disengaged his hand, rose, and, donning a robe, pulled the bell to summon his valet.

"Wilson," he said when the man entered the room, "please arrange for a bath to be drawn for me in here, and one for Her Grace in her dressing room."

"Very good, my lord." Wilson bowed and left.

Rose liked Wilson. The man had been Robert's valet. After his master's death he had asked to stay and valet for Philip. He was the soul of discretion and—no matter where he found her—treated her with genuine respect. He certainly accepted her presence here in Philip's room.

Philip moved round to her side of the large four-poster bed and held a robe out to her.

"Here, my sweet," he said. "You're right. We should be ready and waiting for our guests when they arrive. Cook has planned a light supper in the drawing room as I suspect they will be tired from the journey, and Drake will be eager to see you."

He escorted her to the door linking his master suite to her rooms. Wherever they stayed, he always gave her rooms connecting with his. He never tried to hide her away, or make her feel ashamed that they were lovers.

He pressed a brief kiss on her lips and then gave her a gentle push into her room. "I'll be in the study when you are ready. Collect me on the way to the drawing room and we'll greet our guests together. I promise I'll be out of my sulk by then. Rose"—he hesitated, then continued—"dearest Rose, I *am* truly grateful that you've come all the way to Scotland to be with me for these weeks. I have missed you."

Then he stepped back, letting her close the door.

As she did so, and then called for her maid, Rose inwardly smiled.

I have missed you.

This was why she stayed with him, even while hoping for more. Philip had always owned a piece of her heart. In moments like this he made her feel like the most special woman in the world.

I have missed you.

Not *I love you*. He'd never said he loved her. But then she'd never talked of love, either. It didn't matter. He treated her better than many men treated their wives, or mistresses, and actions spoke louder than any words could.

When the bath was drawn and ready Rose slipped into the soothing heated water. How she wished she were not such a coward. She wished she could tell him what was in her heart, but her years of being the person who ended affairs and tried to ensure no one fell in love with her had taught her the signs.

Philip didn't want her love. He wanted her company, her intelligence, her beauty, and her presence in his bed. That was all.

The truth was that one day he would have to marry. He was, after all, an earl. For a moment, alone in her tub, she wanted to weep. But duchesses didn't weep over hard truths. All she could hope was that, when Philip chose a wife, he chose her. If he didn't, she hoped her heart was strong enough to become an impenetrable fortress, or her world would crumble to dust.

Chapter Two

The next morning, before breakfast, Philip took Sebastian, Henry, and Drake to his favorite fishing spot. After showing the boys what to do—and landing a nice-size salmon in the process—Philip left them on the bank, studying the deep pool with complete concentration, and joined Sebastian on a fallen tree trunk.

Sebastian handed Philip a flask of whisky to ward off the morning chill. Summer days were warm, but near Loch Rannoch the morning could still be cool.

"They won't be happy unless their catch rivals yours," Sebastian said.

"I hope it does." Philip glanced around, enjoying the morning and the boys' enthusiasm. "It seems like only yesterday I was here fishing with Father." *And Robert.* But he couldn't bring himself to say his brother's name.

Sebastian leaned back with a sigh. "I must admit I can't wait to take my son fishing. However, if Beatrice has her way I'll be taking his older sister along, too. So much for a quiet masculine pursuit."

Philip laughed. "Your wife is quite capable of fishing. Why shouldn't your daughter be?" He took a gulp of the warming whisky—and realized the import of Sebastian's words. "Wait. Is this your way of announcing Beatrice is with child again and you are hoping for a son?"

"Yes. And no." Sebastian nipped the flask out of Philip's hand and took a swig. "My only hope is that both mother and baby survive the birth." He flashed Philip a look of mingled pride and worry. "When it's your wife, you'll understand."

Your wife. Philip remained silent. How did he tell his friend there was no wife in his future? No sons to fish with? No daughters to rock? "Well, I'm not married yet, so children are a long way off." He looked over to where the boys huddled and whispered, "Drake, if you keep peering into the water the salmon will see your shadow and retreat."

The boy obediently moved back.

Sebastian grinned. "Speaking of wives. What are your intentions toward Rose? You must know the ladies are expecting a proposal by the end of our time here."

What? Philip jerked to his feet. "Why would they expect that?"

Sebastian shrugged. "You've been together for more than two years. You didn't invite her to Scotland last year. This year you did. The ladies thought—and I did, too—that there was some significance to the invitation."

Philip's gut went cold and he rubbed his hand over his face. Obviously he had not thought the invitation through. He had not seen Rose for eight weeks, so the prospect of spending a couple of weeks at his Scottish hunting lodge with his friends, where society could not judge him or her, had enthralled him. He did not want to come without her *or* Drake. He'd grown very fond of the boy. Since he would never have children of his own, he welcomed the boy's presence. He felt as if he had a family of sorts.

Family? Panic gripped him, and he began to pace.

Did *Rose* expect him to propose? No, of course she didn't. Since her disastrous marriage ended, she'd made it very clear she did not wish to marry again. She was safe. It was that safety that made their relationship work.

He glanced back to the boys and lowered his voice. "This isn't the time or place for this conversation."

Sebastian waved his concern away. "They're completely engrossed. They need a fish."

And Philip needed a drink. He turned to Sebastian and beckoned for the whisky flask. Sebastian handed it over.

After a large gulp of the fiery liquid, Philip blew out a breath. "Rose has made it perfectly clear she is not in need of a husband."

Sebastian laughed and accepted the flask's return. "Well, not in general terms. But what about you specifically? Her response might be different if you asked her."

"Why?" Philip knew his face had gone completely blank. Like his mind.

Sebastian was grinning like a fool. "Philip. Even *you* must know she's never stayed with any lover for this long. Besides, Portia told Beatrice that Rose has been infatuated with you since she was a little girl." He frowned. "Is that why you're holding back? Do you think she would say no?"

Why didn't one of the boys catch a fish and end this hellish conversation? Philip knew he should have ended his affair with Rose long ago, but every time he spent more than a few weeks away from her he . . . he didn't know his reasons, but he could not let her go.

"I'm not ready for marriage yet." He spoke the lie so easily because he'd been saying it to his mother for the past two years—and she, he knew for certain, would not understand his logic or his choice.

"Tosh," Sebastian said. "You're only a year younger than me." His friend hesitated. "Is it her reputation? Do you hold her various lovers against her? Because if so, that's unfair. You've had more than your fair share."

Philip shook his head. "No. It is not that. I understand why she chose to live as she did. After being sold like a broodmare to a man old enough to be her grandfather . . . it's no wonder she wants the freedom to make her own choices now, including lovers."

Sebastian nodded. "I've heard rumors of Roxborough's sexual proclivities. Rose is a brave woman to take the risk again after sharing his bed."

Privately, Philip agreed. Rose had told him only a little but it hadn't been hard to deduce the rest. A man like Roxborough and an eighteen-year-old innocent. No wonder she had been terrified, humiliated, and hurt.

"Then why not marry her?" Sebastian was obviously not going to let it go. "You need an heir and it's obvious you're wonderful together."

"Unlike you, my friend," Philip snapped with a slight edge in his voice, "I have three younger brothers. Any one of them would make a superb earl."

A frown crossed his friend's face, but Sebastian had done no more than open his mouth to speak when Drake let out a whoop.

"I have one!" he shouted. "I have one!"

Quickly, Philip moved to the boy's side. A big salmon could pull the boy into the river.

With one hand firmly on Drake's shoulder, Philip spent the next several minutes supporting the ecstatic child, instructing him in the finer points of reeling in his catch while Sebastian helped Henry—who was dancing excitedly and brandishing the net—land the fish.

The look on Drake's face, Philip decided, was worth every second of the struggle. The child shone with pride, grinning like he'd landed a whale single-handed.

Of course, Henry was now determined to catch one, too. After some argument, he took Drake's "lucky" rod, and after another half an hour, landed a similar-size salmon.

"We should get these to Cook," Drake said, importantly, the moment Henry was finished gloating over his prize. "Because there is nothing as good as fresh salmon for breakfast." And together they raced off toward the house carrying their catch between them in the fishing net.

Much to Philip's annoyance, Sebastian took up their previous conversation.

"If you love Rose," he said, "then marry her. Don't let the past muddy your decisions. You deserve to make a happy future for yourself. Robert would not have wanted you to remain alone. But"—he cleared his throat—"if you are not considering marriage with her, then let her go. It's obvious that she loves you, and it's unfair to let her believe something that will never happen."

"But she doesn't wish to remarry," Philip snapped, goaded by both guilt and rising anger. "It's no secret."

Sebastian nodded. "That is indeed possible. She has no need to marry—except for love. Kirkwood, however, might force her hand. As Drake's guardian he will be thinking of Drake and his reputation. After all, he controls her son, and Rose loves the boy. Kirkwood could make her do virtually anything. I suspect he's waiting to see what becomes of your affair. But if you walk away, I think he'll insist on her remarrying."

The very thought of Rose married to someone else made Philip's stomach clench, and the fiery dragon of possessive jealousy roared awake.

"Well, well," Sebastian said slowly. "So the idea of her marrying someone else is repugnant to you. Then why are you not already wed and setting up your nursery?"

Suddenly furious, Philip swung around on him. "Because not all of us are like you," he snarled. "Not all of us want a wife and sons to carry on the name. I have three brothers. Any one of them is perfectly capable of stepping into my shoes. I don't *need* a wife. I don't *want* a nursery."

Sebastian had stopped walking. Now he stood still, his narrowed gaze fixed on Philip's face. "My God. That's why? Because of Robert? Don't be a stupid bugger, Philip. Robert would want—"

Enough was enough. "Don't you dare preach to me about

what Robert would want." Self-loathing fanned the raging fire of guilt and anger, and his very muscles trembled with the need for violence. "My choice is none of your business. Keep out of it."

For a moment it looked like Sebastian might give him the fight he wanted. But in the end he simply shook his head. "Well, I think you're a fool. However, if you truly do intend the title to pass to Thomas, then it's even more imperative that you let Rose go. She deserves the chance to be happy."

And with that Sebastian stalked off, leaving him in the shade of a large alder tree, fuming.

Slowly, he began to walk back to the hunting lodge, following Sebastian's stiff, angry strides up ahead of him.

Why did he need to tell Rose anything? Why should he let her go? Weren't they happy as they were? Why shouldn't an arrangement to simply remain lovers suit both of them? Sebastian might be right about Kirkwood's plans for Rose, but he was quite capable of dealing with Kirkwood if he ever became a problem.

By the time Philip reached the house his mood had lifted. He entered the entrance hall just as the boys clattered in from delivering their fish to Cook, and the ladies were descending the stairs.

When Drake saw his mother his face lit up and he ran to her.

"Mama, Mama," he cried, almost dancing with excitement. "Father helped me catch a big salmon and we're going to eat it for breakfast."

"Silly," Henry said into the sudden awkward silence. "Lord Cumberland is not your father."

Philip saw Rose's face infuse with color and the boy's smile dimmed, his cheeks flushing crimson.

Then Rose hurried forward and hugged him. "It sounds as though you had an exciting morning. Did you thank Lord Cumberland for the treat?"

"Yes, Mama." Drake, cheeks still flaming, lifted his chin. "I'm sorry, my lord. I made a mistake."

An excited child's mistake, but the sense of desolation and loss in the boy's voice now tugged at Philip's heart. He said the first thing that came to mind, "That's all right, Drake. I'm honored that you think of me that way. You're a son to make any father proud. Now"—he walked over and ruffled the little boy's hair—"let's get cleaned up before breakfast so we can sit down with the ladies like gentlemen and eat that salmon."

He held out his hand. After a moment Drake took it. Then hand in hand the two of them walked up the stairs, the sound of silence trailing after them.

Chapter Three

London, three months later (early November)
My darling,
I promised to take Drake and Henry to see the Bassae Frieze at the British Museum. We would love for you to join us. May I beg an invitation to stay for supper afterward? I shall send my carriage for you at three.
Yours always,
Philip Flagstaff, Earl of Cumberland

Rose's stomach fluttered like that of a young girl receiving her first love letter. How thoughtful of Philip to include Drake in their outing. Of course she wanted to go.

She was aching to see him. After their holiday in Scotland Philip had returned to Devon and she to Cornwall. There had been no opportunity since to discuss their situation in person, and he had written to her only twice in the past months. Of course, he was an earl with huge estates to run and family to look after. His mother, too, still lived on the estate.

But his lack of communication had hurt—and made her feel somehow bereft.

Their time together in Scotland had been enjoyable in every respect but one. Philip was as attentive to her as ever, but he seemed to become more and more withdrawn as the days passed. She could feel him slipping away. Was this how he ended his affairs —simply letting them die away without discussion? Unlikely. He had more honor than that.

There was also an odd tension between him and Sebastian. Rose was sure it was to do with her. She was also sure Beatrice knew what had happened, but Beatrice had given her such sympathetic looks that Rose couldn't bear to swallow her pride and ask, in case the answer was something dreadful.

So she told herself she was imagining foolishness and had pretended all was well. And all had been well—perhaps one of the happiest times she could remember spending with her son and friends.

Drake loved the freedom. In Scotland he had climbed trees, ridden horses, and romped around with Henry without Kirkwood's servants watching his every move and fussing: *You are a duke. Behave like one. You are the last of the Deverill line. Be careful. You have a duty to the family. Remember your obligations.*

She knew Kirkwood was only looking after her son's interests, but it was a terrible burden to place on a young boy and she protected him from it as much as she could. He was a child. He should be able to *be* one.

Philip was treating him like the young boy he was—a visit to the British Museum with his best friend. It warmed her heart— and not only on Drake's behalf. Philip had arrived back in London only the day before and she was thrilled he wanted to see her so soon. Yes. Everything was well between them. She was just allowing her imagination to cut up her peace.

Once he'd heard Lord Cumberland's plans for the afternoon, it had been almost impossible to keep Drake focused on his lessons. By a quarter to three he was haunting the drawing room window like a well-groomed ghost. Not for the first time, Rose worried about Drake's growing hero worship. If—when—their affair ended Drake would miss Philip almost as much as she would.

The sick feeling deep in her stomach returned.

Precisely at three o'clock, Philip's carriage drew up outside the townhouse. As Rose glided down the stairs toward him, the warmth in his smile, the heat in his eyes, and the gentle pressure of his hand as he helped her into the carriage, chased away her doubts.

He was still hers.

While Henry and Drake excitedly chattered together, Philip sat studying her gravely. When she felt heat steal into her cheeks, his mouth curved.

"I love making you blush," he said softly.

She glanced quickly over to where the boys sat. They were so engrossed in their conversation and with peering out the window that they took no notice of the adults.

Philip's gaze settled on her mouth. Embarrassed, delighted, she licked her lips. "You are looking well, my lord," she said.

He reached across the small space and took her hand, lifting it to his lips and pressing a kiss to her gloved knuckles before slowly letting it go. The light touch of his mouth through her gloves burned like a brand.

"I'm all the better for seeing you," he said. "I have missed you, my Rose."

And with those simple words, she was lost. For the past twelve months Rose had fought her feelings. Now she admitted defeat. She had fallen in love, and for the first time since her horrid marriage, she admitted she would marry in a trice if Philip asked her. She wanted him with her every day. She wanted to wake with him in her bed in the morning instead of having to sneak him away before dawn. She wanted to be able to walk proudly on his arm as his wife, without knowing looks from the men, haughty disdain from their wives, and whispers throughout the *ton* about their affair. She wanted to have his children. Most of all, she wanted that.

"I have missed you, too," was all she could manage.

His smile made her knees weaken and her desire soar.

It was a blustery autumn day and the British Museum was filled not only with scholars but also with ordinary people, many with children.

The boys loved the museum. They especially loved the Egyptian mummies. Rose did not love the mummies but she loved watching Drake's and Henry's enthusiasm for the exhibits. She followed them from room to room as Philip filled their heads with history and adventure and fired their imaginations.

He was a natural with children. They responded to him and he really listened to what they had to say. No question was brushed aside. None was too silly. Even Drake's "What would happen if the mummy came to life and chased us?" received thoughtful consideration.

"But it couldn't, could it, sir?" asked Henry, wide-eyed.

"No," Philip answered gravely. Then he smiled and lowered his voice. "But if it did, remember that mummies are dried-up husks. All we'd have to do is throw water on them. They would become soggy and drown."

Of course they believed him. Rose wasn't sure that *she* didn't believe him, and was glad to leave the Ancient Egyptian exhibit. She spent the rest of the visit trying to maintain a sober face as the boys took careful note of each exit in case of mummy attack, and every container in every room was examined as a potential water carrier.

"Wretch," she murmured as Philip drew her arm through his. "If they or I have bad dreams tonight—"

He laughed. "They're made of sterner stuff." He leaned closer. "But you, my sweet, delicate Rose, have me to keep you safe."

The fun atmosphere changed when one of the museum staff asked Philip if his wife would like a chair to rest for a moment. The man was being kind and, of course, had no idea they were not married.

Before Philip could respond, Rose smiled at the man. "I'm

perfectly fine standing, thank you. It was very thoughtful of you to ask."

As they moved on, Henry asked Philip a question. Drake moved closer to Rose and tugged her hand. She leaned down.

"Mama," he whispered. "You are not married to Lord Cumberland, are you?"

Rose swallowed the lump in her throat. "No."

"Oh." Drake looked over to where Philip and Henry were huddled over a display case and said softly, "I would not mind if Lord Cumberland became my father."

What could she say? She had seen the look on Philip's face when the man called her "your wife." It had been panic. Some of the joy of their outing faded and her stomach knotted with worry once more.

"He's a very kind man." She smiled at her son and ruffled his hair. A moment later he squeezed her hand and raced off to join Philip and Henry as they strolled into the next room.

Rose did not follow immediately. She needed space to think.

She could not put off talking to Philip about the future much longer. Drake was growing up, becoming fonder of Philip, and more confused about his place in their lives. She no longer had the answers to satisfy him.

If she weren't so in love with him, she'd force him to talk tonight. But she had not seen him for two months and all she wanted to do tonight was lose herself in his arms. Let him make love to her over and over until he had to leave.

No. She could not discuss the future with him today.

A little voice inside her head reminded her that she'd made that excuse for the last twelve months. There would never be a good day for a talk about their future because it was obvious Philip's choice would break her heart.

Philip didn't want a future that included her.

Philip stretched his feet toward the roaring fire. The day had been perfect and he'd never felt more relaxed. Drake had gone to bed over an hour earlier, and Philip was quite content to sip his brandy and talk with the most beautiful woman in England.

Rose's presence always chased his ghosts away. In her company, the pressure of his role as earl fell from his shoulders and he could simply be himself.

"You look tired."

He opened his eyes and smiled at her. "A little. I'm sorry I'm so quiet but I traveled from Devon in one day. I wanted to see you before I get sucked into business and duties here in London. Grayson is asking support for his new bill."

"What is it about?"

"Are you really interested?"

She nodded. "I'd like to know what Grayson is asking you to support."

"He's trying to gather support for a pension for those either retiring from the army or discharged due to injury. I don't think there is much hope it will even get as far as a reading because he has not yet found a way to raise money to pay for it."

Rose lowered herself to the floor at his feet and rested her head on his thigh. A simple gesture full of trust. "I think that's wonderful. Soldiers give up so much to fight for us, for our children and country. They deserve to be cared for after such sacrifice."

Hers was a female perspective, but he, too, wanted to help.

He'd seen men who had fallen into a trance from the horrors of battle and never come out. Or those who still dived for the ground in terror at a loud noise.

As for him, his nightmares were of watching Robert step into the path of the bayonet meant for him.

In his dreams he always managed to push Robert aside. Always took the mortal blow himself. Felt the numbness, then the agony. The warm blood, the cold rain, the stench from gun smoke and his own entrails. Over all the noise, the screams and gunfire, he'd hear Grayson's shout—

And then, always, the dream would change. Suddenly it was

Robert on the ground, his guts mixing with the mud and rain while he—Philip—fought with sword and pistols, standing over his dying brother while Grayson Devlin slashed his way through the French to his side—

"Don't you agree?" Rose asked.

Philip shoved the memories aside and tossed off his brandy. He reached down and lifted her into his lap. "Yes, I do. But we have to find the money to pay for the pensions, and there just isn't enough money to do everything we need."

She wrapped her arms around his neck and her soft breasts pressed into his chest. "You mean the government would rather fund more wars than look after the heroes who won the last one."

She was very clever, his Rose.

His.

He thought of her as his. Already his body cried out to give her pleasure and to take his own. It hurt him to know he'd then have to creep away before dawn as if what they shared was something to be ashamed of.

He bent his head and kissed her. "Someone had to stop Napoleon. We could all be speaking French by now."

She snuggled into his arms.

He held her tight. If Napoleon had won, Robert's sacrifice would have been in vain. He would never have been able to live with that.

When he shivered, she tipped back her head to look him in the face. "Are you cold?"

"No." In the light of the dying fire he stood, gathered her into his arms, and headed toward the door. "Time for bed."

"You're staying?"

"Of course." He smiled. "I'm tired but not that tired."

Her saucy smile made him harden. Everything about her made his body hum and desire grow until the thought of her consumed him. He'd never want a woman as much as he wanted Rose.

Her lady's maid knew when to be discreet. Philip could

manage very nicely on his own. Undressing Rose, revealing the perfect creamy skin and curvaceous body, was his favorite thing in the world—except of course, for being buried deep inside her.

He kicked the door shut behind him, crossed the room, tossed her onto the bed, and followed her down, trapping her beneath him.

"You can hardly undress me if you keep me pinned to the bed," she teased.

He settled on top of her. "I'm enjoying the softness."

"I'd rather enjoy something hard." Her hands rose, reaching for his cravat.

With a chuckle he caught them, one in each of his, and pressed them back to the coverlet, anchoring them on either side of her head. "You know how much I love undressing you. It's been too long since I have seen this magnificent body. I beg you to indulge me."

Her lips curved. "I'd indulge you in anything you want to do to me. I know you'd only ever give me pleasure."

He met her wicked gaze with one of his own. "Unfair. Now I want to rip your clothes off."

She pressed quick, breathless kisses to his face. "I'm not stopping you."

He couldn't help it. His mouth crushed hers and his need began to race. She was like a drug in his veins. The more he tasted her the more he wanted her. If he was not careful he'd do something foolish—like promise her something he could not give.

His body was primed and ready but he needed to slow things down. He wanted to pleasure her all night. In his current state—and after two months of abstinence—he was a pistol ready to fire.

Dragging a portion of his wits free of her seductive powers took effort. The sensual silk of her mouth, the wicked touch of her tongue, the knowledge of what that hot, wet mouth could do to him—

He drew back, warning her with upraised finger to stay still as he unhooked the fastenings on the front of her gown. "Do all your gowns hook in the front? Very convenient."

"Only the ones I wear for you," she whispered, sending a shiver over his earlobe while her fingers fumbled with his cravat.

He made a strangled sound and tried to ignore her explorations. He could have demanded she stop, but her need for him excited him even more.

Finally, he was peeling off her gown, his hot palms skimming the curves of her shoulders, pushing the silk over and down her arms. He had done this hundreds of times before, but with Rose, each time felt like the first.

In two swift tugs, Philip pulled down the sleeves of her gown, trapping her arms at her sides with the bodice crumpled at her waist, leaving her breasts screened only by the translucent silk of her chemise.

"God, you are a feast for a starving man." He ran a finger over one hardening nipple, and the flare of hunger on her face as she watched him watch her went straight to his cock. "So beautiful."

Her breasts rose and fell in a shuddering laugh. "Then devour me."

His awareness and every last one of his slavering senses locked—intently—on her. On her curvaceous body trapped beneath his. On the utterly absorbing sight of all she was offering him. He barely kept his hands from shaking as they reached up and, gripping her silk chemise, ripped it apart, baring her to his gaze.

Her excited intake of breath made those wonderful breasts lift and fall again, and he could no longer resist. Taking one plump nipple into his mouth, he suckled. Hard.

Slowly, he eased her gown down her body before tossing it on the floor. The torn chemise was next, and finally he sat astride her hips, admiring her creamy expanse of silken skin. A quick glance over his shoulder at her long limbs told him she still wore her stockings. But nothing else.

He turned back and grinned down at her.

"You have me at your mercy. What are you going to do to me?"

She could drive a man wild with that husky voice.

"That would be telling, my darling. I prefer actions to words."

She shivered at his words, her skin puckering in anticipation, and he hadn't even touched her. "Stay still. Stay exactly like this. Don't move."

Pulse racing, he eased off the bed.

Quickly, he shrugged out of his jacket. Then his waistcoat. Almost ripped his shirt in his hurry to pull it over his head.

He smothered a grin when she licked her lips as her gaze locked on his chest.

"Oh, what a shame," she cooed. "Your bronzed glow from summer is fading already. I do have to say, though, that you look wonderful naked. It's a sin to clothe such a muscular body."

He laughed in delight at her teasing. "You'd be happy if I walked around naked? How thoughtful of you. How the ladies of the *ton* would appreciate that."

She pretended to pout. "Would you like that? To have all the ladies slavering over you?"

His little Rose was jealous? His grin widened. "I want only one woman's undivided attention, my sweet. And that woman is you."

Her pout faded to a saucy grin. "You have it. You really have it."

Tossing his shirt aside, he used one hand to undo the buttons of his fall. Impatient, he sat, removed his buckskins, and dispensed with his Hessians. Finally, he untied his drawers and let them drop to the floor.

Then, naked and more than ready for her, he prowled to the bed.

She tensed as he put a knee on the bed, as he leaned over her and pressed kisses to her shoulder.

When his body came to rest on top of her the contact seared him to his core. She deserved to hear words of love. His words. He wanted to say what was in his heart but he couldn't and it killed him. Instead, he swore to show her. To teach her what was in his heart.

He kissed down her neck and across her décolletage while his hands cupped and caressed her bountiful breasts. She parted her long, stocking-clad legs to accommodate him between her thighs, her impatience obvious.

But Philip was in no hurry. He'd dreamed of her for two months, and when a man held his dream woman in his arms he did not miss any opportunity to indulge his desire.

He tweaked one nipple as his mouth found the other and suckled deep. He continued to play with her breasts, licking and sucking and caressing until Rose's moans grew in volume and her breathing hitched and caught. Loving how responsive she was to him, Philip began to kiss his way down her body.

As he sank between her opened thighs the scent of her arousal filled his senses. He could not wait to taste her. He ran his tongue over her open womanhood and felt her tremble beneath his hands. He loved having her open to his mouth, his tongue, and fingers. Tonight he would not take her until she had screamed his name.

He looked up at her face. She was watching him with eyes bright with need. "Shall I stop and fetch a handkerchief to stuff into your mouth so you don't wake the house?"

Her eyes darkened with desire, and she reached under her pillow. "Do your worst," she said huskily, and withdrew a handkerchief.

"My worst?" He shook his head, and as he lowered his mouth he murmured, "Always my best, my dear. Always my best."

On second "best" he drove his tongue inside her—and she came up off the bed.

Soon Philip's mind was empty of anything but the sounds of Rose's pleasure. He licked and sucked, laved and stroked, pressing first one, then two fingers inside her. As her inner lips tightened her cries grew in frequency and volume. Soon she was shaking, her legs gripping his head, her hands thrust deep into his hair, one moment tugging him away, the next pushing him closer. He began to suck and nibble and lick in earnest. On a muffled scream, Rose's body went as taut as a strung wire, and he lapped at her release.

She was still trembling as he kissed his way back up her body, angled his head, and plunged his tongue into her mouth. She was soft and welcoming and all his. He fought the need to drive his throbbing erection deep into her hot, wet body.

Not yet; he'd come too soon.

He gained some relief as he claimed her lips and her tongue, seized her awareness and anchored it in the kiss. He wanted to take her to heaven again—with him, so they could take their pleasure together.

Still locked in the kiss, he lowered his weight to her, careful not to crush her. In response, Rose lifted her legs to wrap around his hips, drawing him to her. He moved slowly, pushing his hard member through her slick folds.

God, it felt so good.

With his free hand, he started to push her arms above her head. But before he could pin them down she slid her hands into his hair, fingers spearing through the thick locks and clenching, clinging, holding him to the kiss. She turned the tables so masterfully, kissed him so wantonly, that he lost track of his mind.

When she compounded her conquest by arching against him, he was fit to burst, and feeling her bare breasts pressed against his chest—so tempting, so alluring—he could not tease her much longer before he lost control.

He wisely surrendered to his instincts.

Boldly, he closed his free hand about one pert breast and drank down her instinctive gasp. But she got her revenge when her small hand slipped between their bodies and wrapped around his pulsing member.

This time it was he who groaned into the silence. He had forgotten that she knew his body as well as he knew hers. She drove him wild. Seduced his senses. Made him hers in a way that left him not merely eager, but hungry for more. So hungry he'd keep coming back, night after night, for however long the magic between them lasted. And it had lasted far longer than he'd ever imagined.

He sent his hand gliding over her body, tracing curves, relearning dips and hollows.

Sweat beaded on his brow. Her sliding hand was magic, so good he had to take charge before she ruined his plan.

He drew back and she understood him perfectly, guiding him to her wet, tight entrance. With a groan that felt as if it came from his soul, he sank into her heat.

They stilled, reveling in the perfection of their joined bodies. He was braced above her, lost in the slow, gentle stroke of her fingers through his hair.

For long moments, eyes closed, he simply savored. If he'd been the King of the Beasts he'd have purred, not roared.

Only Rose could tame him. Only Rose could silence the demons driving him. Only Rose brought him this intensity of pleasure.

She shifted to press even closer. He wrestled her hands to anchor them beside her head. He needed to take control. Needed her to know the pleasure he felt when she was in his arms.

He leaned down. Their lips met—and, as always, they were in perfect accord. He began to thrust and, sensing his mood, she met and matched his rhythm. It was as if their entire beings—mind, body, and senses—revolved entirely about the other. He could have died right then and been contented.

He wanted these sensations to last as long as possible, but desire flared, rich and hot and luscious between them. He withdrew and thrust in again, and his Rose matched his rhythm, caught it, and drummed it back to him until the world spun in a wild dance around them.

Making love with Rose was never the same dance twice. Each time he learned more about her. This time, when he ground against her mound, her legs tightened at his hips and she gave two little gasps. How was it that after two years he still could not get enough of her? How could it be that each time they were together he lost a little more of his heart to her?

The tempo escalated, and they raced together—hearts thundering, lungs laboring, will, intent, and focus all locked unrelentingly on reaching the shining peak.

Soon Philip lost himself in the primal drive, the compulsive friction and exquisite sensations of having her body respond to his. His breathing turned harsh and ragged, the world faded away, and—blind with desperation, arms braced, head hanging—he plundered, finally taking for himself, seeing to his own need.

Dimly, in the distance, he heard Rose scream, felt her body arch up beneath him, her nails sink into his arms. Then, over everything else, the powerful contractions of her sheath told of her unraveling. She tumbled from the peak in the same moment as he leaped toward it in triumph, a roar ripping from him as he pulled free of her body and let his release shudder through him.

They clung to each other as his seed soaked the sheets. The tumultuous sensations caught him, tossing and hurling him like a ship lost on a stormy sea, like a man drowning in pleasure.

Her heart thundered under his ear. Her skin slick with heat and him. She was his perfect, beautiful Rose, and he would never feel like this with any other woman. If he'd been a praying man, he would have prayed that their world would remain as it was. That society would leave them alone. That no one would hurt her again —least of all him.

"Am I crushing you?"

Rose's answer was simply to wrap her arms around him and hold him even closer. Even tighter.

"I love the weight of you—the feel of you atop me." She stretched and yawned. "There is nothing more perfect."

He relaxed on her but moved his body so she didn't bear his full weight. He'd rest, for just a while, because he wasn't leaving this bed before they did *that* again. Soon his eyelids drifted closed. Heavy. So heavy.

"Sleep," she whispered. "I shall wake you later—and this time I shall enjoy doing all the work."

He would dream of all the inventive things she could do to wake him up. She was wickedly skilled with her mouth—and not only in conversation.

He fell asleep with a smile on his face.

Rose watched Philip as exhaustion overcame him. She would let him sleep for a few hours before taking enormous pleasure in waking him.

She moved and felt the damp patch where he'd spilled his seed. Tonight he'd made love to her as if she were the only woman in the world. She'd hoped that maybe—just maybe this time—he might have declared his feelings by spilling his seed deep inside her.

Stop being a coward and ask him. Tell him that you have changed your mind. You want to marry him. You want more children.

But something stopped her. Philip was the type of man who would see what he wanted and hunt it down. If he really wanted her as his wife he would ask her—no, he'd demand it of her.

She feared to confront him, to speak her heart. Because the truth was that if this half-life was all he could give her, she was afraid that she'd accept it and settle for fleeting moments of pleasure, when really she wanted so much more.

So she said nothing, just lay in the dimming firelight stroking his hair and watching as the man she wanted above all others slept.

Chapter Four

Rose knew Philip was busy for the following few days. Then, on the day of Lord and Lady Spencer's ball, he sent a note. It was brief and to the point. He'd meet her there.

She couldn't wait. Part of her hoped that meant he would sneak into her townhouse afterward. Another part reminded her of her decision to question his intentions. Already she was both anticipating their meeting, and dreading it.

Tonight, after the ball, she would find her courage and face her fears. It was time for them both to be honest about their relationship—if one could call it that.

It wasn't as if Philip was openly courting her. A few nights in secret here, a few weeks' holiday together there. Over the course of two years it was hardly a commitment.

The ball was a sad crush, and she was beginning to wonder if she would even see Philip in the crowd when a prickle of heat on her neck alerted her that she was being watched.

She turned her head, and there he was. Philip. Their eyes met and held, and awareness smoldered like a stoked fire between them.

She caught her breath.

He was so handsome. An image of him as he'd looked when she'd been a young girl of fifteen pushed to the forefront of her thoughts. He had been the kind of *handsome* that warranted second and third looks. But she had not realized at the time that, as he matured, his looks would become more masculine, morphing into a stark beauty that stirred her senses. Was it any wonder that first impression upon her fifteen-year-old heart paled in comparison to her feelings for him now?

Would this feeling ever fade?

Her heart thumped painfully in her chest as it occurred to her that tonight might be her last night with him.

"He is exceedingly handsome, is he not?"

Lady Philomena's catty voice jolted Rose from her lustful thoughts.

The impoverished widow hated her, seeing her as a wealthy rival. Rose's husband had left her a large widow's portion. Philomena's had left her barely enough to have a few new gowns made each season. Desperate to land a wealthy husband, Philomena had wanted to get her hooks into Philip but Rose came along.

Really, some women were so blind. Philomena—and many other women of the *ton*—only saw Philip's handsome face, his title, and his wealth. Rose saw all those things, too. But she saw so much more. She saw his hurt, pain, and guilt. She, more than anyone, understood Philip. Perhaps better than he did himself.

"Who is handsome?" Rose pretended nonchalance, but feared everyone had already seen her reaction to Philip.

"Why, Lord Cumberland, of course." Lady Philomena's catlike smile held an edge of malevolence and enjoyment. "Don't you agree? And there are so many fascinating women in the room. Really, the man is spoiled for choice."

The witch was enjoying herself far too much. What had Rose missed? "I'm sure Lord Cumberland is deluged with admirers," Rose said, keeping her tone neutral.

Lady Philomena laughed. "We should know, darling. We

have both shared his bed." Her eyes and voice hardened. Chilled. "He used to share his favors, but then you cast your spell." She studied Rose insolently, slippers to crown. "You stole him from me. Now it's your turn to be tossed aside. He's in the market for a wife."

Gooseflesh prickled her heated skin. Was he? Was this why he'd kept his distance? But she couldn't think about Philip. Not with Lady Philomena watching her like a cat. *Call her bluff; don't let the bitch know you are vulnerable.*

She lifted a shoulder in a casual shrug. "Quite possibly. He has to marry sometime. Heirs are a requirement for an earl."

Rose had the pleasure of seeing her response was not what the woman had been hoping for.

Lady Philomena's eyes narrowed. "So, you really don't wish to remarry."

Rose's light laugh cost her dearly. "What do I need a husband for? A man, yes, one must have a lover, but a husband?" She let the implied question hang in the air.

Lady Philomena lost her catlike smile. She thrust her head forward, teeth bared and eyes flashing. "It's so easy for you, isn't it?" she said. "You're still Duchess of Roxborough. You're young. You're rich. But one day you'll have nothing, and then where will you be?"

Alone. Rose would be alone. She was honest enough to admit she did not wish to end up alone. But she also did not wish to find herself with another husband she could not stand. She already knew how *that* would be. It was far worse than being alone.

The strains of a waltz—the first waltz of the evening—sounded from the orchestra.

"Well, well." The delight in Lady Philomena's voice burned like acid. "It appears your lover has found his future bride."

Startled, Rose followed the direction of Lady Philomena's pointing fan. And all her dreams came tumbling down.

On the other side of the ballroom stood Philip, about to lead a young woman onto the floor. Lady Abigail Somebody-or-other,

Rose thought numbly, the nineteen-year-old beauty reputed to be the leading debutante of the Season.

"I told you so." The victory in Lady Philomena's voice broke through Rose's pain. "He's never danced the waltz with any of the *ton*'s leading debutantes before. He's made his choice—and it isn't you." With that poisoned barb, she turned and rustled away, leaving Rose standing by herself. Like a statue. Mesmerized by the pair as they glided past, the girl gazing adoringly up into Philip's smiling face.

Rose recognized the look. It was how she used to stare at him years ago when she was younger and still innocent. She was no longer innocent. Life and her silly pursuit of *freedom* had seen to that. How could she blame Philip for wanting to possess something so lovely, so untouched, so beautiful?

Philip made a comment and the girl laughed, light and happy. Rose's heart squeezed hard in her chest, squeezed so hard she thought she'd not be able to take another breath—

An arm slipped through hers. "*Smile*," Portia said. "Others are watching." And she gave a little giggle as though Rose had said something funny.

Obediently, Rose smiled and followed her best friend's lead, walking and chatting as though she hadn't a care. As though her heart hadn't been ripped out of her chest. As though her world were not falling apart.

Finally, they reached a quiet spot out of the way of dancers and watchers. Portia drew her down to the seat beside her, and Rose went willingly before her legs folded under her.

"Why?" she whispered.

"I'm sure it's only because Mother is here," Portia said comfortingly. "She has been ringing a fine peal over him for months about getting married and filling his nursery."

Portia's light reply made her feel worse. If Philip wanted to appease his mother, that was one thing. If he wanted to make a public statement that he did not consider *her* a viable option for his countess, that was quite another. Pain lanced through her at that thought. She couldn't just sit there.

She shoved to her feet, not sure how she got her legs to move. If Portia hadn't joined her and quickly slipped an arm around her waist—all the time chatting inconsequentially about fustian nonsense, Rose felt she might have crumpled to the floor in a puddle of tears.

But Portia refused to allow Rose to wilt. She was the Duchess of Roxborough. People might believe that something was amiss, but unless Rose lost control they would not be certain.

So they walked around the whole ballroom, ignoring the speculative glances of the men and the horrified glee of many of the women. Only when the dance had ended did Portia relent and shepherd her over to where Lady Serena and Lady Marisa sat talking together.

"How lovely to see you, Rose," Serena said, and kissed her cheek. "I do hope you're free for dinner on Wednesday night. Just a small gathering."

"That would be lovely," she replied automatically, wondering at the same time if Philip would be there with Lady Abigail. If so, she would send a regretful refusal.

Would she lose the friendship of these women now that her affair with Philip was over? How awful to lose everything in one day. But it would be awkward—to say the least—to have one's ex-lover in the same room as one's future wife.

Her head began to pound and the noise around her sounded odd—like breaking waves—and far too loud. Home. She wanted to go home.

She thought rather badly of him. That Philip should so publicly signal the end of their affair in this manner instead of letting it die away slowly or at least preparing her. She could have put on a brave face with a private and mutual ending to their affair, but to be unprepared, to have to face the end of her love affair this way . . . in front of the *ton* . . .

That was the issue. It had never been a love affair for Philip—merely an affair.

She could feel tears welling.

"I'm so sorry, ladies, I have a terrible headache. If you'll excuse me, I'll ask a servant to call for my carriage."

Serena placed a hand on her arm. "Are you sure you want to leave, Rose? There could be an explanation for his behavior."

So even *they* understood how dishonorable Philip's actions had been.

She shook her head. "I really don't care what people think, but if I don't leave now I might slap his face if I see him." Grief lodged in her throat. Made it hard to speak. "I don't understand. I've never treated any of the men who professed to love me this way."

"I agree with the slap." Portia sounded almost bloodthirsty. "I'd like to kick him in the family jewels. But Serena is right. This is unlike him. There must be something else behind his behavior."

Perhaps. At that moment Rose hurt too much to care. She squeezed Portia's hand. "Thank you. I must go. I'll be fine in the morning, but tonight I need to lick my wounds in private. Walk out with me, Marisa?"

"Of course." Without a moment's hesitation Marisa linked her arm through Rose's and, chatting brightly, escorted her out to her waiting carriage.

After one of the most insipid dances of his life, Philip strode toward the refreshment table. Thank Christ that bloody display was over. It finally dawned on him how difficult it was going to be to misdirect his mother for much longer. She was unlikely to leave the matter of his marital status alone, but after tonight perhaps she would turn her attention to one of his brothers. He needed a drink. Then he needed to find Rose—and sanity.

"I could kick you where it bloody hurts."

Surprised at his sister's vicious whisper, he accepted the snifter of brandy the servant offered and turned to smile down at her.

His smile faded as he recognized her calm mask. Portia only wore that expression when she was furious. "What's wrong?"

She blinked at him. "And for that stupid question I just might get Grayson to bloody thump you, too. Very badly done, brother."

He took a long-suffering sip of the spirit. No doubt he'd need it. "What am I supposed to have done?"

Portia's eyes blazed but her face remained calm. "Are you really so unfeeling? Don't you understand what that waltz with Lady Abigail signaled to everyone here?"

Damn Lady Abigail. And damn his mother's interference. "It signaled that Mother is determined to see me riveted to some chit. You know what she is like. One minute I am talking to her and wishing I were anywhere else, and the next I find myself escorting some vacuous debutante onto the floor. It meant nothing."

"Did it?" Now the polite mask slipped. "It certainly meant something to Rose. And to the *ton*. Everyone now believes you've discarded your mistress to start hunting for a wife. Lady Philomena couldn't wait to rub Rose's face in it."

Philip's heart dropped to the soles of his shoes. A curse on his mother. How could a woman of only five feet, two inches manipulate him into something so stupid? Because, as usual, he hadn't *thought*. And he'd *asked* Rose to come tonight. He went cold. "Goddamn it to hell."

Only as he frantically scanned the room for her did he realize the buzzing groups at the edge of the dance floor were casting covert glances their way. If he was the subject of speculation and gossip, then Rose—

"Where is she? I need to explain—"

"Gone," Portia snapped.

Stunned, Philip swung his gaze back to her. "What?"

"I said she's gone." Portia's cold mask was once again in place. "What did you expect? The *ton* believes you've publicly announced the end of your affair. She's heartbroken that you'd treat her so cruelly."

His fists clenched as he silently cursed his mother—and himself—to kingdom come. He'd known the moment his mother had come over with the simpering Lady Abigail that she was up to something. Why had he not found a way to thwart her? But as always, he hadn't *thought*. All he'd seen was a chance to get his mother off the scent for a while by dancing with a young lady.

The entire set had been bearable only when he imagined it was Rose at his side. Rose's hand he held. Rose's face lifted up to his. That face appeared in his mind's eye now, pale and haunted. Because of him. But he would never have ended their affair this way. Never hurt her like this. She had a place in his heart. If Robert had not died at Waterloo, then perhaps they could have been happy together. She was the only woman he wanted, needed. And yet he couldn't give her what she deserved—his name. *This* was his punishment for causing Robert's death—to grieve the woman he . . . cared for.

Sebastian was right. He was being unfair to Rose. It was time to set her free.

But first, he had to beg her forgiveness for his actions.

He put down his drink and, ignoring both Portia's attempts to stop him and all the avid eyes of the *ton*, he shouldered his way out of the ballroom.

Chapter Five

Philip stormed up the steps to the Duchess of Roxborough's townhouse.

Before he reached the top step, the door was opened by Rose's butler. Booth had recognized his carriage. Normally, Philip drove it round the back out of sight of wagging tongues.

"Her Grace is not at home, my lord." Booth's pointed stare at the Earl of Cumberland's recognizable equipage parked in full view of the street told Philip of his faux pas.

Philip walked back to his carriage, directed the coachman to drive up the street and around to the stables. Frustrated at the wasted time, he raced back to the servants' entrance . . . only to be halted once again by Booth.

"I don't think you understand, my lord," the butler said. "Whether you come by the front or back entrance, Her Grace is not at home."

This was even worse than he'd imagined. "Booth, it is imperative that I speak with Her Grace. I think she may be under a misapprehension. I'm not here to make a scene. I'm here to grovel at her feet."

Philip held his breath as indecision flickered over Booth's face.

"Please, Booth. I inadvertently hurt Her Grace this evening

and I need to explain and apologize. Please let me in. I don't want her upset if I have to force my way through."

He must have sounded as sincere as he felt, because Booth stepped aside and bowed him in. Philip didn't wait for the butler to precede him. He knew the back stairs better than in his own house, and he raced up them. Most of the staff had gone to bed but those still awake ignored him, or turned a blind eye.

A few moments later he was at Rose's bedchamber door. Before he could knock, it opened and her lady's maid stepped out. The woman's forehead dipped into a frown when she saw him, and her lips thinned. Quick as thought, she squared her shoulders and blocked the doorway. "My lord?"

He didn't want to argue with—or explain to—Rose's servants. He was in the wrong but it was Rose to whom he owed an explanation. He gently moved the maid aside and walked through the door, closing it firmly behind him.

The only light in the bedchamber came from the fire burning bright in the grate.

It took him a moment to see Rose. She was curled in her favorite armchair by the fire, twisting a handkerchief in her fingers. She looked so lost his heart almost stopped. As if a lightning bolt hit him, he suddenly realized she didn't merely care for him. She loved him. He could see it in the curve of her body, in her misery, and it broke something inside him that he could not love her back or give her what she wanted, his name. Perhaps if she hadn't loved him they might have been able to stay lovers all their lives. But this travesty was all they could ever have—and now he knew with certainty it would not be enough for her.

She was so lost in misery she did not hear him until he knelt at her feet.

"I'm so sorry, darling," he said. "I'm a bumbling buffoon. I would never do anything to hurt you. I simply didn't think."

Her eyes filled with tears of hurt and disappointment. "It was humiliating, true. But what hurt the most was the possibility you did it to make a point."

He stayed kneeling, his hands on her thighs, gently massaging. "I would never deliberately hurt you. I'd rather drive a dagger through my own heart than cause you such pain."

She caught herself on a sob. "I thought you were announcing you were ready to marry—and it wasn't to me."

Philip snorted at the idea. "I'd never be interested in a young chit like Lady Abigail. Mother cornered me, and it was either make a scene or—" He stopped, looked into her eyes. Waited till she really saw him. "I should have made the scene. I'm immeasurably sorry."

Another tear spilled over. He wiped it gently away with his thumb. "What can I do? How can I fix the situation?"

She sighed and reached out to cup his cheek. A weak smile broke on her luscious lips and she looked fragile in her nightgown and robe curled in on herself. "It's not the situation we have to fix. It's us. The affair. I'm not sure I can do this anymore."

He rocked back on the balls of his feet, his instant reaction to shout "don't leave me." But for once, he thought of someone other than himself and stayed silent.

She gave a wry laugh. "You're relieved. I can see it in your eyes. You're glad I've brought the subject up. You *do* want to end the affair. Is it because you want to marry?"

He took a moment to compose himself by rising and moving another chair closer to her. Then he walked to the side table in the corner and poured himself a glass of the brandy Rose kept there just for him. "I need a drink. Would you like one?"

She nodded.

After he'd handed her a tumbler of the fiery liquid, he sat back and closed his eyes, appreciating the warming alcohol as it dulled his feeling of impending loss. The image of Robert as he lay dying flashed into his head. The guilt and horror of it gave him the strength to do what was right.

He let out a deep breath and looked at her. She was so beautiful, even with red-rimmed eyes. "No." He finally answered her question. "I do not wish to marry."

Disbelief lifted her brows. "You will have to, sometime."

"No. No, I don't."

Now a frown raced across her perfect features. "But you need an heir."

"Do I?"

She took a sip of brandy, considering. "I suppose not. You have three younger brothers." She pondered further. "But why, Philip? Why would you not want a family and children of your own? You'd make a wonderful father. I've seen how good you are with Drake."

He swallowed his misery. "I have my reasons. They're personal." If he told her, she could tell Portia—and then the whole family would know and it would distress them all.

"Too personal to share with me?" She sat up straighter in her chair and her eyes narrowed. "Very well. At the beginning of our affair, I did say I never wanted to remarry. Now I want more—more than a few moments stolen here and there. And then I must consider Drake. He is getting older. Soon he'll be old enough to understand and be embarrassed by his mother's behavior. I can't carry on this way."

He knew she was right. He knew he was being unreasonable. Childish. "But we are wonderful together. I—I love what we have. Why ruin it?"

She sighed. "It's already ruined. We just haven't wanted to accept it. If I did not feel about you the way I do, then what we share would probably be enough. But I want more children, and you make it perfectly clear every time we make love that you do not wish me to have your child."

Philip went cold at the thought of Rose conceiving his child. If she were to become pregnant he would either have to marry her or leave her ruined. A legitimate heir was precisely the reason he could not get married. Thomas or his son had to inherit. Rose's response moments ago was enough to tell him she would not understand or accept his reasons.

Robert chose to buy a major's commission only because he

believed Philip had bought a commission. But Philip had had no money to buy a commission. Instead, through a favor, he'd been given a non-purchase commission as a lieutenant. Philip signed up only because he didn't want to have to tell his wiser, older brother that he'd just lost his year's allowance, and then some, in a daft and what turned out to be a very risky investment.

He'd joined the cavalry out of desperation at his own stupidity, and Robert had paid the price.

So he dangled his glass from his fingers and quirked an eyebrow. "If Robert were still here I could do as I please, and I'd marry you in a heartbeat."

Her mouth twisted in a parody of a smile, and his heart ached in his chest when even that faded. "It's my reputation, isn't it?" she murmured. "You would prefer a virginal Lady Abigail."

The very idea of Lady Abigail made him want to hurl his glass into the fireplace. "Don't be ridiculous."

Her beautiful face filled with anger. "Then tell me *why*. *Why* should we not marry?"

"I can tell you my reasons have nothing to do with you or your reputation." He softened his sharp tone. "It's not you, my sweet. It's just I am not ready to settle down." He grasped at straws, desperate for something she might believe. "The estate takes up so much of my time, and I want to make Robert proud of how I've stepped up to take his place. I never expected to be the earl"—that at least was not a lie—"and there is a lot to learn—and a lot at stake for my family if I fail."

For a moment she said nothing. Then words spilled out of her. "I wish Robert had never gone to war. No. I wish bloody Napoleon had never been born."

"As do I, every day." It was the absolute truth. "But we rarely get what we want, do we?"

"No." She slumped in her chair, blinking back tears. "When I was married to Roxborough I prayed every day that you would ride in and rescue me. It was silly. You didn't even notice me when I was a young girl."

Was that what she thought? He pressed a kiss to her palm. "I noticed you. Every man did. But at first I did not understand what your father was planning. When I did—that you were to marry a duke—I was sure your father would never allow you to marry the second son of a mere earl instead."

She shook her head. "You misunderstand. I prayed you wouldn't care about my father. I just wanted you to come and carry me away." She brushed her fingers over her eyes. "As I said, silly. The foolish dreams of a young, frightened girl." Now she met his gaze. "Just as foolish, it appears, as the dreams I've had for the past year."

"I thought you were just as averse to marriage as I."

"I did say that." She stared at him, head tilted as though she was trying to make sense of him. "It would appear I have changed my mind. Perhaps you will, too, one day."

"No." He had to crush that hope before it took root. "It won't happen."

"Because," she continued as if he hadn't spoken, "if I knew that one day you might change your mind, I could carry on. I could wait."

The wistful despair in her quiet voice made Philip want to weep. She loved him. It took all his willpower not to pull her into his arms and beg her to stay with him. But he could no more do that to her than he could pour out the truth about his vow. "No, my love. That would not be fair—fair to you. If you want to marry again, then you will have to choose another man."

He said no more, refusing to debate what he knew in his bones to be his only honorable course of action. Robert had sacrificed his life for Philip's. He'd sacrifice his for Thomas, for his family's sake.

Rose could hardly breathe through the pain. She'd ended affairs before, but they had rarely lasted more than a few months. She had certainly never fallen in love with any of her paramours—probably because she'd always loved Philip. Now she hoped none of those men had fallen in love with her. She would hate to know she'd caused any man this kind of pain.

Her love for Philip might have started as girlish infatuation with a fairy-tale hero, but over the years she'd fallen for the man—the foolish, pigheaded, arrogant, *stupid* man, sitting across from her.

Finally, he stirred. "Will you really not consider carrying on as we are?"

She studied his handsome features and was sorely tempted. But— "Will you really not consider making me your wife?"

"We don't need marriage. We could be together for the rest of our lives."

The idea was tempting. "You've forgotten Kirkwood. He won't let this go on for much longer. Drake is five—almost six. Kirkwood will expect me to act with more decorum. If I'm lucky he'll let me live quietly at my country estate. If not, he'll insist I find a husband."

She watched Philip's mouth firm and his grip almost shatter the glass he held.

When he stayed silent, she tried again. "If Kirkwood insists on my remarrying, I can't take that step with you in my bed and—even worse—in my heart. I need to be free to find a man who, if he doesn't actually love me, at least cares for me. And I need to be able to care for him. So, I am sorry, I have to refuse your offer."

For one foolish moment she thought he might drop to his knees again and declare that if Kirkwood forced her into marriage then *he* would marry her. But she wasn't a young girl anymore, needing to be saved. She was a grown woman, needing to be sought after because the man she loved could not live without her.

He tensed, and then nodded slowly. "Then we are really over."

"It would appear so."

She sounded calm and rational. She felt as though her world, her heart, was exploding into a million little pieces as she sat there. They were finished. But they'd still have to move in the same circles. She'd have to stand by and watch as he took other lovers—

"I cannot believe this is to be our last night together," he whispered, hoarse with pain. "Please, Rose. Let me make love to you. Just one more time."

She wanted to deny him, to scream that he was being an idiot. But she couldn't. She wanted one more night to cherish and lock into her memory against all the lonely days and nights ahead. She needed one more touch before he left.

She placed her glass on the table beside her and stood. Then she moved to him, pulling up her robe and nightgown as she lowered herself to straddle his thighs. Her breasts brushed against his evening jacket, and she rested her forehead against his.

Philip's arms tightened around her as if he'd never let her go. He began to kiss her face, her brows, her eyelids, as if he, too, was trying to imprint her into his memory. He nibbled at her cheek and chin, gently nipped her lower lip, drawing her mouth open to consume her tongue.

Her breasts as her breath shuddered out, and her fingers dug into his broad shoulders.

He released her briefly to fumble with the tie to her robe, then distracted her again by deepening his kiss, sweeping his tongue into her mouth with possessive ownership.

Frustrated, she had to break the kiss when Philip began to tug her robe from her shoulders. Although she didn't want to stop touching him, she wanted more. She helped him shed her robe, undo the little ties holding her nightgown closed, and bare her body. To his eyes, his hands, and—God Almighty—his talented mouth.

Philip kissed his way down her neck. Her nipples went hard, and as she arched back, his tongue played over them. He licked and suckled her skin, his exquisite mouth sliding along her body.

"You are the most beautiful woman I've ever known," he murmured.

Then he bit down, sucking hard on her breast just above her left nipple. He was marking her at the same time as he was saying goodbye. Marking her heart. Making it ache forever.

"You have too many clothes on," were the only words she could manage.

This time it was he who helped *her* as she struggled to remove his jacket, waistcoat, and shirt.

Finally, she touched skin, glided over sleek muscles. Flickering flame shadows glided over the sleek contours of his skin as if they, too, took joy in his shape. The corded steel of his chest, the hard strength of his sinewy arms, the rippling muscles of his abdomen—they stirred her even more. She memorized every inch of him.

He gazed into her eyes, his own dark and stormy with passion. They smoldered as she reached out and undid the fall of his breeches. Glinted as she grasped the rigid length of his arousal and stroked him.

He throbbed in her hand as he allowed her to play, to incite, and to worship. She leaned in, kissed him deeply, sucking on his tongue, a teasing taste of what she would soon do to the hard length she stroked in her hand.

Not once did he close his eyes as she pleasured him.

Soon she forgot he was watching, entranced by his masculine grace. The solid power of his hardness, so thick in her grasp, told her he was more than ready.

She pushed out of his hold and stood, allowing her nightgown and robe to float to the floor. Standing naked before the fire, the heat in her belly came not from the flames. It came from the longing look in her lover's eyes, his need, his desire.

Holding his heated gaze she lowered to her knees and let her fingers walk up his thighs. The muscles contracted under her touch. As her finger trailed up his erection, his rippled stomach muscles clenched. She leaned closer and blew on the tip of his erection as her hand wrapped around his hardened length.

A drop of moisture appeared at the tip, and she swept her tongue over the head of his penis, tasting him, thrilled as he responded to her touch.

A groan escaped his throat and deepened to a rumble in his chest as she took him fully into her mouth. She alternated between gentle and hard, first licking and then sucking. Giving pleasure. Stoking her own desire until she was lost in the pleasure and response.

Finally, he stopped her with a groan and gathered her back onto his lap. "I want you."

She brushed her cheek hungrily against his. "Darling, I want you, too."

He lifted her and, with his powerful hands at her waist, lowered her onto his pulsating member. She closed her eyes, reveling in the sensation of fullness as she took him into her body. As he filled her to the hilt.

Breathless, squirming, Rose ran her nails down the sculpted wall of his chest, exulting in the flex of his muscles as she began to ride him.

She grasped his nape, took his tongue in her mouth. Joined to each other in ravenous need, she was desperate for completion. And yet, this would be the last time they made love. She wanted to savor the joy, the joy of having him buried deep within her.

His warm fingers cupped her breast, kneaded it, tweaked her nipple.

Breaking the kiss, she leaned back, giving him space to tease and taste to his heart's content, using the unguarded moment to watch him from beneath half-closed eyelids.

His face was set and focused as he struggled to hold off his release until she'd found hers. But she wasn't ready. She wanted this to last all night.

Her thighs gripped his as she took control and began to slow things down. He tried to urge her on by lifting her, but she would not have it. Instead, she used his shoulders to push up and once more watch his face. His eyes had darkened to the color of ink. On a guttural groan he took the other nipple into his mouth and bit down none too gently.

The pain mixed with pleasure eroded her control and she jerked and writhed as if riding a bucking horse. Her moans of need blended with his ragged gasps and the sound became a sensual symphony, and the pleasure was almost unbearable.

She had to close her eyes. She had to— "Oh, God. Oh, Philip, that's it—"

Then she was flying, touching heaven, her body quaking under wave upon wave of mind-numbing pleasure of the Little Death.

She was so caught up in the exquisite moment she hardly registered Philip's roar of release, or that he held her hard down upon his lap as he surged up and up, spilling his seed deep within her.

Did he realize he'd done it? Was he even aware?

They were wrapped in each other's arms, too overcome with the power of their release to move, or focus on what had just happened.

Her heart still pounded—not from exertion, but from pain. This was her last night with the man who would always be her one true love. Her passion. Her joy. Her everything. Would he leave now? Was he already preparing his farewell?

As if Philip read her mind, his arms tightened around her.

"Not yet," he whispered, and then stood, lifting her into his arms, kissing her face, carrying her to her bed, and tumbling onto it. She could feel his erection hardening again deep within her and was thrilled that the night was not yet over. For a few more hours she could still pretend that morning would dawn bright and full of promise.

It would. But not for her. For her, all promise of happiness was gone.

Thank goodness she had Drake.

Chapter Six

It had been three days since Rose had ended her affair with Philip, and life had somehow just continued on as usual. It felt wrong. All she wanted to do was sit by the fire and mope, and yet the cards for balls and invitations for functions kept arriving.

She was about to enter the drawing room with a handful of correspondence when Drake and his nanny descended the stairs.

"Henry's got a boat to sail," he told her. "But I promise I won't get too dirty."

"Have fun. Be good for Nanny," she said and blew him a kiss as she waved goodbye.

In the drawing room she pried open the seal and pulled out a card. It was an invitation from Serena to a small dinner party in a few days' time.

That was the moment when she realized the enormity of the changes she was going to have to make. From now on if she went to a dinner party with all her friends, Philip would probably be there. It would be awkward with everyone watching them, and she couldn't bear to see pity in their eyes.

With a sigh she put the card aside and moved on to the next envelope.

How different losing Philip was to the usual ending of an affair. Typically, she would celebrate by making a list of eligible men and taking her time to assess those she might find intriguing and willing to share herself with.

This time, however, she could not bear to think of sharing any man's bed but Philip's.

At the end of half an hour she'd managed to get through quite a few of the envelopes and selected a number of social occasions to attend. They were mostly ones she thought Philip would be unlikely to have on his list.

A knock sounded on the door and Booth entered. "Lady Blackwood would like to know if you are at home, Your Grace."

"Of course." Rose had known this conversation was coming. "And I suspect we will need some tea"—and under her breath—"or something stronger."

A moment later Portia swept into the room with a big smile on her face, embraced Rose heartily with kisses to both cheeks, and then dropped onto the chaise longue opposite Rose.

"I called for some refreshments," Rose said as Portia spread out her skirts and patted them down. "Will you be visiting for long?"

Portia smiled, a rueful twist of her mouth. "It almost sounds as if you want to get rid of me already. Have you got a previous engagement?"

She felt her face heat. "No engagement. Drake has gone for a walk in the park with Henry and the nannies. I thought I would join them."

It was the first time she had lied to her friend, but she knew if Portia stayed for long the conversation would stray to her brother. Admitting to herself that their affair was over was painful enough. Putting it into actual words—making it public—hammered home the reality that she would never be a real part of Philip's life again.

"Oh." Portia glanced around the room. "When did they leave?"

"Not long ago," Rose said.

"We'll have at least an hour, then." Portia removed her hat and placed it on the seat beside her. "The boys will want to romp all afternoon. Did you receive Serena's invitation? Won't it be fabulous to all be together for a change? Well, I mean, without other company so we can talk freely. I don't think we've caught up on everyone's news properly since we stopped Victoria destroying our husbands and families."

Here it was, the moment Rose had been dreading. She took the coward's way out. "Yes, and it's such a shame I won't be able to attend. Kirkwood has requested a private supper that night. I'm disappointed at the clash but it can't be helped."

"Really?" Portia frowned. "I understood Serena checked the dates with us all before selecting that night."

"She did." Rose crossed the fingers of one hand behind her back and pointed to the stack of open envelopes with the other. "I've only received the news today."

"I hope nothing's wrong. It's not like Lord Kirkwood to require your attention on such short notice."

"I'm sure it will be nothing of note."

Portia clapped a hand to her forehead before declaring, "Gosh, I hope it's nothing to do with Philip's behavior at the ball the other night."

This time it was Rose's turn to frown. "What on earth would Kirkwood have to do with that?"

"You did mention that Lord Kirkwood had suggested you look at remarrying. I suspect he thought Philip might offer. In fact, *I'm* wondering why Philip hasn't. Perhaps Kirkwood took Philip's behavior as a signal he is not considering you for that position. Silly, I know. Philip would never marry the likes of Lady Abigail. He's in love with you."

She tried, she really did, but Portia's words brought forth the pain of loss, and her eyes instantly welled. Desperately, she tried to blink them back before Portia noticed. But her friend noticed everything and immediately pulled a face filled with horror.

"Oh, dear. Lord Kirkwood has not forbidden the match? Is that why both you and Philip were not at Lady Chillingworth's ball last night?"

She couldn't talk through the knot in her throat; she merely shook her head.

"Then what on earth is wrong?" Her eyes narrowed. "The other night my brother took off from that ball as if his breeches were on fire. I thought he'd come to beg your forgiveness."

Rose sniffed and took out a handkerchief. "He did apologize."

Portia sat back, satisfied. "So he should. It was badly done of him. Are you hiding because of his dance with Lady Abigail? Who cares what society thinks? I never have. Philip is yours and you know it, so no more hiding. I missed you at last night's entertainments. Philip attended but stayed only briefly."

Rose hesitated, not knowing what to reveal. She wanted to carry on as if nothing had changed, but she knew Portia would keep pushing and it would not take her long to guess why they were no longer seen together. She'd rather Portia learned the truth in private than in public. Rose might not be able to contain herself if that happened. Here in her drawing room, it didn't matter.

She took a deep breath and said, "Philip and I have agreed to end our affair. I just need some breathing room. That's all."

Portia's mouth dropped open. "*No.* Why?" She looked like she was ready for a fight. "Did you break my brother's heart? I thought you loved him. I thought you'd marry him when he proposed—"

"I would have." This time Rose didn't try to hide her pain. She simply let the tears roll down her face. "But he didn't propose. He doesn't want to marry me."

Portia was by her side in a flash. "I'll poke his eyes out. How dare he prefer a chit like Lady Abigail."

She shook Portia's arms off her. "No. He is not marrying Lady Abigail, either. He told me he has no wish to marry."

Portia's mouth dropped open and then closed, then opened

again. "Many men seem to think marriage a bore but I would have thought my brother had more sense. He will marry eventually. He needs an heir. I thought he'd marry you."

Rose wiped away her tears, feeling somewhat better for having gotten the situation off her chest. "He's adamant. He will not marry. You forget you have brothers—Thomas, it seems, is to inherit, with two more brothers in reserve."

When the maid arrived with the refreshments, Rose set about pouring the tea.

Portia waited until the servant had closed the door behind her. Then she stood, seized the whisky decanter from the sideboard, and poured a little into their cups. Seeing Rose's raised eyebrow, she grimaced. "I feel a little fortification is called for."

Rose couldn't argue.

Once more settled in her seat, Portia sipped her tea, then sighed. "I don't know what to say, Rose. I'm so sorry. Just wait until I see my brother. Of course he'll have to marry."

"No." The last thing she needed was Portia scolding Philip. "Please don't say anything. He has his reasons. I hope one day he'll wake up and realize he's been a fool. I only hope that day is not too late for me." For *them*.

"Well, it's not going to be." Portia's cheeks blazed with crimson. "Just wait until I tell Mother. She'll have something to say to him about his duty to the earldom."

Dear God. That was the last thing she or Philip needed. "Don't do that. I do not wish to betray his confidences." What was said between them was private.

Portia's eyes narrowed suddenly. "What do you mean you hope Philip's coming to his senses isn't too late for you? You do think Kirkwood will want you to remarry?"

She shrugged and sipped her whisky-laced tea. It was the first time since Philip left that she'd felt warm. "I suspect he'll want me to change my ways for Drake's sake if nothing else. I'm only six and twenty. I like intimacy. I enjoy sex. If I remain a widow, it will mean a lonely life."

Portia had lost her angry flush. Now her cheeks went pink. "I enjoy bed sport, too, but only with Grayson. I can't imagine having sex with any other man."

Rose didn't take offense. "I didn't have the luxury of marrying where my heart led so I suspect our experiences in the boudoir have been quite different. I discovered pleasure only after my husband died."

"Does Philip know Lord Kirkwood might insist you remarry?"

She smiled at her friend. "You are not going to let this go, are you? Yes, Philip knows. Lord Kirkwood is a kind man, so I hope he won't force the issue. But he is also very fond of Drake, and soon I suspect he'll tell me to send Drake off to school. Then I will be truly alone."

She blinked back the sting of tears at the thought of seeing her son for only a few months a year. "I can't live my life stuck in the wilds of Cornwall on my own. I want a man in my life. I would like more children. If Kirkwood is concerned about the Deverill name he'll make a push to see that I remarry. He won't compel me to accept a particular man, but he'll expect me to select someone."

Portia's face took on her thinking look. After a few moments of silence and sipping fortified tea, she said, "I can't believe Philip would let you marry someone else. Oh! That's it." She leaned forward in her chair and excitedly placed her teacup on the table with a rattle. "We'll put it about that the Wicked Widow is husband-hunting. I know my brother. I know he loves you. Whatever nonsense is stopping him from proposing, his possessive jealousy will never allow you to marry anyone but him."

But Rose was not so sure. Would the idea of her marrying another man bring Philip to his senses? She knew he cared for her. They were more than compatible in bed—they were combustible. Dared she hope? "He was very determined not to marry."

Portia waved Philip's determination away. "I think I know my own brother. Of course he wants to marry. He loves you. He loves children. There is something more afoot here, I can feel it. You have to make him jealous."

Rose laughed. Could she make him as jealous of another man as she'd been of Lady Abigail? She'd wanted to slap the smile off that perfect, simpering face. "It seems such a childish notion."

Portia scowled. "So you are simply going to give up? I thought you loved him."

"I do," she protested vigorously. "But sometimes love is not enough."

Portia waved that idea away, too. "Love is always enough. More than enough. Love is all that matters."

Rose's heart sank. "Then he does not love me. If he did, he wouldn't have left my bed knowing I might have to marry another."

"Oh, my dear girl." Portia's smile was that of a cunning fox. "*Knowing* and *witnessing* are two very different things. You should have seen Grayson's reaction when he thought I was seriously considering Maitland as a marriage prospect. A rival tends to crystalize a man's view on love very quickly."

Perhaps it was the large amount of whisky in the tea but suddenly Rose's life no longer felt like it was over. Hope—something she'd lost—began to bloom inside her. She put down her teacup and picked up Serena's invitation. "Bugger your brother. I'll attend Serena's dinner *and* bring a charming dinner guest."

Portia's smile in response was just as mischievous. "I shall make sure Philip is there. I'll say Grayson has information on a new market for the Flagstaff wool. He'll be interested in that. And I'll say you are unable to attend. After all,"—she shrugged—"what's a lie between siblings?"

Rose laughed. "You are wicked."

Portia's smile dimmed. "I just want you both to be happy. Why can't you be happy together? I love you both so much."

Emotion welled up in her. "I love you, too."

Portia blinked and glanced over to where her half-full cup sat, contents gently steaming. "If I drink any more tea I won't be able to walk with you to the park, and I want to see that handsome boy of yours."

Rose was more worried about the effects of the whisky. "Thank you, Portia. I don't know if our plan will work but you're right about one thing. It's better than doing nothing." She got to her feet and walked to her friend, pulling her up to stand beside her. "Suddenly I find it's a beautiful day and, after our indulgence, I need some fresh air." She handed Portia her hat. "Shall we?"

"Absolutely, dear girl. And while we walk we shall make up a list of the most desirable single men in London at the moment."

Rose laughed. "I think I'm going to enjoy this experiment a tad more than poor Philip," she called over her shoulder as she went to organize her coat, hat, and gloves.

Portia gave a most unladylike *humph*. "Don't you dare feel sorry for my brother. He's an idiot, and idiots deserve all they get."

Which was true. But as Rose prepared for their outing, she prayed that Philip didn't turn out to be a *stubborn* idiot.

Philip Flagstaff, you are an idiot.

He knew he should not have had that extra bottle of brandy, but he'd dined with Arend and Isobel and they were so damned happy. Watching them together, excited at the approaching birth of their first child, he'd been tempted to leave them to their excitement, race to Rose, tell her he'd made a mistake, and beg her to marry him.

But he hadn't. The last thing he remembered was Arend shoving him—none too gently—into his carriage. He'd have to send a huge bunch of flowers to Isobel as an apology for such boorish behavior.

And he'd lied to them. When Isobel had wanted to know where Rose was he'd told her she was tired and wanted a night in. Neither of them believed him.

Soon his friends would start asking why they were no longer seen together. Why he let a woman like Rose slip away.

Slowly, he sat up and his head began to pound as if a rampaging bull was running through it.

Scrubbing a hand over his face, he reached for the decanter by his bed. His tongue stuck to the roof of his mouth, as dry as stable straw. He took a long slug of spirits, swirled it round his mouth, and then spat it into the privy basin.

His friends would not be his only problem. His mother would take the end of his affair with Rose as a declaration that he was ready to take a wife. How the hell would he stop her parading young debutantes in front of him?

His worst problem, however, would be Portia. His sister would be furious, and she of all of them was unlikely to be fobbed off with high-sounding fustian. She knew how he felt about Rose.

Cursing his sister, his headache, and his life in general, Philip pushed back the covers and rang for his valet. He needed a bath before he escaped to his club for the afternoon. The following week he was expected at Serena's for dinner and he'd better have a plausible reason for the break with Rose by then. At least Rose would not be attending—a prior engagement with Lord Kirkwood concerning Drake's schooling.

Another blow for Rose. Drake was her life, and when Kirkwood took the boy off to school she'd be heartbroken. He wished he could be there to help her through it. But there was nothing now that he could do. Their relationship was over.

An hour later, bathed, groomed, and dressed, Philip spent an hour in his study to clear up correspondence before heading for the club. It was safe enough. His mother was out shopping, and at that time of day Portia would be at home with Jackson, his nine-month-old nephew. He loved the boy even though he reminded him so painfully of Robert. The child had inherited Robert's and Portia's eyes and mouth.

So it was a surprise when, not long after he'd settled in, Portia strode into his study without being announced and without knocking.

"My lord." Merton peered over Portia's shoulder. "Lady Blackwood has come to call."

"I see that," he said. "Thank you, Merton." He waited for his amused butler to close the door before he frowned at Portia. "Your manners have not improved as you have aged."

"Are you calling me old, brother dear?" She took a seat. "Because let me tell you, I have a great number of names I'd like to call *you*. For example." She began counting off on her fingers. "One, stupid. Two, idiot—"

"I hate to be pedantic but they mean the same thing."

"Three, fool." She sighed and her little fists clenched in her lap. "*Oooh,* I'm so angry with you. How could you hurt Rose by telling her such a whisker? Of course you'll marry. You're the earl, for goodness' sake. There's such a thing as responsibility to the name and the title."

His humor fled and he ran a frustrated hand through his hair. Goddamn interfering sisters. Of course Portia would rise to the defense of her friend. But he shouldn't have to explain himself to anyone. "My activities are none of your business. Please just leave it alone." He made his tone cold and hard. "As head of this household I deserve the right to some privacy. I never once poked my nose into your affairs."

"I didn't have affairs."

"Not those sorts of affairs," he conceded. "But I did not try and meddle in your cider business. I did not try to stop you doing what you wished. What makes you think you have the right to interfere in mine?"

Portia drooped in her chair, all the fight gone out of her. "Because since Robert died and you became the earl, I've never seen you as happy as when you're with Rose." She gazed pleadingly at him. "I just want you to be happy, Philip. Rose makes you happy."

He gave her a wan smile. "I love that you care but please respect my—and Rose's—privacy. What is done has been done for the best, and I don't intend to explain my actions to you or anyone. If you love me, then you'll let me be."

"But you're my brother." Her mouth trembled. "And she's my best friend. I was so hoping you'd propose." She sniffed. "Now it's going to be awkward. But I am *not* avoiding her at functions just because you might be there."

God, no. He'd hate that. "I do not expect you to. We have parted friends and I have no intention of cutting Rose, either. We are adults, are we not?"

Portia nodded and perked up. "Speaking of functions, there's a dinner soon at Serena's. Grayson said to tell you he has learned of a new wool market and will share the details then."

Portia had stopped scolding far too quickly. Something was up. "Will Rose be there?"

"Oh, I don't think so. She told me an old beau had come to town and she thought it would be too awkward for everyone. She did not wish to ruin Serena's evening."

An old *beau*? His hackles lifted although he had no right to be annoyed. "I thought she had an engagement with Kirkwood." She might have mourned their relationship for a decent period before looking for another lover. Or had Kirkwood put pressure on her now that he had not come up to scratch?

Damn it all. Why was life so complicated?

"She does, but it won't take all evening. Her beau . . . What's his name?" She tapped her fingers as she thought. "Yes, that's right. Lord Tremain. It's Viscount Tremain."

The stirring of the green-eyed monster in his belly took him by surprise. He had to work to keep his fists relaxed, to keep his jaw from clenching his teeth together. He knew all about Viscount Tremain. Tremain was the man who'd introduced Rose to passion.

"He's in London for the Season." Portia prattled on. "Rumor is he's looking for a wife."

Damn the man to hell and back. But there was no way he'd let his conniving little sister know how much the idea of Rose with

Tremain hurt. "Then I wish him every success. Perhaps he'll ask Rose. She now appears to be keen to remarry."

Portia did not rise to his bait. Instead, she looked sad. "Perhaps he should. She would make a wonderful wife for any man—especially a man who is brave enough to declare his true feelings." With that, Portia rose. "Then I shall see you at Serena's in a few days—and I promise I'll ensure the ladies do not ask you too many awkward questions. However, I should warn you that you won't be very popular with the wives of the Libertine Scholars."

When she'd left the room and shut the door behind her, he thumped his forehead on the desk a few times. Perhaps he should head back to Devon until this died away—but the image of Tremain in Rose's bed put paid to that idea.

He stood and moved to look out the window. Giving up Rose was the hardest thing he'd ever had to do. No, the second hardest. Burying Robert had been harder.

Robert. He had to keep the reason why he would never marry in focus. He was Cumberland. As the earl, his duty was to husband and increase the estate, and then hand it over to his heir in the best condition possible. His duty was to provide for his family. There was no place in his duty for selfish happiness. Not when his selfish desires and actions had such disastrous results.

While his heart wanted to steal Rose away, to keep her for himself, he could not in all conscience do so.

He pulled out his pocket watch. His mother would be home soon. He'd be wise to make himself scarce and leave for his club before she arrived. He'd have bet the best stallion in his stable that if Portia knew about the end of his affair, so would his mother.

As soon as he walked into the lounge at the club and saw Grayson sitting with Wyndall Herbert, Earl of Easterside—Rose's elder brother—he sighed. Finding the two of them together was not a coincidence. They were hardly good friends.

Christ, he did not need this.

As he wove through the room to join them, he noticed many of his friends and acquaintances casting varying looks of pity and humor his way. It would appear news of the incident with Lady Abigail and his appearance alone at Lady Chillingworth's ball had set tongues wagging.

"Blackwood." He nodded to Grayson as he came up. "Easterside. Unusual to see you both here. I hope you're well."

"Take a seat, Cumberland," was Wyndall's terse response.

Grayson made to stand. "Perhaps I should leave you to talk in private."

"Stay," Wyndall demanded. "I may need a second."

"Bloody hell." Philip dropped into a chair and signaled to a servant to bring him a drink. "There is no need for that, Easterside."

"I agree," Grayson said. "Cumberland here is a crack shot."

Wyndall ignored him. "That's not the point. Most of society knows my feelings about my wayward sister, but I thought she had finally settled down. Perhaps was even considering an offer from you. Imagine my horror when I hear instead that not only did you end your connection but did it in such a way as to humiliate her in front of the *ton*. I should call you out for that alone."

By the time he'd finished his tirade, Wyndall was shaking with rage.

Philip kept his tone polite and careful. "I have already apologized to Her Grace for what happened at the ball—which was a result of a lack of attention on my part, and for which I deserve you to plant me a facer. But you are quite wrong that it was my decision to end the connection. I would not have done so. It was Rose's choice. I'm simply abiding by the lady's decision."

That took the wind out of Wyndall's sails. He was silent for a moment. "My apologies. It seems my sister is up to her old tricks. When the devil is Kirkwood going to stop letting her bamboozle him and make her see sense? Why have you not offered marriage? You need an heir and you are of age."

Again his body reacted to the thought of Rose in another man's arms, and his heart beat faster. "No one should be forced to marry when it's not necessary. I am not ready."

"You may have no need of marriage yet, but Rose has cultivated a reputation and I see nothing admirable regarding her behavior. She should think of the boy, of our family." Wyndall glanced at Grayson, then back to Philip. "Your sister was a bit wild, but at least she had the sense to settle down with a fine man."

Grayson drew himself up, eyes flashing. "Keep my wife out of this, if you please."

"Funny," Philip said, "I was about to say the same thing to you. Portia paid me a visit about an hour ago."

"Did she?" Grayson grimaced. "What did you expect when you upset her best friend?"

He could hardly refute that.

Wyndall stood. "Well, I've said my piece. Thank you for your candor. I shall have a word with Kirkwood. It's about time my sister changed her ways. The next man she chooses will be a husband. Good day, gentlemen."

With that, Wyndall took his leave.

When he was gone, Philip let out a breath he didn't even know he was holding.

"Not quite the truth, was it?"

Philip glanced over at Grayson. "I did offer to continue our affair."

"But she was prepared to marry, and marry you. That's quite a concession from the woman who for over five years has refused all offers." Grayson rolled his brandy balloon thoughtfully between his fingers. "I thought you'd jump at the chance."

"Did you?" He grimaced at his friend's raised eyebrow. "I'm not the only man to want to avoid the parson's mousetrap. When we rescued Portia from Egypt you swore black-and-blue she was not the woman for you."

Grayson grinned. "Touché. You'll know when you know. But a word of warning, my friend. Be careful that you don't wake up one day and find you have let the most important person in your life slip away. Women like your sister and Rose, have many options."

"Like Tremain?" He hadn't meant to say the name, but Grayson knew everyone in the city. "Did you know Tremain is back in London?"

Grayson's brows jerked up and almost immediately dipped into a glower. "No. I didn't. I'm amazed he has the balls to show his face. The word is he's gambled away everything his father left him and was chased out of France because of his debts. I suspect he's only here because he's on the lookout for a wealthy wife."

So did Philip. "I thought you'd have heard. It was Portia who told me he was back and paying court to Rose. And, what's more, she took a great deal of pleasure in telling me."

Grayson cursed under his breath. "I know what she's up to. She did this to me with Maitland. And it bloody worked. I wanted to beat my oldest friend black-and-blue."

Philip understood the sentiment. "I'd have no problem beating Tremain black-and-blue for what he did to Lady Claire all those years ago. If he tries to destroy Rose, I'll—"

"What?" Grayson growled. "You'll do what? She is no longer yours to defend."

"She'll *always* be mine to defend."

At Grayson's look of surprise he wished he could take the words back even though they were absolutely true.

"Is that right?" Grayson glanced over at the mantel clock. "I'm due home. But before I go, let me say this. I'd never tell a man whom he should marry, but from your last statement it's clear you still have deep feelings for Rose. So why not offer for her? I doubt she'll refuse you."

Was everyone deaf? "As I keep saying, I have my reasons."

Grayson studied him and lowered his voice. "Are you ill, Philip? If you are, you know you can talk to me."

Not unless being sick with guilt counted as illness. "No. Not that I am aware of anyway. I'm just not ready to take a wife—and I'm not sure I ever will be."

"Rubbish," Grayson said. "If you feel this way, then perhaps Rose is not the woman for you. When you find the right woman, you'll fight to your dying breath to make her yours."

Grayson shoved to his feet and slapped Philip's shoulder as he made to leave. "Ah, well. If you don't feel that way about Rose, then you did the honorable thing by letting her go. But I agree. We should watch Tremain. Rose's widow's portion is significant. Not that I imagine Kirkwood would allow such a match. Have a pleasant evening." And with a nod he left the room.

Philip hadn't considered approaching Kirkwood. Of course he'd be a good ally against Tremain if the rogue was a fortune-hunter. He made a note to call on the older man soon.

But not tonight. As a scrupulous older brother, he had a card game to attend with Maxwell and his friends. His brother's luck with the cards was nothing short of abysmal and he'd begged Philip for some pointers. He'd agreed, but it was, Philip knew, a waste of his time. Maxwell had never liked to back down from a challenge, and the most important lesson a successful gambler learned early was to know when to fold.

Chapter Seven

It was, Rose decided, going to be a very long evening. The Hollanders' ball was in full swing. The music grated on her ears. The inane conversations around her chafed at her spirit.

And as for Conrad, Viscount Tremain . . .

"Rose," he said in a voice that was far too loud, "you are by far the most beautiful woman here, my dear, no matter that you are no longer in your first flush of youth."

Rose gritted her teeth. "Why, thank you, Conrad."

The wretched man had just praised and insulted her in the same breath. Really, he was beginning to wear on her patience.

She wondered at her younger self's naivety. Yes, he *was* still incredibly handsome, but his looks weren't the only thing that had attracted her after Roxborough's death. At one-and-twenty, she had succumbed to Tremain's lures because he was the first man to be kind to her. Or that was what she had thought at the time. Looking back, she understood it wasn't kindness that had driven him, but ego. He wanted to be the first to seduce the young widow.

Now she saw how—at every window or mirror they passed—Tremain would glance at himself in their surface, trying to catch his reflection. To make sure his dark hair was groomed to perfection, that the latest French fashions and his breeches showed off trim calves and strong thighs to best advantage. That he was tall enough to be imposing, that his jacket fit without a wrinkle.

His face was classical Greek, with a long nose over full lips and high cheekbones. Jet-black lashes set off the blue of his eyes.

But when Rose looked closely into those eyes she saw only conceit. He knew how good he looked. He expected to be worshipped and adored. How had she never noticed before how vain he was?

Now Rose had learned that Philip would not be putting in an appearance. It was all too much. Her head ached and she just wanted to go home. Drake had a cough and she was worried.

She smiled, willing herself to appear calm and collected. "If you don't mind, Conrad, I'm in need of a private chat with Lady Jersey. Would you be kind and dance with one of the young ladies who is not as popular this evening?"

Outraged conceit lifted his chin in a haughty refusal. "I—they are—"

"You're the most handsome man here. Everyone will think very highly of such kindness."

"Of course." He'd grasped the prospect of looking good in the *ton*'s eye very quickly. "I shall find you later to escort you in to supper."

"Of course. Thank you."

Relieved, she quickly made her way through the throng, trying to ignore the rumbles and murmurs.

The evening was heading toward a total disaster. While Portia's idea of allowing a select few gossips to learn that the Wicked Widow was looking for a husband held merit, Rose's encouragement of Tremain had been shortsighted. The man was a bore. In a few more minutes—and before the next set ended and Tremain returned—she would plead a headache, call for her carriage, and go home.

The doors to the terrace stood open, allowing the chill

evening air to cool the heated rooms. To get away from Tremain, she'd risk the cold outside to clear her head. She pulled her wrap tightly around her shoulders, stepped out onto the dimly lit terrace—and into the fragrance of cheroot smoke. Philip liked to smoke and she missed the aroma scenting the air of her home already.

"I had not realized that ending our affair would cause such a stir."

Philip. She whirled to face him as he stepped out of the gloom. "I'm sorry. I didn't realize you were out here."

He moved close and ran his finger down her cheek, gazing silently at her as she stood there, mesmerized. "You are the most beautiful woman I've ever known."

She licked her lips. His eyes flared with heat. "Beauty fades."

"In my eyes yours never will."

"You shouldn't say such things." She didn't want the rush of emotions engendered by the seductive tone of his voice. "Why are you doing this to me?"

He stepped back. "I miss you."

She missed him, too—so very much it hurt. "Do you?"

"Very much. Won't you reconsider my offer?"

Temptation was a living, breathing thing inside her. *Be strong. Be strong.* "Won't you reconsider mine?"

Such longing raced over his handsome features. "If only I could."

"You could if you chose." They both knew it was the truth. "You're choosing not to."

His face settled into a cool mask. "And you're here with Tremain. Why Tremain of all men?"

"He's an old friend."

"Old lover."

"A long time ago." Was there a flash of jealousy in his voice? "Now only a friend."

"One who needs to marry."

Not jealousy but definitely something. "Perhaps he wants to marry."

"Wants?" Philip threw back his head and laughed. "Hardly. He's in dun territory. He was thrown out of France because of his gambling debts. Even your brother has despaired of him."

Rose wished she could slap him for his heartlessness. As for Tremain . . . She fumed at the man's colossal ego. No wonder he was pleased that she was considering a second marriage. Did he really think he stood a chance with her? She'd take care to nip that delusion in the bud immediately.

"Well," she said as carelessly as she could manage, "at least something good has come from tonight. Thank you for the warning. I can cross a second man off my list of potential husbands. However"— she eyed him thoughtfully—"if you plan to catalog the flaws of every man I happen to have on my arm in the future I shall find you extremely tedious." A muscle worked in his jaw. "If women did not overlook a few faults in a man, none would ever take a husband."

"So you really do mean to marry."

Had he doubted it? "I thought I made my intentions clear. As clear as you made yours."

He moved closer. "Perhaps I can make you change *your* mind." The heat from his body warmed her against the chill of the November night. "I know your body as well as I know my own. You still desire me."

As he spoke his mouth came closer, closer.

She could have put her hand up to stop him, but she was weak. She closed her eyes to ease the headache now pounding behind them, and breathed in his scent as his lips pressed gently, deliciously, to hers. When she opened for him, denying him nothing, she was pulled into strong arms and held against a hard body as his mouth consumed her.

Any other man and she would have had the strength to push him away, to let go, to move on with her life. But Philip? Philip owned her heart, and her heart was not willing to let him walk away.

The kiss deepened. The cold brick of the wall pressed into her back as he moved into her, as his hands swept down her body, cupping her breasts, and tweaking her hardened nipples. She moaned into his mouth. His hand slid farther down, over her hip, gathering up her skirts.

When he ran his long fingers up her bare thigh above her gartered stockings she widened her stance to give him better access to the part of her that was wet and throbbing with need.

But just as she was about to beg for his touch, he withdrew his hand. Let her skirts fall. Broke the kiss. Stepped back.

She looked around, wildly, thinking he'd stopped because he heard someone approaching. But they were alone in the cold night air. "Why did you stop?"

"Because I've proved my point."

She didn't understand. "I beg your pardon."

"And so you should." He looked into her eyes, jaw tight. "I could have taken you here, up against this wall, and you would not have cared who might have walked out and seen us. How can you think of marrying another when it is my body you crave, my bed you belong in?"

She wanted to slap him—hard. But he spoke the truth. Until she'd purged him from her life, she couldn't move on. Her bluff had been well and truly called.

"You knew."

His bared teeth gleamed white in the dimness. "Portia is a terrible conspirator. She came to visit me, and then Grayson mentioned something and I came to a conclusion. This kiss just clarified it. I won't change my mind about marriage, ever. I will continue our affair if that is what you choose."

The sadness in his smile almost broke her. "I miss you, Rose. I always will. If you decide to remarry, it might kill me but it will not change my mind."

The finality in his words told her she'd lost, and in that moment her heart broke.

She did not wish to spend the rest of her life alone or as some man's mistress. She wanted a husband, a family. She wanted more children—legitimate, acknowledged, and loved.

"I can see your answer in your face," Philip said. He sounded quiet. Sad. "I will not bother you again, my darling. I shall do my best to avoid engagements you might attend until I return to Devon for Christmas."

She wanted to wail, to scream that this couldn't be the end. She closed her eyes to fight the pain and when she opened them he was gone.

Her head pounded and a wave of nausea swept over her. She wanted to go home. Home to Cornwall. Soon it would be Christmas and they always spent Christmas there. She would leave London early on the excuse she wanted to get Drake away from London for the sake of his health.

She would try and make the celebration a happy one for her son.

He was what mattered most.

The next morning Rose received a missive from Lord Kirkwood, asking after Drake and saying he would call on them that afternoon. He must have heard about the boy's cough. She replied that she would be delighted to see him.

Drake still had a cough and was excused from lessons with his tutor. However, he must have been feeling better because he got annoyed, as bored little boys do when they are told they cannot go to the park or to visit friends.

So after breakfast Rose took him into the drawing room with her. There they snuggled down before the fire while she read part of his favorite story, *Robinson Crusoe*. Drake had a vivid imagination and was soon romping around the room, wanting to build a fort to keep out marauding cannibals. Entering into the spirit of the game, Rose helped him pull some of the chairs together and drape a few throws from the window seat over them to create a defensive structure.

"When is Lord Cumberland coming to pay a call?" Drake wanted to know as they huddled together, cocooned in their fort. "I have not seen him since he took Henry and me to the museum. He said one day we should ride together in the park. I want to ride a real horse. Penny's only a pony."

Oh, Lord. Rose had forgotten it was not only she who would miss Philip. "Lord Cumberland has had to return to Devon, Drake. But he asked me to give you a big hug and a tickle. Like this."

As her fingers found his stomach, Drake burst into laughter, squiggling in her arms. "Stop! Oh, stop, Mother."

She let him be.

He rolled over onto his side. "When will I next see him? Could we not stop at Devon before we go to Cornwall?"

This was so unfair. "I don't think so, my sweet boy. We have to get home in time for Christmas. We don't want to make that cough of yours worse."

"I haven't coughed all morning," he said proudly.

He was right, and she pressed a kiss to his forehead. "Lord Kirkwood is coming to call this afternoon. We cannot greet him in a fort. Let's tidy up before we shock him."

Drake sighed, but crawled out from under the throws. "I like Lord Kirkwood, Mother, but not as much as Lord Cumberland. Henry said Lord Cumberland might become my father. I think I would like that. I didn't want to share you with anyone, but Lord Kirkwood explained I'm to go to Eton next September and I don't want you to be alone."

Bless him. "I won't be alone." She'd only be lonely. "I have many, many friends, and I will be waiting each week for your letters."

"But are you going to marry Lord Cumberland?"

She didn't want to dash his hopes. Not yet. "A lady has to wait until she is asked."

Drake gave a little hop of excitement. "That's easily fixed. I shall ask my tutor to help me write to Lord Cumberland and I'll suggest he ask you. He would be lucky to have you as his wife and he would also have me to look after, too. I know he's a sensible man."

Heart aching with love and tenderness and loss, it was all Rose could do to smile. "Do you?"

"Of course." Drake took the folded throws she gave him and walked quickly to place them back on the window seat. "He prefers fishing and hunting to working in his study. He told me so himself."

"I see." She smiled at her son's logic. "One day you will have to spend a great deal of time working in your study."

Drake smiled. "But not yet. Lord Cumberland said I have to learn how to be a boy first." His brow furrowed. "I thought that funny because I *am* a boy. I don't need to learn to be one."

She ruffled his hair, hardly able to argue with that reasoning. "Then let us finish tidying this up, my *boy*"—his cheeky grin made her laugh—"and then we'll see if Cook will give us scones and tea."

An hour later she was wiping jam from Drake's sticky hands when Lord Kirkwood was announced.

"How are you, Your Grace?" Kirkwood bowed to Drake. "I hear you have been under the weather. You look fighting fit to me."

Drake returned the bow. "I feel perfectly fine, sir, thank you. But Mother worries about me. She fusses."

Kirkwood smiled and relaxed. "That is what mothers do, my boy, they fuss. And do you know what? We let them."

"Yes, sir," Drake said and flashed a conspiratorial smile at Rose.

She laughed. "Then I shall stop fussing and say I think it's time you went upstairs and read the book Mr. Magnus suggested —as you are feeling so much better. Lord Kirkwood and I have much to discuss."

"Yes, Mother." Drake's smile faded as he started out of the room. When he reached the door he turned back. "I will practice my letters by writing Lord Cumberland that note we discussed."

"Of course." She could hardly tell him not to do so in front of Kirkwood. She'd just have to intercept it before it was sent. "What a grand idea."

Once Drake had left them and Booth had served Kirkwood's requested brandy, they chatted politely for a few minutes. She asked after his health, how his son, Francis was, and the ease of his journey. He inquired after *her* health and her plans for the festive season. When the social niceties had been observed Kirkwood finally came to the point.

"My dear, I have heard that you and Lord Cumberland have parted ways. To say I was surprised would be an understatement. I really thought you'd met a man who could make you settle down and remarry."

What could she say? That she had met the right man?

But Kirkwood did not wait for her reply. "This cannot go on, Rose. I understood your need to have some freedom, but I believed you and Cumberland had an understanding. It's obvious the man loves you. I was waiting for him to propose. And yet you have turned him away."

It took all of Rose's self-control to speak calmly. "I would have married Philip if he'd asked, my lord, but he does not wish to marry me."

Disbelief flashed across Kirkwood's face. "Then the man's a fool if he thinks someone like Lady Abigail would make a better wife than you. I did warn you, however, that your reputation might cause a problem in finding a suitable match."

Of course Kirkwood would assume it was her reputation that Philip found wanting.

"You misunderstand, sir," she said. "Lord Cumberland does not wish to marry, but I do. That disagreement was the cause for our parting."

The brandy snifter stopped in its journey to Kirkwood's lips. "What?"

"Seeing him stand up with Lady Abigail confirmed my feelings for him. Unfortunately, his lordship seems to have an aversion to marriage."

"Don't be ridiculous," Kirkwood spluttered. "An earl does not have the freedom to avoid marriage. It is his obligation to provide an heir. His duty." He shook his head. "No, no. There must be another reason."

She agreed. But what could it be?

"It will be your reputation." Kirkwood seemed determined for Philip's rejection to be her fault. "Of course he wouldn't come out and say so. It's time to do something about it."

"Excuse me?" About what?

Kirkwood didn't seem to have heard her icy question. "Your behavior has cost you Cumberland. That's too bad, but not the end of the world. Now we must put our heads together and come up with a list of suitable men willing to overlook your past. Drake will start at Eton next September. I want you married by then."

"No." Her jaw ached as she fought not to give way to her anger at his callous arranging of her life. Her breakup with Philip had nothing to do with her reputation and everything to do with a man who had a separate agenda.

"I beg your pardon?" Kirkwood stared at her.

"While I will willingly take your advice regarding gentlemen I might find suitable, I shall certainly not be bullied into a second marriage or given a time limit on my freedom to choose him myself. And your assumption that Cumberland needs to provide an heir for the earldom is incorrect. When I told him I had changed my mind, that I would like to remarry and have more children, he said it wouldn't be with him as he has younger brothers and no need or desire to produce another heir. It appears he stayed with me because of my well-known desire to remain as I am."

God, even the memory of that conversation hurt.

But if she was hurt, Kirkwood was speechless. Finally, after he'd sat in silence for several moments, Kirkwood said, slowly, "What Cumberland says is true. Thomas is a fine young man—very much like Robert both in looks and personality. Robert had a strategic mind whereas Philip always seemed to muddle through in a clumsy way. I always said it was a damn shame that Robert didn't let the bayonet find its intended target."

Rose's fingers clenched into fists in her lap. "That is a dreadful thing to say." But fury with Kirkwood warred with a growing realization in her mind. Was Philip's obsession all to do with Robert? She knew he blamed himself for Robert's death. Was this some form of atonement? Did Philip think Thomas more deserving than he? "Philip has his faults, but I love him."

Kirkwood blinked and seemed to realize he'd spoken more honestly than he ought. "I'm sorry, Rose. My observation was unkind. Perhaps Philip's actions are his way of honorably ensuring the title and estates pass to Thomas. I must say I admire him more if this is so."

"Why?" Men were absolutely incomprehensible. "Why admire him? He's wasting his life—a life Robert died protecting."

"Because Philip is correct." Kirkwood gazed down into his brandy. "Robert would never have taken a commission if Philip had not enlisted—and Philip had no choice but to go into the army. His last investment came to grief and he lost everything Robert had given him. I hope he's learned caution since then, or God knows what state the Flagstaff finances will be in when—if—Thomas does inherit." Kirkwood considered her. "At least his refusal to marry you proves he wasn't after your money."

Was that cold comfort really supposed to make her feel better? It didn't. Her body hummed under angry tension. *Philip, Philip, Philip.* She was more disappointed in him now than when she'd thought he simply disliked marriage. Imagine throwing what they had away because of Robert. It hurt more to know he put some stupid version of honor ahead of her.

But at least she now had ammunition to fight with. "So you

really think he would choose not to have a family just so Thomas or Thomas's future son can inherit?"

Kirkwood considered for a moment. "If Philip loved his brother, yes. He might not be of Robert's ilk, but he had enough sense of honor not to go cap in hand to Robert for money to bail him out when his investments failed. He enlisted instead. If I were in Philip's position, and felt responsible for my brother's death, I might be inclined to do the same thing."

Rose had not been privy to the knowledge that Philip had made a bad investment and lost everything before he enlisted. She'd never stopped to think about why he'd gone to war. She'd assumed it was because he felt it his duty to fight Napoleon.

How would *she* feel if her actions got Portia, or someone she loved injured or killed? She'd never forgive herself—

Oh! She clapped her hand over her mouth. *Oh, Philip! He must be eaten up with guilt.* She wanted to call for her carriage and race off to console him. But what good would that do?

"You are thinking," Kirkwood said, "about how you can make him change his mind. Women struggle to understand a man's code of honor, so let me just say this: Asking a man to choose between his honor and his love is like asking him which arm he wants removed. The answer is neither."

"So I should just give up?" She was full of grief and fury at the same time. "I don't believe that. I want to help him. He deserves to be happy. *I* deserve to be happy. Philip makes me happy." When he wasn't making her miserable. "Living with this guilt day after day can't be healthy, either."

"True." Kirkwood watched her through veiled eyes. "What a pity he never got you with child. He'd marry you then, by God, or I'd call him out myself. I might be old but I'm excellent with a rapier or a pistol."

She tried not to imagine the meeting. Kirkwood would be no match for Philip. "Are you prepared to give me time to see if I can change his mind?"

He inclined his head. "Of course, my dear. Now I understand

you want to marry—and your preference is for Cumberland—then I will do everything I can to help you win him."

Was that a good thing? She eyed him warily. "You won't interfere, will you?"

His lips curved. "My darling girl. When have I ever interfered?"

"If you thought I would settle down and marry, you'd interfere to hell and back." The words seemed to pop out of her mouth without her volition, and she flushed.

"Language, my dear," he scolded, but with a laugh. "Very well. I will give you until next September. If Cumberland hasn't seen sense by then we shall put our heads together and find a man worthy of you. Now, I must go." He placed his glass on the table and rose to his feet—still sprightly, she noticed, for a man of nine-and-fifty. "You and Drake will spend the New Year celebrations at my estate, of course. I'm planning a rather large house party. I'm sure I can find room for one more name on the list—and ensure he accepts."

For some reason his kindness made tears prick behind Rose's eyes. She stood up and kissed his cheek. "Thank you, my lord. You really have been most kind to me. More than I deserve."

His own eyes turned soft and slightly sad. "My darling girl. Your father—God rest his soul—although my friend, was a selfish man. Had I been fortunate enough to have a daughter, I would never have allowed her marriage to Roxborough—or any other man of his age."

She knew he spoke the truth. "If you'd had a daughter, she would have loved you deeply."

"Thank you," he choked out and then cleared his throat. "Goodbye, my dear." He lifted her hand to his lips and kissed it just as Booth arrived to show him out.

Alone once more, Rose sank into the chaise longue, mind in a whirl.

Philip and Robert. Kirkwood might be completely wrong

about Philip's motives, but it was the first thing she'd heard that made sense.

Suddenly, the idea of fleeing London held no appeal. But she needed help. Whom did she know who could help her understand Philip's situation? Not Portia. Not a woman. She needed a man's perspective. Suddenly, her eyes popped open. Of course! *Hadley Fullerton, the Duke of Claymore.* Hadley's brother had stepped in front of a bullet meant for him, and Hadley, too, had gone from second son to Duke of Claymore.

She would talk with Hadley and hopefully he would know what to do.

She glanced at the grandfather clock. Yes, there was time to change her mind. She would go to Serena's dinner, after all. Quickly, she crossed the room to the desk and took out a sheet of paper. When the short note was written and sealed, she rang for Booth.

"See this is delivered to Lady Serena, please, and have my carriage ready at nine."

He bowed. "Very good, Your Grace."

She smiled, suddenly eager for the evening. She would spend it watching Philip, perhaps asking a few pertinent questions to see if Kirkwood's theory held merit. If it did, then she would enlist Hadley's help and fight for Philip—and herself.

Her smile faded. And it *would* be a fight. She did not underestimate how hard it would be to make Philip see sense. Guilt was like a coat of armor. She needed to find a weapon that could pierce through it and yet keep Philip whole. After that, she would find out if he truly loved her.

Wouldn't it be ironic? To help him release his guilt over Robert's death, only to learn he didn't truly love her?

But that was for another time. Tonight she wanted to find out only one thing: Was there hope?

Chapter Eight

When Philip walked into Christian Trent, Earl of Markham's, London residence on the night of Lady Serena's dinner, he was not alone. Portia had told him Rose would not be in attendance, and as he did not wish to face an inquisition from his friends over the end of his affair, he'd brought Lady Philomena as his guest.

The others would hardly grill him if he had another woman in attendance. She would also do well to make up the numbers since Rose's absence would mean the party would be one female short.

His conscience prickled. Portia had said Rose was packing to return to Cornwall because Drake was unwell. He hoped the lad was not seriously ill. He was very fond of the boy and if the situation had not been so fraught, he would have visited, taking Drake a gift with which to pass his time while he recuperated. He must ask Portia how serious his illness was. If any harm came to her son, Rose would be devastated.

So imagine his horror when, after he and Lady Philomena were announced, he walked into the room to find a dozen dismayed faces and, seated next to Serena and looking so beautiful he almost forgot to breathe, Rose herself.

He was going to wring his sister's neck because a quick count of the others in the room told him Rose had come on her own. Now he had placed her in a very difficult social position and felt like a complete cad.

The shocked silence did not last long. Serena, ever the gracious hostess, stepped forward to welcome Lady Philomena, and suddenly everyone began talking at once.

Lady Philomena had allowed Serena to draw her into the room but not before sending him an angry look over her shoulder. He wanted the ground to open up and swallow him. One look at Rose confirmed she was wearing the tight smile he knew to be a telltale sign of hurt.

Caught between a desire to apologize and an impulse to make his and Philomena's excuses and leave, he could hardly believe it when Rose invited Philomena to join her on the couch.

He shot Christian a desperate look as his friend came up to him, holding out a glass of whisky. Christian shook his head and handed him the spirits. Philip tossed it back and held out the glass for more.

Christian refilled it. "Don't get drunk, you fool," he growled under cover of the conversation. "I am not going to clean up your mess. What the hell were you thinking?"

"I was thinking," Philip growled back, "that Rose would not be here."

"And that meant you were free to bring Lady Philomena?" Christian shook his head and smiled so no one could tell that Philip was being berated like a schoolboy. "To a dinner specifically for close friends?"

"And just what would have happened if I'd come alone, for God's sake? The ladies would have castrated me."

Christian bared his teeth. "The night is not yet over."

Grayson arrived at his side. "Would you two please join us? Christian, we can reprimand him later. Philip, the least you can do is be a gentleman about this and smooth the situation over as Rose is doing. But I could bloody punch you." And with that he returned to take a seat next to his wife.

Philip, whisky in hand, moved closer to the others in time to hear Philomena say to Rose, "I heard your boy was unwell, Your Grace. I hope it's nothing serious."

Her question appeared genuine.

"Thank you for your concern, Lady Philomena," Rose said. "He has a bad cough, but it does seem to be improving. I may still leave town early to ensure we are safely in Cornwall before it snows. I'm told it is a possibility." She looked in Philip's direction as she spoke.

Philomena nodded. "Very wise."

Rose turned to Beatrice. "Drake is driving me mad, asking when he can see Henry, but I thought it best to wait. I don't wish to spread the cough around your family."

"Henry wants to see Drake, too," Beatrice said. "It'll be such a shame if they cannot catch up before the festive season. Perhaps, when he is better, you will send him to spend a few weeks with us. Knowing there is a treat in the future might help them both bear the separation now."

Rose smiled. "What a wonderful idea. That would be lovely. I know you must not be looking forward to sending Henry to school but I'm so glad he and Drake will attend Eton together. At least they won't be alone."

As the ladies began to talk about their children and schools, and to marvel at Isobel's condition, Philip began to relax.

Rose wore her duchess face—the one she presented to the world but not in their bedchamber. He shifted in his seat. He didn't want to think about Rose in her bedchamber, because when he did, blood raced south.

He cursed and crossed his legs.

He'd known walking away from her would be hard. He'd had no idea how lonely he would feel. It wasn't as though they saw each other that often. When they were both in town they usually shared a bed every night. When he was at his estate he might not see her for two months or more. But never in that time did he take —or even consider—another woman.

He looked over to where Lady Philomena was in conversation with Beatrice. Philomena was beautiful in a hard kind of way. Life had not been kind to her, nor had it been that kind to Rose.

However, Rose had managed not to allow her past to pull her down into despair. Having money would make that easier. Lady Philomena had virtually nothing but her looks. She most certainly needed a wealthy, indulgent husband.

On a sigh he accepted that Philomena—of all the women he could have brought this evening—was the worst choice. After that damned fiasco with the debutante—what was her name again?—she might begin to think he was looking for a wife. And Philomena as his countess would never happen.

Maitland came and dropped down beside him. "I looked at those investments coming due, and you are right, Philip. I think it's time to move out of those commodities and into some others I've been tracking. Why don't you come over in the next couple of days and we can discuss it?"

"Thank you, I will." His gratitude to Maitland knew no bounds. His Grace had taken the time to help explain what to do, and how he should be looking at his family's investment portfolio. It was his lack of investment skills that had seen him lose his money, enlist in the army, and ultimately cost Robert his life.

"I must say you are really coming to grips with the markets. Soon you won't need me at all."

Which was high praise from Maitland, who was an investment king. "I am sure I shall always need your advice."

A little later Sebastian joined them. Soon the men were completely divorced from the women's conversation. But Philip could not help glancing their way. In spite of the polite conversation and the occasional smiles and gentle laughter, Portia was frowning and abstracted, and Rose's mouth was still taut.

"Did I tell you I bought a hunting lodge not far from yours in Scotland, Philip?" Sebastian said. "I don't think we have thanked you enough for such a wonderful stay. Henry and Drake had such fun, and I know it has meant they have formed a strong bond. I can't wait to be up there next summer with the two boys."

Philip made a noncommittal noise, but his heart sank. Great. Now Rose would be near his hunting lodge each summer. If she remarried, her new husband would be there, too. And their children.

"I saw Maxwell the other night." Arend filled the awkward silence. "He was with a few friends at Foster's gambling den. He was betting pretty heavily, encouraged by Lord Farquhar. Are you keeping an eye on him? Farquhar is trouble. He loves watching those with more money but less sense than him lose. I wonder if Foster has him on the payroll—bringing unsuspecting and naive young fools to his den."

Philip sat up, suddenly completely alert. He had meant to have a talk with his younger brother but with everything happening with Rose he wasn't 'in the right frame of mind. "I accompanied him and his friends the other night and it did seem he was struggling to use good judgment on when to stop. I must admit I have been concerned. It's very unlike Maxwell."

"Well, if you are heading back to Devon, encourage Maxwell to go with you. He needs to keep away from Farquhar for a while." Arend paused, and his face closed as it did when he was about to issue a threat. "And I'd leave fairly soon yourself. You've hurt Rose enough."

Philip had known he'd lose the women's goodwill. He had not expected such a backlash from a man he considered a friend.

"I shall leave when I'm good and ready," he said.

Arend bared his teeth. "I could make you ready."

Philip didn't give a fuck what Arend thought. All he cared about was that Rose had been hurt because he should have walked away long ago, but he was weak and now it had come to this. The woman he loved was in love with him—and he had nothing left to offer her.

"Come now, gentlemen," Hadley said. "I'm sure Philip has a good reason for his actions. I certainly won't judge—until he explains himself after dinner. Then we might pummel him a bit." It was said very calmly but Philip knew he was serious.

The rest of the conversation around him faded as he watched Rose and Serena stand and excuse themselves and the women. Where were they going? Was she leaving? Surely she would have made her farewells. But if she intended to slip quietly out— He told himself he was a fool, but when he'd counted to one hundred and she still wasn't back, he couldn't sit and make polite conversation any longer. With an apology to the others he rose and escaped the room. He didn't give a damn what anyone thought. He had to talk with Rose.

If Rose's shoulders knotted and lifted any higher they would be permanently stuck to her ears. Her stomach had begun to churn and she'd started to feel nauseated the moment Philip had arrived with Lady Philomena.

How could he?

Philomena of all women. An ex-lover. Was this his retaliation for Tremain? Yes, she'd taken Tremain to the ball, but Philip had said he knew why—to make him jealous. Had he brought that woman to Serena's home hoping Portia would tell her and she'd get a taste of her own medicine?

For the hundredth time that evening she cursed herself for being fool enough to come here and put herself through this pain. Her hands itched to slap him. How *dare* he bring someone else— a stranger—to an informal dinner of their friends?

She could feel him watching her. Or perhaps he was watching Philomena, whom she'd stupidly suggested sit beside her.

At least Philomena seemed as uncomfortable as she and had done her best to ease the tension in the room.

Rose chatted as vivaciously as she could until she could bear it no longer. Then, using the excuse that she had brought something for Serena's daughter, Lily, and wanted to give it to her before she went to sleep, she asked if a servant could accompany her to Lily's room. Serena, knowing it to be a ruse, offered to take her upstairs herself.

Once in the privacy of the hallway, Serena led her not upstairs but to her husband's study. "Take your time. Compose yourself in here. You know I will not be offended if you decide to go home. I'll say you got a message that Drake is not well."

Rose whirled on her friend. "And run away? It is not *I* who should retreat. How could he? I could shoot him."

"I don't believe he knew you were coming."

She sank into a chair. "I am so sorry for placing you in such an embarrassing position. It didn't occur to me that he'd bring a guest." She tried not to see the compassion in Serena's eyes. Failed. "This is how it's going to be from now on, isn't it? I didn't believe he'd move on so soon."

"I won't excuse his behavior," Serena said. "However, people deal with their hurt or pain in many ways. I suspect—"

Whatever Serena had been going to say flew out of Rose's mind when the door opened and Philip stood there in all his beauty.

"If you'd excuse me, Lady Serena," he said formally. "I'd like a private word with Her Grace."

Serena looked at Rose and, when Rose nodded permission, said, "You may have five minutes' privacy, Lord Cumberland. Then I will return and you will leave." And she swept from the room.

Rose stood up, unwilling to have him tower over her while she remained seated. He still towered over her, however. He stepped closer, opened his mouth to speak—and something inside Rose snapped. She felt it. A sharp jolt of fury. Her hand whipped out, fast as a snake, and she slapped his face. Then, shocked and embarrassed by her lack of control, she turned away in horror.

"I deserved that."

"Yes, you did." She turned back. "If you set out to hurt me tonight—or to prove your point about moving on—I congratulate you. You have done so."

"I did neither on purpose." His cheek was reddening where she had struck him. "Portia said you'd decided not to attend tonight. I brought Philomena to maintain some distance during the evening. They would hardly quiz me about us with a stranger in our midst."

"Why would that concern you? Unless you fear the answers?"

His mouth firmed. "I do not. But the answer I give will be so obvious a lie it will show me in a bad light."

That surprised her. "What would you say?"

He looked down into her face and his mouth softened. "I would say that we are not suited."

Pain lanced into her chest like a red-hot poker. Damned if she was going to let him walk away this time without admitting to the truth. "Enough is enough, Philip. For two years we have shared every moment together that we could both spare. You and I—of all people—could build a happy life together. To say anything else would be a lie indeed."

He shoved frustrated fingers through his hair. "Grabbing moments together is not living together, Rose. You have a son. I have a mother. We would have to combine our households."

Her hackles lifted. "Don't you dare imply my son stands between us. He adores you."

He rubbed his neck. "Of course he doesn't stand between us. That is not what I meant."

"Then tell me what you mean. No lies. No pretty words. I want plain, unadorned truth. Give me the real reason marriage is so abhorrent to you. Or is it only marriage to me that is distasteful and you are trying to be kind?"

A mixture of emotions crossed his face, flickering like firelight. "You won't understand. How could you? You have no idea what I live through every day. It's hard enough to see you and know—*God.*" He swung away, and then swung back, eyes wild. "Do you really think I would not want to touch you, to kiss you, to make love to you? God, Rose, I miss you so."

And then she was in his arms. "I miss you, too, you *idiot*," was all she managed before she was kissing him, and he was kissing her back as if he could not live without her.

But Rose was fighting for her happiness in earnest knowing Serena would soon be back, and she still did not have her answer.

She placed one last, lingering kiss on Philip's mouth and stepped away from him. "You say I won't understand," she said gently. "You're wrong. I understand very well. You believe you do not have the right to love and to be happy, to have a wife and legitimate sons, to see the title pass to your children and your children's children, because Robert is dead and you blame yourself for his death."

He turned into a statue, not moving, barely breathing.

"You say I don't know," she whispered. "But I do, my love. I know you. I know you better than you know yourself, and Robert would have *never* wanted to see you live this half-life you've condemned yourself to, and deep down you know it."

Still he didn't speak. Didn't move. She wasn't sure he even breathed.

And then, a log fell apart in the grate, breaking the spell. He turned on his heel, and a moment later she was standing in the middle of the study. Alone.

Chapter Nine

Rose had never seen Philip look so lost. So desolate. The sound of the door closing behind him brought her to herself and she collapsed into a chair.

He wanted her. He missed her.

She should feel triumphant. He was not dismissing her because of her reputation, or because he loved another, or because he hated the idea of family and marriage. Kirkwood's theory was correct. But that knowledge was cold comfort. How was she now to make Philip see he was being a pigheaded fool?

The door burst open and Serena swept in, eyes bright with concern. "Rose, what happened? Are you all right? Philip has taken Lady Philomena and left. He said he received an urgent message and you would explain."

Rose drew in a weary breath and stood, although her legs were still uncertain. She hated lying but she couldn't share Philip's secrets even with Serena. She loved him. She had to respect his confidences.

"I am fine, my dear friend. Yes, Philip received a message"—that was true enough—"and I was just gathering my thoughts before I returned to the drawing room."

"I can make your apologies if you wish to leave," Serena said, eyes brimming. "No one would blame you."

She stood, smoothing a hand over her hair and clothes. "No. I think I would like to forget Philip for one evening and enjoy a lovely dinner with my friends."

"Good." Serena hooked an arm through hers. "That sounds like a sensible plan."

When they entered the drawing room together every pair of eyes turned her way.

She faced them, chin up, shoulders braced. "If it's all right with you, I do not want to talk about Philip Flagstaff, Earl of Cumberland, this evening. If that is not acceptable, I shall leave."

"Philip?" Christian approached and hugged her like a brother. "Philip who?"

Rose let herself relax into him. "Thank you," she whispered.

And as Christian turned her toward the chaise longue and the other women, the butler called them all to dinner.

Rose knew it was the height of rudeness to call on anyone unannounced. But to call on a gentleman, a married gentleman, when everyone knew she was the Wicked Widow and looking for a new paramour, was perhaps a worse crime. However, she doubted anyone would imagine the recently married Duke of Claymore would be open to any kind of dalliance. She hoped not.

It was why she was calling in the middle of the afternoon.

When the duke's butler announced her and stood aside to let her enter Hadley's study, the duke's eyes rounded in surprise.

"Your Grace," he said. "This is an unexpected pleasure." She took the chair he indicated. "Thurston, some tea?"

"Certainly, Your Grace." Thurston took his leave, closing the door behind him.

Hadley raised an eyebrow. "My wife is not at home at present."

Of course he would be at a complete loss as to why she was there. How did she begin? "I know. And I apologize. I'm so sorry to come here unannounced but I need some advice on a very delicate matter."

A guarded look came into his eyes as he took the high-backed chair near her. "I will, of course, give you every possible assistance."

She wished she had not come. But it was too late now. "You were at Lady Serena's last night so you know the situation between Lord Cumberland and myself."

He nodded, looking even more uncomfortable than she felt.

"What you may not know, is that Lord Cumberland's decision is not simply that he does not wish to marry *me*"—she cleared her throat—"but that he intends to never marry at all."

Hadley nodded slowly. "Unfortunate, but I still do not see how I can help. If you are looking to me to make him change his mind, I believe you would do better to discuss that with Grayson or Arend. I'm more of an acquaintance than friend."

Before she could reply a maid entered, bearing the refreshments tray. She waited for her to leave and then at a nod from Hadley poured them both a cup.

"Are you not curious," she said, handing him one of the fragile cups, "why an earl would choose not to marry—ever?"

Hadley's teacup stopped halfway to his lips. "It's unusual, certainly. Most men with a title know their position in society comes with obligations. He said *never*?"

She nodded, sipping her tea, waiting for the liquid to warm her.

"He does have three brothers."

"Yes, he does." She took a deep breath. "Would it surprise you to learn he thinks he does not deserve the title, or have the right to hand it down to his son? That he believes it should go to Thomas, or Thomas's son."

Hadley understood immediately. "Ah." He rubbed his head. "I'm still not sure how you think I can help."

She carefully placed her teacup on the table. "I believe—and some comments Lord Cumberland has made confirm this—that he does not wish to marry and sire an heir because he feels responsible for Robert's death, and that he should not prosper from such an action."

"Oh." The light went on in Hadley's eyes. "And you wish to ask me how I dealt with the guilt of my brother's death. Or perhaps you think I could talk to Philip?"

She sat back in her chair, ashamed for asking. "I really don't know what I want from you. Perhaps only hope. You have married." She sighed and rubbed a tired hand over her eyes. "It seems such a pity that a man who loves children—and, I think, loves me—would waste his life out of guilt. But I don't know how to make him see sense. He cannot bring Robert back."

She was close to tears when she finished, and when Hadley spoke, his words were softhearted and laced with pity. "No two situations are ever alike. While I was full of sorrow at Augustus's death and admit feeling responsible, I had actually been running the Claymore estates since my father died. So no, I did not feel guilty for inheriting the title. Philip's story is very different."

She lifted her head to look at him and tears welled in her eyes.

"Come now. There's no need for tears." He took her hand. "It does not mean Philip can't learn to live with his guilt. I don't think such a thing ever leaves one, but it is possible to live a full life—including marriage and children."

Hope awoke in her breast and she dashed away her tears. But his next words had that hope plummeting again.

"You can certainly help him, but badgering him is not the answer. He must come to the realization on his own."

"How?" She leaned forward. "How can I help him come to this realization?"

Hadley scratched his head. "That's the tricky part. He has to want something else more than he wants to wallow in his guilt. He has to find a reason to let it settle. He won't lose his sense of guilt entirely but he has to want to learn how to live with it."

Her heart sank. She had no idea what Philip might want that was more important to him than to do what he considered the honorable thing and leave the title to Thomas. It was obvious that *she* was not important enough. He'd walked away from her without a fight.

"I'm sorry," Hadley said gently. "It's not what you wanted to hear."

"No." She gave him a smile that shimmered with suppressed emotion. "But at least I know what I am up against."

His face relaxed. "I am pleased you are not giving up. After two years I can already see a change in Philip. Maitland says his investment skills have grown. He's learned from his mistakes, and the Cumberland estates are thriving. He's no longer aimless. Having the title, having a goal, has focused him. I am sure—with the right encouragement—he could come to accept that his life matters as much as Robert's did."

There was nothing much to say after that. She finished her tea and thanked Hadley for his help, and left.

As her town carriage took her home her mind raced from one idea to the next. She did not know what to do now. She'd hardly slept since the affair had ended, and she was exhausted. She would go to Cornwall early, have Christmas with Drake, and then travel north to Gloucestershire to Kirkwood's estate for the New Year. Perhaps some distance would give both her and Philip time to think about what they really wanted.

The carriage drew to a halt and she was handed down. The front door was already open and Booth waited for her. But his grim face told her something was wrong.

She rushed up the steps. "Is it Drake?"

"His Grace is well," Booth said. "He's safely upstairs with his tutor. However, you have a guest who refuses to leave, Your Grace."

Not Philip. Booth would hardly appear so grim if it was Philip waiting for her. "Who?"

"Viscount Tremain, Your Grace."

When she walked into her drawing room Tremain was standing by the fire.

She didn't wait for him to speak. "What do you think you are doing, Conrad?" she said. "This is my home, not yours. I give orders to my servants. You do not. Now state your business and then leave. I'm tired and wish to see my son before I retire."

"Is that any way to greet your lover?" His face broke into the seductive smile that usually had women melting. "I have been waiting for your return, my dear." He moved toward her, obviously intending to pull her into his arms.

She sidestepped him neatly. "We are not lovers, Conrad," she said. "Not now. Not ever again. I thought I had made that clear the other night. So answer my question. Why are you here?"

His smile wavered and there was a flash of anger in his eyes. "I did not think you meant it. You are looking for a husband. I want a wife. I think we would suit."

She considered. As she had been the one to approach him, she owed him an explanation. "I do want to marry, and I have a man in mind. But I'm sorry, that man is not you."

His smile died. "Lord Cumberland."

She did not answer. "However, ever since I became aware of your financial difficulties I have been considering how best to help you. May I suggest Mr. Hemllison's daughter? She has a dowry of thirty thousand pounds, and her father wants a title. Having met the young woman, I think you deserve each other."

He stared at her, incredulous. "You *know* I am without funds?"

She inclined her head. "Of course."

"Who told you?" When she said nothing, his face went dark. "Cumberland. Damned dog in the manger. He doesn't want you, but he has to poke his nose in where it no longer belongs."

"It will always belong." Rose watched his jaw go tight and his fists clench and release. He didn't frighten her. His pretensions were intolerable. "Kindly leave, or I shall call my servants and have you removed. You are no longer welcome in my home. My staff will be instructed to refuse you entrance."

Tremain took a step forward, eyes blazing. "He won't marry

you. He has no need of your money. He can have his pick of young debutantes. Lady Abigail is the prime example."

The truth hurt, but she'd had enough histrionics for one night. "Lady Abigail is certainly a charming young lady. Please leave."

He stalked past her, but as he reached the door he turned back. "A word of advice. Don't waste your life waiting for him. If he has given you your congé he's not coming back. What fool will settle for another man's leftovers when he can have a wealthy young virgin at the drop of a handkerchief?"

With that insult he strode out and slammed the door after him.

Rose lowered herself into a chair before her legs folded under her. Cruel or not, Conrad might well be correct—for Conrad. But Philip wasn't anything like Conrad. Philip had a heart. She just had to think of a way to make Philip listen to his heart instead of his guilt.

Chapter Ten

If the man guarding the door to Foster's den of iniquity didn't stand aside, Philip knew precisely where his first blow would land.

This was the third night he'd had to rescue his brother. Maxwell was drunk again but still gambling too deeply, being played for a fool.

When the boy sobered up in the morning they were going to have a talk. This behavior had to stop. It was so unlike Maxwell. Something had to be wrong. He'd take the young fool back to Devon for Christmas if he had to tie him to his horse behind his carriage.

In the meantime, Philip's fist itched to pummel something or someone. The guard at the gambling hell would be an excellent place to start. But to his disappointment the man stepped back and allowed him to enter.

Once inside, he made his way through the corridor, hazed with smoke, to the gaming room. As he entered, a young girl—naked underneath her sheer negligee—handed him a brimming glass of what was probably considered whisky and purred, "Are you here to play cards? Or to play with me?"

She was a pretty thing, and his gut twisted at the sight of

bruising on her arms. For many, the world was not a kind or lucky place. Pity for her—and anger against the world in which she was trapped—hit him hard in his chest. Gently, Philip put her aside and made his way farther into the room.

He saw his brother—and the cause of Maxwell's plight. Farquhar.

Farquhar stood over Maxwell, whispering in his ear and fingering the boy's coin on the table. Maxwell slumped in his chair, the cards around him, dejection in every line of his body. It didn't take a genius to see that, once again, Maxwell's luck had run out.

This time, however, Philip had had enough. Three strides and he was at the table.

Farquhar looked up. "Cumberland?"

It was all the bastard had time to say before Philip's fist crashed into his jaw. The power of the blow sang up Philip's arm as Farquhar staggered back into the table. Cards and glasses flew everywhere as the table collapsed under the man's weight. Farquhar landed on the floor on top of splintered wood and shattered glass. He didn't get up.

No one said a word. Not as Philip helped Maxwell to his feet. Not as he draped his brother's arm around his neck. Not as he half carried and half dragged the young fool out and poured him into his carriage.

At thirty, Philip could barely remember what he'd done at one-and-twenty, and he understood that Maxwell wanted—needed—to sow his wild oats. This wasn't a harmless sowing. This was squandering and devastation.

When they arrived at his London residence Philip ordered his footmen to take Maxwell upstairs, draw him a bath, and fetch him some coffee. He wanted his brother sober, not as drunk as a wheelbarrow, before they left for Devon at first light to join his mother and Douglas.

As for Philip, without Rose, London no longer satisfied him. Maxwell needed a repairing lease, and to cut ties with Farquhar.

He needed to cut ties with Rose. God. He missed her. He missed her beyond words.

But Rose was no longer his problem. Maxwell was. As head of the family it was Philip's responsibility to ferret out what was going on with the young fat-wit and deal with it before the demons driving him led him down a road he'd regret for the rest of his life.

For an instant, as Philip ascended the stairs behind the footmen and Maxwell, a glimmer of light flickered in his mind. No. The idea that Philip was the right person to lead this family was laughable. Thomas was not much younger than he and was nothing like Maxwell—he was a replica of Robert.

The glimmer flicked brighter. But *he'd* been young, too, had he not? He'd needed a few years and Robert's guidance to mature. Would he make the mistakes now that he'd made three years ago? The ones that caused him to enlist. The ones that got Robert killed?

"Phil—Philip—I almost won tonight. I swear."

At Maxwell's slurred speech, the glimmer flickered. Died. Maxwell, unlike Philip at that age, was only hurting himself.

When they reached the bedroom the footmen carried Maxwell to the bathing chamber. Then Philip dismissed the men and began to undress his brother.

Lost in a drunken stupor, Maxwell didn't resist. Finally, with the bath drawn and his brother naked, Philip hauled him up and dropped him bodily into the tub. Max came up sputtering but Philip was ruthless. He dunked Maxwell's head under the water five more times, and soon he was as wet as his brother, because Maxwell fought back, arms flailing furiously while he cursed like a sailor.

When Merton arrived with coffee Philip poured it down Maxwell's throat. Soon Maxwell was—if not completely sober—at least able to string a sentence together.

"Put on a nightshirt and robe," Philip instructed him.

"Merton will bring fresh coffee and some toast. You need more than brandy in your stomach. I'll be back in a minute."

Philip went to his room, changed into dry clothes, and returned to his brother's room to find him sitting by the fire sipping what smelled like coffee.

He looked up when Philip came in, his face a mask of sorrow. "I'm sorry."

"You're my brother." Philip dropped into the chair next to him. "Never feel you cannot come to me and tell me if you are in trouble, or if something is bothering you. If I had done that with Robert I might never have made the mistakes that got him killed."

Maxwell hung his head and Philip pretended not to notice tears trickling down his face.

"I owe Foster a lot of money," Maxwell said, gruff and ashamed. "I keep trying to win it back but just when I've had a few wins, my damned luck changes and I lose everything—and more."

No one won in a gambling hell—except the house. "How much do you owe him?"

Maxwell lifted his head and distress joined with shame. "Th-three thousand pounds."

Philip breathed deep. Three thousand was a lot of money but, thanks to Maitland's tutoring and investment advice, not enough to cause the family any harm. "I'll take care of it. But in return you will promise never to return to Foster's, and also to cut Farquhar loose. The man is using you. Foster pays him to lure young fools to his den and then fleece them of their coin."

"Thank you. And I promise. But—" Maxwell hesitated. Flushed.

"There's something else?" Philip asked, holding his breath.

His brother nodded. "A woman."

Philip cursed. There was always a woman. *Please do not say she is with child.*

"She works at the den." Maxwell spoke quickly. "Her name's Faith. He hurts her, Philip, and she doesn't want to be there."

The child with the bruises? "Are you in love with her?"

Maxwell shook his head. "No, no, it's not like that. I—I feel sorry for her. I promised I'd get her enough money to leave. You see? That's why I *had* to win. I also went to ensure she was not hurt—or hurt more than usual."

Philip sat forward and leaned his elbows on his knees. The boy had a soft heart and a softer head. "She could be fleecing you, too."

"I don't think so. She wants to leave so badly that one night when I had ventured upstairs with one of the ladies, I caught her trying to jump from the top floor of the house. I have to help her, Philip. I promised."

"Then you shall." Philip's mouth firmed. "We'll go first thing in the morning, pay your debt, and remove Faith from the premises. If she truly wants to leave such a life there are jobs in Flagstaff Castle."

"Thank you." Maxwell let his head rest back on the chair and closed his eyes. "I am sorry, Philip. I should have confided in you sooner. I would not have lost so much money."

Money they could replace. Life they could not. "Remember that next time you're in the suds, and don't wait so long. Come to me before your problems get so big you can't see a way out. The cost of trying to do everything on your own is high." He got to his feet, walked over to his brother, and placed a friendly hand on his shoulder. "Now get some sleep. We have an early start, and a long day tomorrow."

He was almost at the door when Maxwell spoke. "Robert would be proud of you, Philip. You've become a wise and honorable earl."

His body tensed as guilt rose up to choke him. "I'd rather Robert were in my place, as he should have been."

"But he's not," Maxwell said. "And the family's lucky to have you to fill his shoes. Thank you."

Philip closed his eyes against the pain. "I don't deserve your praise." Or his thanks. "Robert's shoes are hard to fill, and duty is not something to take lightly."

"I know. I will come to you in the future if I get out of my depth. I promise I shall swallow my pride."

Philip believed him. "Yes, I'm sure you will." He wished he had sought out help.

With that he left the room and went to get some sleep.

Your Grace,

I thought you might wish to know that Lord Cumberland has indeed moved on. He was seen this morning paying for a young prostitute named Faith. He took her into his carriage and then he departed London for his estates. Faith is with him.

As stated, a man never goes back for leftovers.

Lord Tremain.

Rose screwed up the note, wishing it were Tremain's neck instead of paper. He would have taken great pleasure in imagining her hurt at such news—and his news *did* hurt. The words stabbed like knives and made her heart bleed. Yet she refused to believe them. Philip would not have moved on so quickly and surely he would never take a woman like this home to Flagstaff Castle.

Even if he had, she refused to cry. She had to accept that what Philip did was now his business alone. He'd made that quite clear by simply walking out on her. However, he would not take a prostitute to his estate in Devon with the family in residence, although he might put her in a cottage on the estate.

She squared her shoulders, walked to the fire, and tossed the note into the flames. Then she returned to her writing desk and finished writing her Christmas cards.

In the morning they would leave for Cornwall. She would spend the two weeks before the New Year thinking about what she could do to bring Philip to his senses.

If he came to Kirkwood's house party and stayed, she would have an opportunity to talk with him. She still had no idea what he might want more than to be a martyr for Robert. She only hoped that, surrounded by her friends, she would find an answer.

Chapter Eleven

Christmas had been a quiet but joyous affair. The highlight for Rose—and for Drake, too—had been the gift from Philip to Drake—a young gelding named Crusoe.

In his note to the boy, Philip had explained Crusoe was looking for a fine young man to be his first owner. He was a good jumper and very partial to apples but had a few tricks—like standing on people's feet or trying to unseat his rider under the trees.

The bad weather had meant Drake had only been able to ride the horse around the stable yard. So it was no surprise that the boy begged to be able to take Crusoe to Lord Kirkwood's so that he might go riding with Lord Cumberland—and, of course, thank him—in person.

The thoughtfulness of the gift gave Rose hope. It seemed unconscionable that Philip would continue to refuse to have children of his own. If only she could make him see what a wonderful father he would be.

Drake had been almost impossible to manage the last few days because he was so excited about seeing Henry again, as well as Lord Cumberland. Sebastian and Beatrice were on Kirkwood's guest list. So were the other Libertine Scholars—all except Arend and Isobel. As Isobel was due to give birth in a few weeks, Arend had decided they would remain at his estate near York.

On the day before they were due to leave for Wiltshire, Rose sat at her writing desk going over her lists. Surely she didn't need to take as much as this to Lord Kirkwood's—although the manor could be quite cold even despite the fires his staff kept burning all day and all night. Drake's cough seemed to have disappeared. She did not wish to risk it returning.

Picking up her quill, she tried to see what on earth she could leave behind.

She was about to scratch off the second fox stole from the list when her lady's maid entered, carrying two of her hatboxes.

"We are going to need at least three carriages to carry everything on your list, Elaine," Rose said laughingly. "Is there anything we can leave behind?"

"There is nothing on that list you will not need." Elaine shrugged. "Or could possibly need. We should be prepared for anything."

Rose nodded. "This is why traveling is such a chore. It's hard to know what one will require and therefore what one should take —or leave behind."

"There is something that needs to be *added* to the list."

Rose groaned. "I can't imagine what."

Elaine gave her a shrewd look. "Your rags. I've had them ready for the last two weeks. I thought your monthly courses would've come by now."

All the air rushed from Rose's lungs, leaving her dizzy. With shaking hands, she set the list down on her writing desk. "That can't be right. Are you sure?"

"I keep your schedule," Elaine said. "You've been as regular as clockwork, except of course, when you were expecting Drake."

Rose let one hand slide to her stomach. "You think I'm with child."

She couldn't help the smile that curved her lips. The prospect of having Philip's child thrilled her. She let herself bathe in her happiness, refusing to let the thought of what Philip might think ruin her joy.

"I can see you are extremely happy about the possibility," Elaine said.

"Yes, I am. But, Elaine, we must keep this between ourselves. If I *am* with child it's very early on. There is no point in raising hopes"—or causing problems—"until we know for certain."

"Shall I ask the doctor to call? I could say that you'd like him to attend His Grace one last time before we travel."

Rose shook her head. "No. You know how gossip works. I believe none of my staff would talk, but I cannot vouch for the doctor. No one must learn of my condition until I speak to Lord Cumberland."

She knew exactly when his seed had taken root. How ironic, that on the very night they called an end to their affair, she became with child. Surely it was a sign that fate had decreed they should be together as man and wife.

"He will have to marry you now."

She could not deny it. However, nor could she help but wish that Philip had chosen to marry her instead of being forced to do so.

Anyway, it was early days yet. She needn't tell Philip immediately. She could still use her time at the New Year's house party to influence Philip. To show his sacrifice in its true light of a martyrdom Robert would never have condoned, rather than a symbol of duty and love.

"At least they are one less thing to pack," Rose said weakly.

Elaine smiled. "I still have the last of your gowns to pack. I assume you wish to wear the lilac gown, and the fox fur cape and throws. And don't you worry, Your Grace. I'll make sure His Grace is wrapped up like a mummy."

With that, Elaine left the room.

The moment she was alone, Rose forgot all about her list.

Instead, she stood, walked to the window, and gazed out on

the Roxborough estate. She had stood here once before, not quite twenty years old, having just learned she was carrying a child. All she could see before her then was a lonely, unbearable, slave-like life.

It wasn't that Lord Roxborough was an ogre. He was simply thoughtless. When he came to her bed, it was under the cover of darkness, they both kept their night rails on, and it was over quickly, for which she sincerely thanked God. Roxborough had no idea how to arouse a woman—saw no use for Rose at all except as a vehicle to give him a son—and the couplings were always painful.

Learning then that she was with child, her first thought had been that there was now no further reason for her husband to come to her bed and she would be free of that awful torture. And she was right. It was almost as if he saw the bedding of her as distasteful. He never set foot in her room again.

Her second thought had been to pray for a son. If she bore Roxborough a son she would *never* have to share her husband's bed again. She gave no thought to the child she carried except as a means to an end, and all through her pregnancy she struggled to form any bond with the life growing inside her.

She had no idea Drake would change her life.

When she did hold her baby in her arms for the first time, love consumed her. She had not expected to feel so much. For the first time since her marriage, she cared for someone other than herself. Everything she had been through, she would've endured again, if it meant a chance to cradle this child—this beautiful baby—in her arms.

And fate had stepped in a second time that day. Upon learning Rose had borne him a son, the Duke of Roxborough ordered the preparation of a party for the entire estate, toasted his son's good health, smoked an imported cigar, tossed back a glass of whisky—and then collapsed and died from apoplexy.

For Rose, the birth of her son had been an exhausting but perfect day.

Now she stood here again, a child growing within her. This time her heart was light, her smile was sincere. She rested a palm on her flat belly, already embracing the life growing inside her. This was Philip's child. Hers and Philip's. She did not care whether she had a girl or a boy. Either would be perfect, because it would be part of Philip. When they married there would be time aplenty to provide him his heir.

Luckily, the snow held off for Rose's journey to Wiltshire. They had to overnight in Devon, and when Drake asked why they didn't stay with Lord Cumberland she simply said Lord Cumberland had already left to go to Lord Kirkwood's. This seemed to pacify him.

Instead, they stayed at a small coaching inn just north of the Cumberland estate. She stayed there regularly when Philip wanted to see her but—because Portia was not in residence—she was unable to stay at Flagstaff Castle. They would meet here in secret.

She knew the innkeeper and his wife, Margaret, well, and it would appear town gossip spread quickly.

"I was very sorry to hear that you and Lord Cumberland— that is to say—that you are not such good friends anymore." Margaret was not fishing for gossip. She really was commiserating with Rose over the breakup of their relationship.

"We are still friends," Rose told her, truthfully. "But for the moment, perhaps not as close as we were."

"His Lordship was in here about a sennight ago." Margaret stood, wringing her hands as if she wanted to impart information but didn't know whether she should.

"Was he? I hope he is well."

"He was well, Your Grace. It was the young lady with him. They called her Faith. It was obvious to me that she was with child. Apparently, she's been given one of the cottages on the south side of the estate and works at the big house."

Faith. Where had Rose heard that name before? And then she remembered Faith was the name of the prostitute Tremain had written to her about.

It took Rose an effort not to let her shock show on her face. "Are you saying it's Lord Cumberland's child?"

For almost two years, Philip had made sure he never got her with child. He insisted on her using a sponge, or he would use a French letter, or he would simply spill his seed outside her body. But in only a few months since the ending of their affair he had managed to get a young girl with child.

Rose knew accidents happened, or couples got caught up in the moment. That's how she now found herself with child. Philip had been so overcome with desire he had broken his own rule with no encouragement from her.

Margaret shrugged. "Who can say? He did seem to take a great amount of interest in her well-being. I—I just thought you needed to know. His lordship left for Lord Kirkwood's estate yesterday. I know that's where you're heading, too."

"I appreciate your concern." Rose was now desperate to get away from the woman. "I know Lord Cumberland is an excellent employer who takes good care of his staff whether in his homes or on his estate. It does not surprise me that he's shown special kindness to a woman who is with child, and on her own. But thank you for telling me."

And with a smile and a nod she turned and made her way upstairs to the rooms set aside for her, Drake, and Elaine.

She could not believe Philip would have moved on to another lover so soon, but then men had needs. And if he was not in love with her, why wouldn't he have found someone else? Looking back she was a fool to think he would marry her. Not once had he lied or misled her. He'd never professed love.

How ironic though. For a man who did not wish to become a father, it would appear Philip was to become a father twice over. She felt a twinge of sorrow for young Faith. There was no chance that Philip would marry her. At least Rose did not have to compete with a lady of her social standing. She shuddered to think what Philip would have done if he'd had to choose between her and, for example, Lady Philomena.

She knew Philip would choose her.

But he hasn't chosen you. He let you walk out of his life.

Pride was little comfort when a woman found herself in her condition.

Kirkwood would never allow her to have a child out of wedlock. If Philip—God forbid—refused to marry her, Kirkwood would marry her willy-nilly to any man, simply to preserve the Deverill name.

But Philip would never be so dishonorable. Once he learned of her condition he would be honor-bound to offer for her. And while the situation did not sit easy on her conscience, she had not, after all, deliberately set out to entrap him. If anything it was his mistake, and she would damn well make sure she—and her child—did not pay the price of that mistake.

Society might tolerate the Duchess of Roxborough as the Wicked Widow. They would not, however, tolerate the Duchess of Roxborough bearing a bastard as evidence of her wanton behavior.

She would not wish society's scorn to come down upon any child—and she couldn't believe, *refused* to believe, that Philip would, either.

Philip looked forward to spending a few days at Lord Kirkwood's estate. It had nothing to do with the fact that Rose would be there, too.

He lay now in a hot tub, scrubbing off the day's ride before heading downstairs for dinner. Rose would arrive tomorrow. He had one more night in which to get his jumbled emotions under control.

He *missed* her.

Having his family around him over Christmas had kept some of his loneliness at bay. But he missed her—and not only in his bed. She was probably the only person he truly shared himself with.

No, that was a lie. He only shared *part* of himself with her. However, she now knew everything about him. He should've realized she would worry and tug at the tangled skein of his excuses until she unraveled them and found the truth. It had, after all, been she who'd understood his guilt and sorrow when they'd stood together at Robert's graveside.

Perhaps that was why he'd accepted Kirkwood's invitation. A part of him wanted to grab at any excuse to let go of the guilt he bore over Robert's death. He wanted Rose to change his mind.

Well, it wasn't going to happen, but he would always be her friend. It was time to build on that decision.

On his ride that morning with the other men, Maxwell had finally confessed that he found law boring, and had no desire to continue his studies. He enjoyed being outside working on the land with both crops and animals. He really wanted to be a gentleman farmer.

Philip was more than relieved to find out the cause of Maxwell's behavior and why he was gambling and drinking himself stupid. He understood his brother's unhappiness, and together the two set about working out what Maxwell would do with his life.

The Flagstaffs had a second estate on the border between Dorset and Hampshire. Part of the estate was home to Portia's apple orchard.

Philip had heard that one of the local squires wanted to sell a large sheep farm close by—in fact, he had the man's letter of offer for sale on his desk. He'd originally decided to turn it down because he thought their Dorset farm manager could not handle much more. But it would be the perfect property to allow Maxwell to learn to do what he loved best.

Now, instead of coming with him to Kirkwood's, Maxwell was on his way to Dorset. If Maxwell liked what he saw, and could agree on a price he was prepared to pay, the family would buy the neighboring farm for Maxwell and merge it with the Dorset farm and orchards.

It had been the perfect Christmas present for both Maxwell and himself. Philip no longer had to worry about the youngest Flagstaff. His brother had not been this animated in a long while.

He now understood how Robert must have felt every time Philip made a mistake. Robert would have wanted to protect him, help him, and try and lead him down the right path, just as Philip fought to do for Maxwell. That is why Robert enlisted. He loved Philip and he wanted to protect him. If anything, becoming the earl had made Philip realize that his actions *had* led to Robert's death. He was definitely to blame. There was such a fine line between guidance and overprotection, and it was easy to slip over the edge either way.

An hour later Philip had bathed, dressed, and descended the stairs to join the rest of the guests for drinks before dinner. Only two other couples were in the room when he entered: Portia and Grayson, and Lord and Lady Jersey. He bid the latter couple hello and then sauntered over to where his sister and her husband sat.

Portia had remained at her husband's estate in Somerset for Christmas with their little boy, Jackson. It had been Philip's first Christmas without Portia.

Grayson rose and shook his hand before searching for drinks for them both.

She stood and held out her arms.

It warmed his heart to see his sister so happy and he returned her embrace with genuine affection. "It's good to see you," he said and pressed a kiss to her forehead. "I hope the journey wasn't too much for Jackson."

She smiled. "He has his father's constitution. I expect you to visit with your nephew in the morning."

"I look forward to it. I have a present for him."

"He's too young for presents," she teased.

"A man is never too young to receive his first bottle of fine whisky," Philip said, straight-faced. "By the time he comes of age it will be perfect to uncork and drink with his uncle."

Portia threw herself back into his arms and laughed. "What a thoughtful gift. I just have to make sure his father doesn't drink it in the meantime."

"Oh, I bought a flask for Grayson, too."

"I could kiss you again. Come and sit and tell me about Christmas. Grayson and I plan to go on to Flagstaff Castle after this to see Mother, Maxwell, and Douglas. Tell me, did Douglas come home for Christmas?"

"He did not. He stayed in Scotland. And, of course, Thomas sent gifts from India. However cleverly Maxwell and I kept Mother amused, I know she misses you and Jackson."

Portia squeezed his hand. "Then I will stay for a whole month. Grayson is indulgent. Will Maxwell be home?"

"No. He is off in Dorset. Inspecting Squire Hornridge's farm. It's up for sale."

Her eyes narrowed, considering. "Isn't that property near our farm?"

"Yes, and Maxwell is looking for an estate to manage. It seems law is not to our brother's taste, after all."

Portia's eyes welled. "So you are buying him a farm. You are such a wonderful brother. I knew he wasn't happy, but you men are such trials to your womenfolk. You won't talk about your emotions or problems." She stopped and then softly said, "Just as you will not share why you are purposely making Rose and yourself unhappy."

"Portia," he warned. "Don't spoil our first night together in several weeks."

Her smile faded. "But Rose arrives tomorrow—and I don't want to be caught between my best friend and my brother."

"That won't happen," he said, hoping it was true.

"I couldn't live through another night like Serena's dinner party. Please tell me you have come here alone."

Did she think he kept a harem? "Of course I came alone. I would not have brought Lady Philomena to that dinner, either, had you not lied to me."

She elbowed him in his stomach. "I did not lie. Rose had told us all she was unable to attend, then changed her mind and only told Serena. There was no reason why she should have told me, after all. I wasn't the hostess."

Philip didn't think she was lying. Portia appeared to be genuinely upset about that evening. "Portia, please. Promise me you won't interfere in my relationships. I want to prove to Rose that we can be seen together without it being awkward. I also want to prove to the *ton* that the end of our affair was mutual and amicable, and that I am *definitely* not hunting for a wife."

"But if you *were,* would Rose be on the list? I'd hate to think you were a prig and had excluded her because of her past. Your own reputation is not precisely lily-white—and Rose does not deserve to be treated like some bit of muslin."

"Stop it, Portia." He knew what his conniving sister was doing. She was trying to get him to admit he still had feelings for Rose. Were he ever going to marry, Rose's name would be the *only* one on his list. "I know you mean well, but you don't understand the situation. Please stop. You'll only end up hurting Rose. And neither of us wants that."

She must have heard something in his tone, because she sighed. "It's hard to sit back and watch something so beautiful implode. Especially when I love you both so much." His mouth firmed. "All right. Although I want to pull caps with you, I shall be a good sister, keep my opinions to myself, and try not to meddle."

He frowned. "Try?"

She sighed. "Extremely hard."

It was the best he was going to get. "Thank you."

"However." She pinned him with a far-from-friendly look. "One day, when we are both old and gray, you *will* tell me what happened. And if you don't have a very good reason for breaking up with Rose, I shall ring a fine peal over you, I give you my word."

Before he could reply, a few more couples entered the room, and they had to stand to greet them. As Portia drifted off to talk with Beatrice and Marisa, he studied their husbands. They were all carrying on various conversations, but each man was fully aware of his own wife—where she was, if she was happy, whether she was comfortable. They watched their women with pride, with love, with possessiveness, and he had never envied men more in his life.

Philip used to think that God had sent Rose to him that day by Robert's graveside to save him from his guilt and misery. But He hadn't. Instead, Rose had been his punishment—to touch what he could never hold, to taste what he could never possess. To understand what loss truly meant.

As he looked at the loving couples around him, he realized the next few days were going to be the hardest of his life.

Chapter Twelve

By the time her entourage made the three-day journey to Wiltshire, Rose was exhausted. It was close to midnight when they arrived, which she hoped would mean she would not see Philip until the following day, after she'd had a chance to bathe, rest, and fortify herself.

Kirkwood personally came to welcome her and Drake, and she hated to imagine what he must have thought of her state of exhaustion, because he quickly organized for Drake to be taken to his room and sent her immediately to her own.

Elaine, too, must have been fagged to death, but she still rang for a bath. Once it was organized, Rose shooed her off to her bed.

"The tub can stay as it is for one night," she said firmly, "and I'm quite capable of drying myself and hopping into bed."

Elaine didn't need to be told twice. "Thank you, Your Grace. I shall check that His Grace is settled first. Good night."

Rose removed her dusty, grimy traveling gown, eased herself into the water and closed her eyes. When she found herself starting to doze she decided to keep them open. She would hate to fall asleep and drown in the tub.

Her pregnancy was probably the reason this trip had seemed longer than usual. The queasiness had started the previous morning. Whether the nausea stemmed from her condition or her trepidation at seeing Philip, she wasn't sure. She hoped she wasn't going to be too sick. It would not take her friends long to make an accurate guess as to why she felt so bad.

Another yawn almost cracked her jaw. Determined to wash her hair, she dunked her head under the water. She would sit in the chair by the fire and brush it as it dried. She didn't care if she fell asleep in the chair. She could rest tomorrow.

While she hid from Philip.

But as she washed the soap from her hair she knew she couldn't hide forever. A wave of nausea washed over her and she placed her hand on her stomach, caressing it gently.

How would she tell him? How angry would he be?

At that moment she didn't care how he took the news. She was thrilled. She'd found something that would make the man she loved forego his ridiculous plan to remain unmarried and childless.

Philip paced his bedchamber like a caged lion.

Rose's carriage had driven up close to midnight. It was now just after two in the morning. He wanted to see her. He knew it was a bad idea, but he wanted their first meeting to be private. He wanted to ascertain how she was, ensure his presence here did not embarrass her, and see how she wished to act when together in public.

He still didn't understand why he'd accepted Kirkwood's invitation. He told himself it was because at some point he and Rose were going to have to mix in society, and it would scotch rumors if they could demonstrate their mutual decision to end their affair and yet remain friends.

His heart, however, told him something different.

Thankfully, not all the guests had arrived yet. He waited until those who made up the party had retired for the night. Finally—and before he could change his mind—he slipped into the corridor.

He had made it his business to discover which suite had been assigned to Rose, so he wasted no time dallying in the corridor. Without bothering to knock he slipped quietly into her room.

A lantern glowed on the dresser by her bed, and the fire still burned bright in the grate. The bed was empty, and it was only when he walked around one of the high-back chairs near the fire, that he found Rose, curled up fast asleep, her hair spread across her shoulders like a shawl.

He saw the open door to her bathing chamber. Noted that the tub was still full of water. She'd bathed and then, being too tired to wait for her hair to dry before slipping into bed, she'd succumbed to sleep.

Gently, he touched her flowing tresses that glinted gold in the firelight.

She was so beautiful. He used to love lying in bed watching her sleep. Her expression was always peaceful, so peaceful he wondered what she dreamed about. He envied her sleep that was never interrupted by nightmares.

He stood looking down at her, undecided whether he should wake her. She looked exhausted.

He frowned. Her face was too pale, and there were dark shadows under her eyes. If he left her sleeping by the fire, she'd have a kink in her neck in the morning. Besides, once the coals burned low the room would become cold. It wasn't snowing outside, but the morning brought heavy frosts.

It was probably best she got some rest. This time together was going to be difficult enough for both of them. Any conversation would just have to wait until tomorrow.

Carefully, he lifted her into his arms. She must be tired, he thought, for she barely stirred—and then only to nuzzle into his chest. He stood there holding her, torn between taking her to her own bed and carrying her down the corridor to his.

Finally, on a muttered curse he walked to her bed and drew back the covers. Then he laid her gently on the cold sheets, tucked her in as if she were a child, and placed a kiss to her head.

She snuggled deep into the downy bed, pulling the covers

tight around her to ward off the chill. She mumbled something, but he wasn't close enough to hear it.

Did she still dream about him, as he dreamed of her?

He had no idea how long he stood looking down at her, but finally it dawned on him that the fire was burning low and he should return to his room.

He took the coal bucket and stoked up the fire so that it would burn all night and keep the room toasty warm. Then, like a ghost in the night, he slipped out of her room, and back to his cold, lonely bed.

As he lay in the dark, indecision racked him. If he wasn't strong this week, he might make a huge mistake. Rose was temptation incarnate.

He missed her more than he'd missed any of his previous lovers, but then he'd never stayed with any other woman as long as he had stayed with Rose.

While he missed their physical union, it was her smile, the way she always greeted him as though he were the most important man on earth, and the way he could converse with her about anything. She had a sharp mind, a quick wit, and was not afraid to share her opinions on his estate business and politics. She was also tenderhearted and understood his inner worries and thoughts.

And she was just down the corridor.

In a bed.

Alone.

His body throbbed with need—the need to simply hold her. To sleep with her in his arms. To wake up to her smile and . . . And what, then? At the end of this week he would only have to go through the pain of walking away all over again.

On a growl of frustration, he rolled over and closed his eyes. With Rose not far away he hoped he'd have sensual dreams tonight, instead of his normal nightmares.

"Mother, wake up. It's light outside. May I have your permission to go riding with Lord Coldhurst and Henry? Please?"

Rose had been having the loveliest dream. She and Drake were breakfasting at Flagstaff Castle with Philip, who was crooning to her big fat stomach. One happy family. She didn't want to wake up.

"Mother, please wake up."

She cracked open one eye. A very excited Drake hopped up and down next to her bed, holding hands with Elaine.

"Sorry, Your Grace," Elaine murmured. "Lord Coldhurst would only take him on his new horse if you said it was all right."

On a sigh, Rose rolled onto her back and tried to pull her arm from under the covers only to find it caught up in her robe. Why was she still wearing her robe? And then a memory, like a dream, flashed into her head—strong, familiar arms carrying her and laying her in bed.

Philip had come to see her last night. She shivered from the warmth that he'd come to her so soon.

"Please, Mother," Drake begged. "Lord Cumberland is riding, too. I have to show him how well I can ride Crusoe."

She pushed up and managed to disentangle herself enough to sit up. "As long as you don't try to show off. And you must follow Lord Coldhurst's instructions to the letter."

"I will. I promise." He jumped up and down excitedly. "Thank you, Mama!" He leaped on the bed and gave her a smacking kiss before racing out the door.

Rose flopped back onto the bed as a wave of nausea engulfed her. She battled the bile but it was going to win.

She rolled over just as Elaine slipped in beside her with a basin. Then she threw up what little she had in her stomach until all she could do was dry retch until the spasm passed.

"I'll get you some tea and toast," Elaine said practically. "You need something in your stomach."

Rose nodded through her misery. "If I recall, I was sick with Drake for almost two months."

Elaine pursed her lips before saying, "That's not too bad. Some women are sick the whole way through."

The very idea exhausted her. "I think I'll rest today. Please tell Lord Kirkwood I'm exhausted from the journey."

Elaine handed the basin to the maid who had entered to see to the fire, and asked her to empty it, clean it, and return with two more. "I'll personally see to your breakfast, Your Grace. I remember what you could manage."

Once the women had gone, Rose lay back and closed her eyes. Her stomach rolled and pitched as though she were on a ship—and now all she could think about was how to tell Philip.

He'd come to her rooms last night. What did that signify? What had Kirkwood said to get him to come for the week? Or had he come for her? She wondered if he would hate her for getting with child. It was hardly her fault, and as far as she was concerned it was the best thing that had ever happened to her.

Portia stopped the maid in the corridor. She could smell the sour odor of vomit from the basin the girl carried as she drew near. "Is someone ill?"

The maid curtseyed. "Yes, your ladyship. Her Grace has been sick all morning."

Portia grabbed the maid's arm. "It's nothing serious, is it?" she asked, concern for her friend making her pulse jump and bounce.

The maid smiled. "Oh, no, my lady. From what her lady's maid was saying, Her Grace was this sick last time she was with child."

Portia's world began to skip and slide but for only a moment. Then delicious happiness engulfed her and she hugged her newfound knowledge close.

Rose was with child. It could only be Philip's.

This was perfect. Now the pigheaded idiot would not be able to walk away. He'd have no choice but to marry Rose and they would live happily ever after.

Portia wanted to go and hug her friend, to laugh, and cry, and plot, and plan together. But it was best to pretend ignorance. Philip should be the first person Rose told.

That thought arrested her. What if Philip *already* knew and that was why he'd agreed to come? Or what if Kirkwood knew and he'd *made* Philip come?

Surely Philip would be excited about becoming a father?

A small doubt crept into her head. No. She shook the doubt away. No. Philip was a good man. He would absolutely do the honorable thing.

Oh, dear. She would have to keep this secret and she was never very good at keeping secrets. She hoped Rose revealed all soon.

In the meantime, she would pretend that everything was fine, that Rose was in perfect health, and no one—*no one*—would be more surprised than she when Philip led Rose forward and presented her as his future countess.

Chapter Thirteen

On his return from breakfast, Philip paced his room after a second night of frustration, which burned as bright as his anger. Bloody Tremain had arrived last night. Why Lord Kirkwood allowed his presence here he could not comprehend. But it was Rose he was concerned for. She had not appeared for breakfast for the second morning in a row. Apparently, she was unwell. She had looked very pale and tired the other night and he wanted to see her and assure himself about her state of health.

But Elaine was guarding her like a lioness guarding her cub.

He was not known for his patience but if Rose really wanted to see him, she would have bade Elaine let him enter. He would have to wait. Causing a scene by demanding to see her would not do her reputation any good, and may start rumors that they had reignited their affair.

You could, a little voice on his shoulder urged. He pushed the tantalizing thought away; it was best to leave things as they were.

He sighed and wondered what he would feel when Rose eventually did marry. To watch the only woman he wanted marry another would be a just punishment for causing Robert's death.

This was going to be a long week, and he still had no idea why he'd come. Perhaps to ensure Rose was not moping but moving on with her life, and to ensure that Tremain didn't talk Kirkwood into letting him marry Rose. His meeting with Kirkwood yesterday appeased his mind; both men agreed Tremain was not for Rose. Lord Kirkwood was very disappointed in his decision not to offer for Rose, especially when Philip kept his reasons to himself. He decided that once he'd seen Rose and ensured she was not really ill, he would leave.

He'd promised to spend some time with Drake before he did leave. There was to be a treasure hunt today but the weather had turned rather nasty. He looked out the window at the heavy rain falling and realized it was not the day to be outside. Especially if Rose was unwell.

Just then Wilson knocked and entered with his pressed trousers. "Lord Kirkwood's butler says to inform you the treasure hunt will be held in the house. With over one hundred rooms, it's almost the same size as the grounds."

"I thought as much. Not much else to do on a day like today. It's preferable to charades. Can you imagine Lady Pothers trying to mime?"

Wilson nodded. "I will try and think of a reason to call for you should you ever be stuck playing charades."

Philip smiled. "I should double your pay, my good man."

On that jovial note he made his way downstairs to mix with the other guests before the instructions were given out.

He met Portia and Grayson in the hall and together they made their way to the drawing room.

"Have you spoken to Rose this morning?" he asked.

"I popped in briefly. She's still under the weather. Tired from her journey."

His sister's chirpy reply allayed some of his fear. "Are you sure she's not dangerously ill?"

Portia laughed this time and his fear slipped away. "Why, brother dear, it almost sounds as if you are worried."

"Of course I'm worried."

"Portia, please do not harass your brother," was all Grayson would say before striding off to walk in front of them.

"Sorry, Philip, that was rather mean of me." Portia put her hand through his arm as they walked. "Rose is fine. More than fine, and she'll talk with you when she's ready."

"I was hoping to talk with her in private before we faced the other guests. I don't want there to be any awkwardness."

"I'm pretty sure she has more to think about than how the guests will perceive the two of you." Portia giggled.

"What are you not telling me, sister dear? I know you. You are far too gleeful this morning, given Rose's illness."

That made Portia giggle more.

"If I don't get an answer I'm turning around and going straight to Rose's room, decorum be damned."

Philip was about to turn around when he spied movement on the stairs below. Rose was there, holding Drake's hand, greeting Grayson. She looked beautiful as usual. Her hair was pulled back in an intricate pattern, winding around her head with curly wisps floating around her face like little fairies. She looked ethereal. The delicate lines of her face emphasized her high cheekbones, and although she still looked pale, her eyes flashed with warmth and humor, and the worry holding his muscles tight eased.

When she saw him the warmth in her eyes deepened and a fire lit. It took all his self-control not to step forward and pull her into his arms. He returned her smile, while bowing low over her hand.

"Your Grace, a pleasure to see you as always."

He could sense those in the drawing room straining to hear the interaction.

Rose surprised him by taking his arm and leading him into the room. "Lord Cumberland, I hope you and your family are well. How is your mother? Did you have a happy Christmas?"

As they conversed the other guests grew bored and settled into their own conversations.

Philip wanted to ask her more intimate questions, like how she was feeling. She was still very pale, but before he could, Lord

Kirkwood called for silence. He began putting everyone into teams for the treasure hunt.

"I have broken the group into three teams and I've tried to make it fair. At least one person who is familiar with my house in each team."

Philip barely listened as Kirkwood prattled on. He kept looking at the woman sitting beside him with her son, and wished that he'd been a better man. If he had only made better decisions, Robert would never have gone to war and he wouldn't feel as if he were suffocating under a mantle of guilt so heavy it was a wonder his shoulders did not break.

Through his painful memories he heard Rose's name being called. Was Kirkwood trying to annoy him? She was in a group that comprised Tremain and Grayson. At least his friend would keep an eye on her.

Then he heard his name. He was paired with Drake and Henry. He inwardly smiled. He would enjoy this rainy-day game. Drake knew every inch of this house. With Kirkwood as his guardian the boy spent many a holiday here. Philip loved to win and he was sure the boys would find the treasure.

The treasure hunt was a list of riddles. If you found the answer to the first riddle you got the next riddle and so on until you found the ultimate prize.

Riddle one went like this . . .

Find me with some bars so neat

I stop open flight but not a tweet

When you find me you will admire

My structure made of sculptured wire

"That one is easy," Drake pronounced. "It's—"

Philip clamped a hand over his mouth, saying, "Don't make it too easy for the others. We want to win."

Drake nodded his head.

"Let's go into the dining room and we can talk freely."

The boys raced on ahead of him so excited. He looked across at Rose and saw her stand on tiptoes and whisper in Grayson's ear. She, too, knew this house. It made him smile seeing how excited she was.

Once in the dining room, Drake, almost bursting with impatience, said, "It's a birdcage."

Henry squealed. "That's it. You're so clever, Drake."

The boys made to rush off.

"But which birdcage? There is more than one," Philip said.

"That's why we need to start moving. There are many to check."

"But why don't we think for a few moments and try to work out which cage it might be and start there?" Philip suggested.

The boys nodded at his words. Soon they began discussing where, if they were Lord Kirkwood, they would hide the next clue. It couldn't be too hard as it was simply the beginning of the hunt. It also wouldn't be too easy or everyone would arrive at the second clue at the same time.

They decided to start not in the orangery like most of the guests would but at Lord Kirkwood's favorite birdcage, the one in his study. It contained a pair of yellow canaries.

They guessed right. The two boys could barely contain themselves when they realized they were the first to receive the second riddle.

A pile of words
Jackets of hordes
Take a quick look
In the place of the book

"The treasure hunt will be over in no time if the riddles are this easy," Henry said.

"Come on, let's hurry. I can hear someone coming."

As Drake flung open the door there stood Rose. A smile crossed her lips when she saw her son and widened upon seeing Philip.

"You three will make an indelible team, but watch out. We are close behind."

And on the word *behind* Tremain came up behind her and

slipped his hands around her waist and ushered her into the study. Philip's jealousy rose swiftly and fiercely. His hand began to curl into a fist, ready to smash into Tremain's face when it suddenly occurred to him that he had no right. For all he knew Rose welcomed Tremain's attentions.

He quickly stepped back out of the pair's way and followed the boys, who sidestepped Grayson and took off toward the library.

Soon the clues led them from the bottom of the house to the top of the house and back down again. Almost two hours later and the current riddle was making the three of them think.

Up and down, and up and down
you climb these every day.
You've likely seen the clue on these,
but passed it anyway.

The boys understood the riddle meant the stairs, but the riddle also said they had been walking up and down them the last two hours. They had never seen the next clue.

He let the boys ponder on this. To him it was either the attic stairs or the servants' stairs. The boys decided to split up. Henry would take the servants' stairs and Drake would slip up past the nursery to the attic stairs. Philip chose to wait there on the third floor landing. From there he could catch sight of the other guests as they searched. He couldn't help wanting to catch glimpses of Rose.

He leaned farther over the banister as he spotted the trio coming out of one of the bedchambers that held the ninth clue. They were a bit behind. A smile engulfed him as he noted how Rose stepped to the other side of Grayson so that Tremain was not near her.

He had just stepped back in case she looked up and glimpsed him spying on her, when a high-pitched scream filled the air.

Drake.

Philip took off at a sprint up the stairs, and as he came to the bottom of the attic steps his heart jumped into his mouth and the blood in his veins struggled to flow as it turned to ice.

He raced to the prone form and only breathed once he saw Drake was still alive and simply had had the wind knocked out of him. It looked as if the lad had fallen down the stairs. He had hit his head and the skin had split but Drake appeared to be more shocked than anything. He scooped him up in his arms and made his way down to the landing where many concerned faces greeted him. When Rose saw Drake she gave a cry and crumbled to the floor in a dead faint. Philip cursed under his breath.

Grayson, thank goodness, got to her first, leaving Tremain scowling. His friend scooped up Rose, and the two of them pushed through all the concerned guests to make their way to Rose's chambers.

Kirkwood was right behind him as he laid the still-crying Drake on the bed next to Rose. He was calling for his mother.

"Keep everyone out of here, and George, fetch the doctor," Kirkwood ordered.

"He's downstairs, my lord. He was to see Her Grace this afternoon."

Philip's eyes immediately went to Rose's form lying on the bed beside her son. She was stirring. Her face was more pale than yesterday, if that was possible.

"What happened?" Kirkwood barked at him.

He turned to face his lordship. "I'm not sure. The boy was checking the stairs near the attic and then I heard him scream. It looks like he's fallen down the attic stairs. I found him at the bottom."

"Why weren't you with him? Why did you let him out of your sight?"

Kirkwood's words echoed the words said to him by his father as a young boy when he'd lost Portia, and that familiar feeling of guilt and worthlessness hit him.

Rose lifted her head and sent a cursory glance at Kirkwood.

"It's only an accident, my lord. A small boy cannot be watched every minute of the day."

Rose's defense of his actions made him feel even worse. He should have taken more care.

When Kirkwood began arguing with Rose, Grayson pulled at his arm and they left the room.

The doctor saw to Drake first; Rose had insisted.

The little boy was shaken and for some reason did not want to go back to the treasure hunt.

She sent the doctor downstairs to have a cup of tea while she talked to him. She still needed the doctor to examine her to confirm what she already knew. She was with child.

Once mother and son were alone, he flung himself into her arms and began to cry.

"What is the matter, Drake? Are you hurting? Is it your arm? Your leg?"

He merely shook his head.

"What is it, sweetheart? How did you trip?"

"I didn't trip." He pulled out of her embrace to look at her, and his face was full of fear. "Someone pushed me."

Her hand tightened on her son's shoulder, pulling him close once more as rage and fear in equal mix engulfed her.

"Tell me exactly what happened."

"I was checking the attic stairs and when I reached the top the door was open. So I went into the attic but could not find a clue, and as I turned to go back down the stairs, and run back to Lord Cumberland, I felt a hand at my back. Before I could turn my head, the hand shoved me and I was falling."

Rose immediately called out for Elaine, who was hovering nearby. "Fetch Lord Cumberland for me, please. No one else, you understand?"

"Yes, Your Grace."

She kissed Drake's head and asked once more with hope that the boy was wrong, "You are not imagining this and you didn't simply trip?"

"No, Mother."

The fear in her son's eyes made her stomach crawl. Drake was not one for making up fancies.

"We shall get to the bottom of this. I promise." And she let him cuddle against her.

Soon there was a knock and Philip was there, concern evident in his face.

"Without letting Kirkwood or any of the guests know, can you go and check the attic for me?" At Philip's questioning look, she told him, "Drake says someone pushed him down the stairs."

Horror etched its way across Philip's handsome face. "I'll look right this instant." With that he left the room, striding for the stairs.

She had never loved him more than in that moment. He had not told her that the boy was being fanciful or not believed Drake's version of the events.

Elaine arrived back with some warm chocolate for Drake, who was still very shaken up, and a cup of tea and a scone for her. She was still feeling queasy herself.

They did not have to wait long. Philip was back but it was obvious he did not wish to talk in front of Drake. Her arms went around her child. She did not want to let him out of her sight.

Elaine looked between them. "Why don't I take Drake to find Henry? His friend is very worried about him. I shall suggest Lord Coldhurst watch them both."

"Thank you, Elaine."

"Do I have to go, Mother? Can't I stay here with you?"

Just then Henry and Lord Coldhurst stuck their heads around the door.

"Sorry, Your Grace. Henry would not wait to see if his friend was all right."

Philip crossed to Sebastian and whispered, "Can you take the boy with you and watch over him? It seems trouble is afoot."

Sebastian called to Drake, "Why don't you come and play with Henry and me? Since the treasure hunt has been called off, we are building a battlefield with toy soldiers and horses in the nursery. I can teach you both about strategy."

Drake looked tentatively at his mother before nodding and slipping off the bed.

He gave Rose one last lingering look and that was when the fear eating her guts was replaced by anger. How dare anyone scare her son like this, let alone harm him?

She waited for the door to close before turning to Philip. "What did you find?"

Instead of answering her he approached the bed and sat on the edge next to her. He took her hand in his. "How are you is more to the point? At least you have some color back in your cheeks."

She looked away, hiding tears. She wanted to scream that she was feeling incredibly ill and that seeing him here and not being able to touch him, kiss him, and then Drake being hurt—It was all too much. "I'm fine. Please, just tell me."

On a sigh Philip brushed a curl off her face and said, "The dust on the floor just inside the door to the attic showed Drake's small boot prints and a large set of footprints, too. Whoever went up there was not looking through the trunks, though. The prints only went in partway, far enough to allow him, or her, to hide behind a crate."

Her breath caught and strangled in her throat. Finally, she choked out, "Are you saying someone was lying in wait up there?"

Philip rubbed his nape. "It looks like it, but it might not have been Drake they were waiting for. How was the person up there to know Drake would go looking in the attic? Drake was there purely by chance. It could have been Henry or one of the other guests. The person hiding in the attic could have been waiting for anyone. What if he had been expecting someone else and he simply made a mistake?"

The knots of tension in her neck eased. "I suppose."

"Besides, who would want to harm a little boy? Especially a duke. No one benefits." He swung toward her. "Do they?"

Rose thought hard for a moment. The title would obviously die away as there were no male heirs in the Deverill family outside Drake, but the estates and money would go to her. That was the marriage contract and will her father had insisted on. He was not giving his only daughter to an old man who would die long before her without giving her protection. Her father at least thought about her financial well-being if not her physical one.

"You are correct. No one benefits but me. With no male other than Drake, the title dies and I inherit everything."

"Then I think we should keep an eye on the boy but think about who the real target might have been." He stood and looked down at her and she wondered what he was thinking. Did he miss her as much as she missed him? Or was he happy to move on?

She pushed up off the bed, willing her stomach to stop rolling. "Thank you. Thank you for caring about Drake."

He stood motionless, just looking at her, and she grew hot under his gaze. Finally, he said, "I care about both of you. Are you well?"

Euphoria at his concern swamped her body and pushed the nausea away. "I'm fine, Philip. I was simply a little tired."

He took a hard look at her. She must not have looked too weary because he smiled and said, "I should get back to the others. I'll talk with Sebastian and Grayson and set the men to looking into this incident."

"Thank you. Before you go I was wondering if we could take a walk in the orangery after dinner tonight. I have something I'd like to discuss with you." His face took on a guarded look and her courage began to falter.

"Can we not discuss it now?"

She shook her head. "You've already been in my bedchamber too long. Tongues will begin to talk if you do not appear downstairs shortly."

He nodded. "Of course. I would hate to have gossips get the wrong idea of our meeting here."

His words kicked her in the stomach, and the nausea she'd

tried to keep at bay began to rise. She needed him to leave. "Of course." She stood and fought the wave of dizziness. "Shall we say ten in the orangery, then?" And she guided him toward the door, practically pushing him into the hall.

"Certainly. I shall slip away and meet you at ten." He hesitated in the doorway. "Are you sure you are all right? You've gone awfully pale again."

"I just want to go and find Drake and reassure myself he is not still scared. I want him to know I'm here for him and I'd never let anyone hurt him." Philip had to go now or she'd throw up all over his boots.

"I'll find the men and we shall start our investigation. But be assured, Drake will be protected at all times. It pays to be careful."

It was rude, she knew, but she merely said, "Thank you," and shut the door in his face as she turned and ran for the chamber pot.

Chapter Fourteen

"Drake was pushed?" Sebastian stood with the billiard cue suspended over the table. "And I thought it was going to be a boring house party."

Philip and the three Libertine Scholars in residence—Sebastian, Grayson, and, as of that morning, Maitland—had retired to the billiards room for some privacy under the guise of a billiards game.

Maitland frowned. "Don't be so casual, Sebastian. It is serious. No wonder you wanted to talk to us, Philip. But why? It appears that no one gains from the boy's death except his mother. It does not make sense."

"I agree," Philip said. "Therefore, I wonder if Drake was a mistake and someone else is the real target. I think we need to keep an eye on everyone."

"That's a tall order," Grayson murmured. "We should alert Lord Kirkwood. He might have a better idea about which of his guests could be the target."

Philip shook his head and lined the white ball up behind the red. "Rose made me promise not to tell him. According to her, he already smothers the lad. If he hears Drake was pushed, Rose is afraid he will exercise his right as guardian and she won't be allowed to take Drake home."

The white ball hit the red with a decisive *crack* and sent the red racing toward the corner pocket.

"Nice shot," Sebastian said as it disappeared into the pocket. "Then I suggest we ask our wives to assist us. They are the most discreet interrogators I know."

Everyone laughed—somewhat ruefully— at Sebastian's tongue-in-cheek suggestion. But Philip was open to all the help he could get. "Good idea." He handed his cue to Grayson. "We four keep our eyes and ears open and set the ladies to do the same. We only have five days."

Rose should have rested before dinner but she wanted to be certain Drake was safe and recovering from his fear after his accident. So she spent the afternoon with Henry and Drake, reading and watching the boys play before the fire in the library and talking with the wives of the other Libertine Scholars.

She was relieved to see that Drake seemed to all but forget his fall as the day went on. Perhaps Philip was right and she was worrying over nothing. It was probably a case of mistaken identity. More likely it was one member of Kirkwood's staff playing a silly prank on another, and it had gone wrong. Who else but one of Kirkwood's household would go to the attic?

All the same, for her peace of mind, Wilson, Philip's valet, had agreed to sleep in the nursery with the boys each night. That had eased her fears slightly. Now she just had the meeting with Philip to worry about. And Portia.

Portia had been acting very oddly, watching her with a secret smile on her face. It occurred to Rose that her friend might have guessed her secret, but she hoped not. While she loved Portia like a sister, she did not want interference from anyone to ruin her moment with Philip.

How would she broach the subject tonight? She knew she'd stumble to get the words out no matter how simple the truth was —*Philip, you are about to be a father.*

"Lost in thought, Rose?" Beatrice's gentle question pulled her back to the present. "Don't worry. We will get to the bottom of this distressing business."

She smiled, willing herself to appear at ease. "Yes, of course."

"Are you heading back to Cornwall after this?" Marisa asked. "Or will you go up to London?"

She didn't know how to answer that question. It would, of course, depend on Philip's reaction and the plans they made for the future. Obtaining a special license would be easier in London.

"I think I'll take Drake on to London. I know it's a little early, but the trip back to Cornwall is so long. The Season starts late January and I promised I'd help Lady Helen."

The reference to Marisa's younger sister and her coming out veered the conversation away from more dangerous topics. Soon the women were excitedly chatting about the coming Season, Helen's part in it, and Marisa's plans and excitement.

Rose, loving the chance to be involved, promised to help by introducing Helen to her dressmaker. She had not experienced a Season of her own. Her father had married her to Roxborough on the day she turned eighteen. Helen was so lucky to have a brother who would let her choose her own husband.

Eventually, Wilson came in to collect the boys, and Beatrice rose. "This is delightful and we'll continue it later. But Helen's gowns are for the future. Our need is more urgent. We'd best ready ourselves for dinner, ladies."

Chattering like a flock of birds, the ladies went upstairs together.

When Rose entered her bedchamber she saw that Elaine had arranged her gown for the evening on the bed. But Elaine herself was nowhere to be seen.

As she neared the bed, excitement, not nausea, fluttered in her stomach. On the pillow lay a white rose, and under it, a note. Philip always left a white rose with his notes.

Smiling, she crossed the room, picked up the rose, and lifted it to her nose. It had a wonderful scent. He must have picked it in the orangery because roses did not bud in mid-winter. A good sign. One that showed he was looking forward to their meeting later that night.

Still smiling, she picked up the folded but unsealed note.

Her silly, love-struck grin faded as she read.

If you want your young duke to live
The name of your babe's father you will not give
Lord Cumberland you cannot tell
Or you'll hear the death toll of the bell

A cold sweat popped upon her skin and she sank to her knees, the note trembling in her hand. Drake had been the intended target.

She leaned forward, resting her head on the edge of the bed as panic built inside her until she could barely breathe.

Had Elaine betrayed her and spoken out of turn? No. Elaine had been with her since Rose had turned fourteen. She loved Drake and had appeared genuinely concerned at his fall. Rose could not believe Elaine would be party to anything that threatened either of them.

What was she to do? She needed help, but who could help her? Who could she trust? Whoever was behind this horror was watching her closely. How else would they know of her condition? She daren't tell Philip now, not until—until when? Until the baby was born? How could she possibly hide that she was with child for six months? Then how could she explain a baby to Drake, to society, oh, God, to Lord Kirkwood?

Her immediate reaction was to pack up and leave the party. But where would they go?

In that moment she understood just how alone she really was. There was no one to help her. To confide in. To care—

That had been her choice. When her husband had died, she had brazenly declared that she did not need another husband, but as her relationship with Philip developed, she realized that declaration had been a way to protect her life. She could not bear to be married off to another man who did not care for her or love her. If she was ever to marry, she knew it would have to be for love, and the only man her heart cried out for was Philip.

One of the only men who never asked for her hand in marriage.

On a sob she crushed the note in her fist and beat the bed, trying to think what to do.

"Your bath is ready, Your—" Elaine broke off and then ran to her side. "Oh, my lady, what's wrong?"

"Nothing." Rose fought for control. "It's nothing. But I want Drake to sleep with me, in my bed tonight. Will you fetch him for me, please, and stay with him until I retire after dinner? Wilson can watch Henry. I'll feel better if I watch my son myself."

"Of course, Your Grace." Elaine spoke soothingly, obviously realizing how upset she was. "Shall I fetch Lord Cumberland?"

"No!" She forced herself to be calm. To think. "No. I want to be alone." She got to her feet, keeping the note crushed in her fist. "But while you're watching Drake this evening I'd like you to pack for us. Do it secretly, Elaine. And only what is necessary to enable us to reach London. Tell no one, do you understand?"

She had no idea what she would tell Kirkwood. If she told him anything. "We'll leave before the rest of the household is up and can send for everything else once we are safely in London." She did not want to be on the road at nightfall.

"We are leaving?" Elaine sounded blank. "But I thought—oh, my lady, is His Grace in danger?"

She couldn't answer the question. "I would simply feel safer in my own house." It was true.

"Shouldn't you wait to see what Lord Cumberland—" Elaine stopped, apparently recognizing Rose's unyielding look. "Yes, Your Grace, I shall pack lightly enough that our leaving can be discreet." She turned to go, but then turned back, her face a mask of anger. "I never believed Lord Cumberland would be so dishonorable. He's not worthy of you, my lady. Not worthy at all." And with that she stalked from the room.

Oh, God. Rose wanted to weep. Elaine thought she'd told

Philip of her condition and he'd rebuked her. And she was supposed to meet Philip tonight to tell him of her condition. Impossible now.

The note was still crushed in her fist. She opened her fingers and stared again at the words. She'd moved to the fire and was about to throw it in the flames, damning it to hell, when something stopped her. Lord Markham might be able to help her. He, or one of the others, might recognize the writing—or find someone who did. She flattened the paper out, refolded it, and stuffed it in her reticule.

All she could think to do now was to put distance between herself and whoever wrote the note. If someone followed her to London, he or she was the likely culprit. Then she could safely tell Philip and the other Libertine Scholars. They had experience at this sort of thing. But she could not risk telling them here. Not with an unknown enemy watching and listening.

Nor would she continue to risk Drake's life with staff she did not trust and in a house that harbored an enemy. Once she was safe in her own home she would call Lord Markham. The earl was the biggest sheep farmer in Dorset and the most profitable. He was not present here, but it was well known that he helped her with advice on estate business. No one would wonder that he and his wife should attend her. There was no connection there to this house party.

And Philip.

Her dream of a happy life with Philip was not ruined, she reminded herself. It was merely on hold. Drake's safety had to come first. But she couldn't face Philip, not tonight. She would send Elaine to the orangery with a message that she had a headache. Tonight she would sleep with her son safely by her side, and before dawn they would slip quietly away.

She glanced at the clock on the mantel. There was now very little time to bathe and dress before dinner.

She bathed and dressed in a whirling daze that sent her head spinning.

It was still spinning when she sat down to dinner. Thank God she'd been seated next to Philip. He would not expect her to make polite conversation after her fright that afternoon. She could sit quietly, watch the other guests, and try to ascertain who would do this to her and why.

Her gaze fell on Viscount Tremain. Conrad had not taken her refusal to marry him well but he was here courting Lucy Hemllison as Rose had suggested. Mr. Hemllison was fawning all over Viscount Tremain, happy with the match, so she doubted Conrad had the motive or stomach to torment her.

She moved her attention down the table, analyzing each guest, until her gaze fell on Lady Philomena.

Now, there was someone with a possible motive to keep Rose and Philip apart. The delusional woman thought Rose was the one stopping Philip from falling at her feet, when it was actually Philip who could not stand the woman. Lady Philomena might have been a poisonous bitch on occasion, but did she have the brains to instigate a plan this devious? Rose doubted it.

Lady Philomena had not looked at Philip at all. In fact, the only person she laughed with, talked with, and showered attention on was Lord Kirkwood—a widower, an elderly widower. So Lady Philomena was setting her sights on an older man who would leave her with position, title, and money? Clever woman. And to Rose's surprise, it seemed Lord Kirkwood was enjoying the attention. She saw his hand slide over Lady Philomena's and give it a gentle squeeze.

Well, if it made Lord Kirkwood happy, where was the harm? He had lost his wife many years ago, his only son was grown and led his own life, and she knew how lonely life could be. Lady Philomena was not a bad person, merely desperate, and as poor as a church mouse. Lady Philomena could not do better than Lord Kirkwood. It was frustrating, but Rose had to admit Lady Philomena did not seem to have a motive, either.

As for the others at the table, she did not know any of them well enough to guess their motives. And there would have to be a very strong motive to do something as evil as the attempted murder of a child.

Philip sat beside Rose at dinner, but for all the attention she gave him he might as well have been a statue. Yes, they were no longer lovers, but he'd hoped they would always be good friends. Tonight, however, he felt as though a stone wall had risen between them, and he'd begun to dread the prospect of their meeting in the orangery later that night.

Could it be that she had already accepted—or wanted to accept—a proposal from someone else? They had been apart over two months now. Something was worrying her. She'd worried her bottom lip almost raw, and she'd hardly smiled or conversed with him—or anyone—all night.

She had, however, not taken her eyes off Tremain all night. Surely she bloody would not! No. She was not setting her cap at Tremain. She couldn't be that desperate. But the jealousy eating his insides had turned his dinner to ashes in his mouth.

Philip had spent the afternoon discreetly making inquiries of the staff.

When he asked if anyone had been sent to clean in the attic, everyone had said no. But there was one young maid whose cheeks had flushed crimson and who could not meet his eyes. He was certain she was lying, but nothing he said or did made her change her story.

When he told the others about her, Sebastian suggested she might be in league with one of the guests, so they set up a schedule to keep an eye on her. As she was unlikely to use the main stairs they decided to watch the back stairs leading to the servants' bedchambers. Philip took that duty for himself. He would get very little sleep, but better that than to have Rose frightened or Drake hurt. He'd come to care very much for the boy.

Tremain might have fooled others into thinking he was serious about the Hemllison heiress, but a spendthrift and gambler would hate to be tied to a father-in-law's purse strings.

The viscount would prefer Rose as a wife. Her jointure was already large. If Drake were to die, she would be wealthy beyond his wildest dreams. Yes, instinct screamed that Tremain was behind Drake's danger. What he could not yet fathom was why Kirkwood had invited the man. That invitation, to Philip, made Kirkwood a suspect, too.

He wanted answers, and he'd find them and make Rose safe before he left to return to his life of service to the Cumberland title and estates.

When the women rose to leave the men to their port, Philip decided it was time to push Tremain to reveal his true intent. When Mr. Hemllison moved to sit with Kirkwood and Sebastian, he stood and walked down the other end of the long table and took the seat next to Tremain.

"I must say I'm surprised to see you on the guest list, Tremain."

A smile that could only be described as triumphant spread across Tremain's lips. "I could say the same. I thought Kirkwood would have called you out for walking away from Her Grace." His smile faded. "Unless, of course, he invited you to browbeat you into a proposal. It's not a secret he wants to curb Her Grace's wanton ways."

Philip's fist itched. "Be careful, Tremain. Her Grace's ways are none of your concern."

At the reminder of his failure, Tremain's eyes lit with anger. "Nor yours." He nodded toward where Mr. Hemllison sat. "I have my eye on a better catch. What's your excuse for being here?"

He had asked himself that when he first set foot in the house, but Tremain had no right to question his motives. "I'm not sure you'll like any arrangement with Hemllison. I've heard that, upon his daughter's marriage, he'll only pay a quarterly allowance to her husband. It seems Mr. Hemllison believes he can get his daughter her title while keeping his future son-in-law on a very tight leash."

Tremain's tight jaw twitched and his bored veneer slipped. "You sit there, all high and mighty, looking down on me. You, too, were in dun territory once. But you were clever enough to talk your elder brother into going to war. And you came home alone. How very convenient!"

Red rage filled Philip's vision and he was out of his chair before Tremain had finished. His first punch took Tremain in the mouth, splitting his knuckles and singing up his arm. His next would have taken the bastard to the floor—had he not been grabbed from behind and held.

"Stop it, you fool," Maitland snapped in his ear.

Philip tried to shake him off, blind with guilt and sorrow. And then Kirkwood was there, too, anger scoring white lines around his mouth.

"Gentlemen," he said. "And I use the word loosely. You will contain yourselves."

Philip didn't want to contain himself. He wanted to challenge Tremain to a duel for his words. But he couldn't. Not without revealing his shame to the world.

"Lord Tremain," Kirkwood said. "Go and see to your hurts."

Philip only had a moment to take satisfaction in Tremain's split lip before Kirkwood swung his way. "As for you, Cumberland"—the man's anger blazed like wildfire—"apologize this instant."

Philip looked around, but Tremain had already left the room with Sebastian close behind.

"To me," Kirkwood said. "I will not have ill-bred brawling in my home. Apologize immediately, or leave."

Philip shook off Maitland's restraining hand. "I apologize unreservedly for my offense, Lord Kirkwood," he said stiffly.

His lordship nodded. "My study. Ten sharp. We need to talk." He did not wait for Philip to agree but raised his voice. "Gentlemen. I believe it's time to join the ladies." The glare he sent Philip's way as he ushered everyone out was as sharp as a dagger.

Maitland waited until he and Philip were alone in the room before he spoke. "That was unwise. Tremain wanted a reaction and he got it. What came over you?"

Philip could not meet his eye. Nor could he tell Maitland the truth. So he lied. "He mentioned Rose."

Sebastian strode back into the room. "I say, what have I missed?"

"Cumberland took a swing at Tremain," Maitland said. "Lord Kirkwood is not amused."

Sebastian laughed. "I wish I had seen that." His countenance grew serious. "Guess who our little maid rushed to help?"

"Tremain." Philip's hands curled into fists. "I knew it."

Maitland sank onto one of the dining chairs. "He has to be behind Drake's fall. But to what end?"

Philip could tell him now. "Because if Drake dies before he produces an heir, everything—the entire Roxborough estate—goes to Rose. That was her father's condition before he agreed to the marriage. So if Rose inherits everything, what are the odds that any husband will take control of the assets?"

The men glanced around at each other, worry creasing their faces.

"How many people know of this?" Maitland said.

Philip wished he knew. "I don't think anyone knows—except Kirkwood, of course. As Drake's guardian he must know. I only learned of it today from Rose herself."

"Could Tremain?" Grayson asked.

Philip shrugged. "I have no idea. But if he does, I would not put anything past him. Drake needs to be watched." The clock on the mantel chimed ten as he spoke. "If you will excuse me, gentlemen, I have somewhere I must be. Shall we pick up the conversation in the morning?"

Excitement, fear, sorrow and—as usual—guilt were Philip's companions on his journey to the orangery. He made another vow. Drake would not end up in the cold ground, dead before his time, like Robert. Philip could not marry Rose but he would protect both her and her son.

The fragrance in the orangery was intense enough to make it

impossible for him to distinguish her floral perfume from the flowers around him.

He made his way through the plants until he heard rustling up ahead. But when he rounded a palm he found not Rose but her maid instead.

His gut churned and he raced forward. "Is Her Grace all right? The boy?"

"Perfectly, my lord." The woman looked like she would have preferred to spit and hiss like an angry cat rather than conduct a calm conversation. "She bids me to say she has a headache and will not be able to keep her appointment with you. She is also worried about His Grace. He will sleep in her room tonight."

"I see." But he didn't. The maid seemed upset with him, which was hardly surprising. She'd been with Rose for many years and would know it was Philip who had walked away.

Apparently, those few words were all Rose had sent him because the woman turned to go.

Philip stopped her. "One moment. I have news about His Grace's accident." But with the child sleeping in her room he could hardly visit her tonight. "Please tell Her Grace I wish to see her tomorrow."

The maid stopped. Now she turned back, and her face was coldly furious. "See her? Why don't you just write another note? To treat her that way—I had thought better of you. Her Grace deserves better than you."

On those cryptic words she continued on her way.

Note? "What note?" he called, but she did not stop.

If he hadn't already caused such a scandal tonight by planting Tremain a facer he'd have gone straight up to Rose's room. Drake would also be there. Damn it all. He would have to wait until morning.

The maid might never forgive him for ending his affair with her mistress, but he hoped one day Rose would understand and do so. It would be unlikely. Only one responsible for another's death could understand his vow. How could anyone else?

What others thought did not matter. It was his vow and his alone. He would know. Robert would know. God would know.

He hoped it would be enough. When he saw Robert once more he hoped he would have atoned for his selfish acts. He hoped Robert would be proud of him.

Chapter Fifteen

"What do you mean Her Grace is gone?"

Philip glared at the maid the next morning as she was cleaning the empty bedchamber.

"I don't know, my lord. Her Grace and the young duke left at dawn."

He stopped scowling. There was no point in frightening the poor girl, and he wouldn't get the answers he wanted from a maid.

Kirkwood must know what was going on. It was not yet ten, but he turned on his heel and made for Kirkwood's study.

Why had Rose fled? And why had she not come to him for help. *Because you've made it clear she's not important enough to you.* The blood pounded in his head, and trepidation gripped him. On the open road she and Drake were an easy target.

There was another possibility, of course.

He turned away from Kirkwood's study and strode toward the dining room. To his relief, Tremain was not only still in residence, but also sitting at the table breaking his fast with Mr. Hemllison.

Philip's immediate concern for Rose eased slightly. Tremain would not be carelessly plowing through kippers if he'd assisted

Rose to leave. And Philip was not about to tell the man anything, either, just in case.

Mr. Hemllison saw him before he could slip away, so Philip entered and walked directly to Tremain. "Tremain, my sincere apologies for my behavior last night. I had too much brandy."

Tremain's surprise was evident but he recalled his manners. "Apology accepted, my lord. I may have overstepped good manners myself."

The two men shook hands.

"Why don't you join us for breakfast, my lord?" Mr. Hemllison said.

Philip smiled at the man and said, "Thank you, sir. I would, but Lord Kirkwood is expecting me. I look forward to the hunt later this afternoon. Gentlemen." With that he slipped away.

As he made his way to Kirkwood's study, he considered Tremain.

Could Tremain know about the contents of Roxborough's will? If so, how? And would the man have stomach enough to put a plan like this into action? He was desperate, yes. But Mr. Hemllison seemed willing for Tremain to court his daughter—so why risk his neck by plotting murder?

The more Philip thought about it the less likely it appeared that Tremain was their man. The fact that he had no other suspect made his gut tighten.

As soon as he'd spoken to Kirkwood he would go after Rose.

Something had made her bolt. What? And why?

He knocked on the study door and Kirkwood bade him enter. Kirkwood was standing at the end of the room, looking out the window.

"What did you say to Rose to make her leave?"

Philip counted to ten. "If you are referring to Her Grace I have not seen her since dinner last night—during which she barely spoke a word to me, or I to her."

Kirkwood swung to face him. "But you must have some idea why she left."

He was about to admit what they had learned about Drake's fall, about someone being in the attic and pushing him, but some instinct held him back. "I do not. It appears I'm no longer in her confidence."

Kirkwood studied Philip for a moment but seemed to accept his answer. "Please sit."

Philip took his seat and studied the man he'd always held in very high regard.

Kirkwood had been kind to Rose. He had allowed her more freedom than many men would in his position. A persistent thought entered his head and took root. Why had Kirkwood allowed Rose such freedom? Was it because she'd sworn never to remarry?

"I invited you to this hunting party for a reason, Cumberland. It was not to punch Viscount Tremain."

"No, my lord. I'm sorry."

"It was because I'm concerned for Rose's future. Brandy?" Kirkwood gestured to a decanter, Philip nodded, and Kirkwood poured them each a glass. "You were together for two years. Everyone thought you'd propose to her. I know she wants to marry you. So I'd like to understand why you have ended your affair."

He'd more than half expected something like this. "I believe that is between Her Grace and me, sir."

Kirkwood tapped his fingers on the desk. "Let me be perfectly clear. Drake will be sent to school in the fall. I have told Rose she is to remarry by then. I'm telling you in case you wish to change your mind, because once she marries you will lose her forever—and forever is a long time. Believe me. I know."

It was as if someone had shoved a sword through Philip's heart. While she remained a widow, he could pretend their friendship would go on forever as it was. But once she married, she would be out of his life completely.

It was a truth he really did not want to face. "Thank you for your concern, Lord Kirkwood. However, I have made my decision and will keep my own counsel as to the reasons." He started to rise.

Kirkwood nodded. "Forgive an old man's interference, but I'd hate to think that events surrounding Robert's death are stopping you from reaching for your own happiness."

The sly old fox. Philip sank back into his chair. Had Rose told him? Surely not.

"It's a long and lonely life without a wife and children," Kirkwood said quietly. "I knew and liked your brother. Robert would not expect this of you."

Everyone knew and liked Robert. "Probably not, but I expect certain things of myself. I have a lot to make right."

To Philip's surprise, Kirkwood nodded. "No doubt. Just be certain of the strength of your vow. Once Rose remarries, I do not want to hear of you rekindling your affair."

Philip remained in his seat but it was an effort. "I may be many things, my lord, but I have never been an adulterer."

Kirkwood raised his hands in surrender. "It is a warning. I'll not have the reputation of Drake's mother questioned."

"I would never do anything to hurt Her Grace or the boy."

"Then I think it best—if this is the way you truly intend to go on—that you stay away from both Her Grace and young Roxborough. Let her move on and find happiness."

He could respect Kirkwood for wanting to protect Drake and Rose. But a sudden idea leaped into his brain. Wouldn't Drake's guardian—and old Roxborough's good friend—know the terms of the late earl's will? Of course he would. And this was his house filled with his servants all doing whatever they were told to protect his interests.

Suddenly, Philip had another suspect on his list. Was Kirkwood up to something sinister? Surely not. The man had no need of money. Kirkwood was one of the wealthiest men in England.

Philip realized he'd been silent too long. "I'm sorry, my lord. I'm a little confused. I have been trying to stay away from her. I've been encouraging her to move on. It was at your insistence I came to this event."

"I know." Kirkwood smiled as if he was indulging a child. "I'd promised Rose I would invite you. I think she hoped to make one last appeal."

Philip doubted that because she'd left without conversing with him at all. "Then I believe we understand each other, and it would be best for me to take my leave. Thank you for your kind invitation. I'm grateful for the opportunity to clear the air between us." He rose to his feet as he spoke.

Kirkwood inclined his head. "I hope you heed my advice. I will be a formidable enemy if you continue to cause Rose problems."

How odd. Why would Kirkwood threaten him when Philip had already made his intentions clear? Something wasn't right. But he didn't rise to Kirkwood's bait. He simply bowed and left the room.

Philip strode into his room and called for Wilson. "Ask the Libertine Scholars to attend me in my bedchamber. Then start packing. I have some letters to write. Then we are off to London."

Quickly, he wrote a note to Christian, who was still in London. If Rose was there he wanted Christian to organize men to stand guard on her home.

When he was finished he gave it to Wilson. "Deliver it into the hands of one of my people yourself. Don't send it via Kirkwood's servants."

"Yes, my lord," Wilson said and stood aside to let Sebastian, Maitland, and Grayson enter.

"Rose left first thing this morning," he told them. "I'm off to London now to find out why. Maitland, I have a favor to ask."

"Anything to help."

"Everyone in the financial markets knows you. Can you discreetly look into Lord Kirkwood's finances?"

Maitland, who had been leaning against one of the four posts of the bed, straightened. "You think Kirkwood is involved? I've heard no rumors."

"Murder is usually about revenge or money. I'm merely trying to understand who benefits from Drake's death. Revenge seems unlikely. It has to be about the money."

"So how does Kirkwood get his hands on Roxborough's money?" Grayson asked. "If Drake dies it goes to Rose."

"Who does it go to if Rose dies while still a widow?" Philip saw the reaction on their faces and added, "He wanted me here to see if I had changed my mind about marrying Rose."

Sebastian bared his teeth. "Have you?"

"That's not the point. Why is Kirkwood so interested? At first I'd put it down to the fact he genuinely cares for her. But then after he told me to leave her alone, he threatened me. Why? Something doesn't add up."

"He's right," Sebastian said. "If you don't wish to marry her then you do need to leave her alone."

Philip wanted to hit something. "I'm not about to leave her alone when someone's trying to hurt Drake. So do you think I'm mad suggesting we look at Kirkwood? It makes more sense if it is him. He could have had servants hiding all over the house watching to see where Drake went. It just so happened he went to the attic alone. That's what is troubling me. How would anyone know Drake might go to the attic?"

Maitland was nodding enthusiastically. "That sounds infinitely logical. Kirkwood could have had several men or women waiting to hurt Drake. He really is the only one. No one looks at servants."

Grayson spoke up. "I think we have to investigate him. He would be the one to know the full details of Roxborough's will and Rose's marriage settlement."

Philip rolled his shoulders. "Then I'm off to London. There is no point staying now that Rose is not here and it would look suspicious if I did. But we can't all leave." He thought a moment. "Except for Maitland. He needs to talk with those in the financial markets. Could you think of a reason to leave tomorrow? The rest of you will have to stay the week. I've written to Christian and asked him to put a guard on Rose and I'll seek his counsel."

Maitland looked as if he was deep in thought. Finally, he clicked his fingers. "When you get to town send me a letter. I'll say it's a summons from the Prince Regent. Kirkwood won't think that's odd. Prinny called me away from a dinner that Kirkwood was attending in July."

"Brilliant," Philip said, clapping him on the back. "Now get out of here so I can finish packing."

"Not yet," Grayson said. "We may learn Kirkwood is behind Drake's accident but finding proof that would void his guardianship will be difficult, if not impossible." He hesitated. "The only way might be to catch him in the act, and that means using Drake as bait. I can't see Rose agreeing to that."

God, no. But if she knew the stakes? "Leave Rose to me. She'll want Kirkwood stopped. In the fall Drake starts at Eton, then no one can protect him. She needs Kirkwood's guardianship broken before then."

"Then we'll break it," Grayson said.

"Good luck," Sebastian said just before he stepped through the door. "Once I'm back in London I'll do anything to help. Drake and Henry are best friends and it will be easy to guard them."

Philip understood his sentiment. "I understand that you're worried about your son and of course Drake, but I won't let anyone hurt either boy, I promise you that."

Sebastian shook his head. "Sometimes life has a way of taking our good intentions and destroying them. Don't promise an outcome you have no control over—and one that no one would hold you to anyway. We will guard them as best as we can but we know the risks that someone could still get to them. Sometimes fate has other plans for those we love no matter how hard we try to protect them."

Once Sebastian had closed the door, Philip stood still in the middle of the room playing that fateful day on the battlefield over in his head. What could he have done differently? Did fate play a hand in Robert's death?

He relived that day and saw Robert fighting a Frenchman, watched in slow motion as the enemy pulled him from his mount. Philip had ridden over the top of anyone in the way of reaching Robert. But that had been his mistake. Robert was doing fine on his own and was just about to remount but Philip, so intent on saving his brother, did not see the Frenchman on his left, but Robert did. Robert stepped in front of Philip's horse and took the killing blow meant for him. He sat frozen watching as Robert slipped to the ground and Grayson's pistol killed the enemy.

"My lord," Wilson said from the door. "Your mount is ready. I'll take everything in your carriage and see you in London."

"Thank you." And as he rode on to London he prayed his interference in Drake's situation did not get anyone he loved killed.

Christian Trent, Lord Markham, called on Rose not long after she arrived in London. She told him about Drake's accident and Philip's suspicions, and was relieved—not to mention a little annoyed—to learn that Philip had also sent word, and asked him to post guards for her—and Drake's—safety.

She promised not to leave the house without an escort, and to watch Drake closely. She trusted the staff in her home completely; they had been with her for over six years, and they loved Drake.

When Christian told her Philip was on his way from Wiltshire, she almost told him to tell Philip to stay away. But that would raise more questions that she couldn't answer.

As he was leaving, however, Christian gave her a head-to-toe study and frowned. Being a gentleman, he made no comment about the tightness of her dress but there was a glimmer of suspicion in his eyes. Rose pretended not to be self-conscious about his scrutiny or his probable conclusions. Soon she'd begin to show and there'd be no hiding her condition then—unless her dressmaker could work a miracle.

Alone once more, Rose sank onto the chaise longue. She felt exhausted and sick and just wanted to break down and cry.

Everything was such a mess, and she was running out of time to convince Philip that he loved her and should marry her.

Her fear was that he would learn of her condition first and insist on their marriage out of a sense of duty. How long would it be before his resentment at being forced to do something he so vehemently opposed destroyed whatever feelings they shared now?

Then there was the note itself. She could not risk telling anyone about the note until the writer, their enemy, was caught. Therefore, she could not tell Philip about the child. That meant hiding her news for a few weeks.

Why was everything such a mess? Philip deserved to be happy. She deserved to be happy. They deserved to be happy together.

And, because she deserved to be happy, she cried.

She'd just recovered enough to curl up on the chaise longue with tea, scones, and a novel when the door to the library crashed open to reveal Philip.

He stood in the doorway, smelling of horse and covered in mud, which was dripping from his greatcoat onto her Persian rug.

"For goodness' sake, Philip," she scolded, only just rescuing her teacup before it slipped through her fingers.

"The Earl of Cumberland, Your Grace," Booth said, with none of his usual sedateness.

"I can see that, Booth. Thank you." She placed the teacup carefully on its saucer and then turned her attention back to Philip. "Please take his lordship upstairs and provide him with a change of clothing before he ruins my floor. When he's presentable I shall meet him in the drawing room."

Philip's glower deepened but when he looked down and saw the mess he was making he had the grace to bow to her, turn around, and follow Booth from the room.

Rose wasn't sure how to feel. Philip appeared to be angry. Was it because she'd left when Drake was in danger, or because she'd left without telling him?

Who knew? She didn't, and at that moment, she didn't care.

It was time to make him realize that he could not have his cake and eat it, too. He was not her master. Nor her lover anymore.

She took time over tidying herself before making her way to the drawing room where fresh tea and a decanter of brandy waited for her.

Philip—his temper apparently under control—returned a moment later, without his greatcoat, and with clean boots and buckskins. While it hadn't snowed for a few days it was still cold outside. At Rose's silent gesture he took the chair by the roaring fire.

The moment Booth and the other servants left the room, Philip spoke. "You left without telling me."

"I did." And if he was angry, well, so was she. "But before we discuss anything further, I would like to point out that you no longer have the run of my house. In the future, you will not barge in unannounced. What if I had been—entertaining?" She would let him wonder what sort of entertainment she might have had planned.

His cheeks flushed. "I hardly imagined you'd be stupid enough to entertain when there is an enemy out there, determined to hurt your son." He took a deep breath. "But I shall of course be more—appropriate in the future."

"Thank you. Now, I assume you have learned something pertinent since you rushed in here as if your breeches were on fire."

The shock on Philip's face made her want to laugh out loud. She'd never been so brusque with him.

"You left without telling me."

"So you said." And he'd sounded so aggrieved. "I don't believe I need your permission to do anything. You are not my husband."

Something that could have been pain flashed in those blue

eyes. "That is not what I meant, and you know it. What protection did you have on the road?"

"I had enough." He didn't need to know her business. "Especially since I was as sure as I could be that I was leaving the enemy behind. Was I wrong? Besides, I thought if anyone came after me, we would know who the villain was."

He took a swallow of brandy. "You could have confided in me. Or am I your enemy, too?"

"Oh, Philip." Why did he not see? "I can't continue to live my life relying on you. And how am I to find a husband if I'm running to you for everything? I was faithful to Roxborough. I'll be faithful to my next husband. I don't want anyone—especially not the man I marry—to see you as a rival or to have cause to doubt the truth of my marriage vows."

A muscle tightened in his cheek. "So you still wish to marry?"

She tried to stifle her impatience but was not successful. "Yes. Is there any point in going over this ground once more? We have had this discussion. Have you changed your position? Do you also want children?"

A look of such longing crossed his face that she wanted to beat at his chest until he admitted his desire. But it was not the way. He had to learn how to forgive himself. To recognize that, while sometimes fate intervened, war was dangerous. Philip might have saved Robert that day only to have him killed in the next battle, or after a fall from his horse, or in duel, or from a lung ailment. There was only one certainty in life—that everybody died.

He didn't answer her question. "You left without knowing the danger you are in. I was worried."

Of course he was. In many ways he was such a good man. "You were worried for us—Drake and me. I know. But I can't continue to rely on you. I've asked Christian to look into Tremain—"

Philip shook his head. "I don't think it's Tremain."

"But it has to be." She rubbed her nape. "There's no other possibility."

"Yes, there is." Philip's words were soft and almost gentle. "There's Kirkwood."

Her blood turned to ice in her veins. "No." Nausea swam in her stomach.

But even as she denied it, Rose saw the logic. How would Tremain know she was with child? On the other hand, she was staying in Kirkwood's home. That Kirkwood knew would make more sense. Nothing went on in his house without his knowledge. And servants talked. He'd have put two and two together and realized what her sickness indicated. He'd written the note?

"Now you understand why I'm so concerned," Philip said. "The marquess is a powerful man."

"But Kirkwood?" Philip had to be mistaken. "He's Drake's guardian. What is there to gain from his death?"

It worried Philip how pale she'd become at the thought of Kirkwood as her enemy. He moved to sit beside her and drew her trembling body into his arms, while he told her his theory.

She did not refute anything he said. "I'm not sure how he could possibly get me to marry him."

Philip hugged her tighter. "Not marry Kirkwood, perhaps. But what about his son? He's two years younger than you, and still a bachelor. What happens to Roxborough's assets if both you and Drake die before you remarry?"

She turned, if possible, even paler. "Now I am really going to be sick. I'm not sure. I never took much notice. But I think it all reverts to Kirkwood—or his son, should Kirkwood die." Her eyes widened. "He wants me dead, too. Why now?"

"I suspect it's because you and I are no more. Your talk about remarrying means he has to act now."

"Oh." She breathed in, then out again, slowly and with care. "When will Maitland learn about his finances?"

"It will take a few days. Maitland won't be back in London until tomorrow at the earliest." Should he make his move now?

One glance at her almost bloodless cheeks decided for him. "I think it best if I stay here until we find our evidence."

She stiffened in his arms. "Is that wise? If word gets out that you are living here my reputation might not recover."

"If that happens, I'll do the honorable thing. Our getting married is the most sensible outcome anyway. He can't win then."

A tear slid down her cheek. Then another. "Oh, my darling, that will not do. I can't marry a man I love when he does not love me. Besides, you don't really want to marry me—and knowing that would eventually break my heart."

Not love her? "I do love you."

She shook her head. "You might think you do, and maybe—in your own way—you do. But you don't love me enough. If you did, you would put me first—even before Robert's ghost and your guilt. A woman in love never wants to be second best."

When he did not deny her words the hope in her eyes faded. But he couldn't give her false hope. She was right. Robert and his vow came before anything he desired. It had to.

She withdrew from his embrace and he felt that withdrawal to his soul. He hadn't understood that losing her would feel like his heart was turning to ice.

"I assume you have a plan," she said, smoothing down her skirts. "If Maitland finds Kirkwood's finances are not what we have been led to believe."

He nodded. "I have an idea. But I'd like to speak to the others before I outline what it is."

"Yes, of course."

She sounded abstracted and held herself stiffly, hands pressed to her stomach. "I know this is a lot to take in, but I swear I'll protect you and Drake."

She smiled up at him, her hands still on her stomach. "Thank you. You really are a fine man. I'm sorry. I just wish that when I see you my heart didn't feel like it was about to break."

She stood and pulled the bell. A moment later Booth entered. "Lord Cumberland will be staying with us for a few days. Please have the Garden Room readied for him. And Booth, please ensure that news is kept within these walls."

"Of course, Your Grace. Should anyone ask, I shall say you have a second cousin staying."

"Thank you." She turned to Philip. "It will be hard to keep Drake quiet. He will be excited to see you. You probably heard him when you arrived. He's in the ballroom playing the piano. Why don't you go and see him?"

Philip stood, feeling bereft, as though they were strangers. Polite strangers. "Shall I see you at dinner?"

She nodded. "Yes. We'll dine early, but I'm sure you won't mind. You must be as tired from traveling as I."

When she left the room Philip gulped down a tumbler full of brandy. Was his offer to stay his way of getting around his vow to Robert to never pass the title to his son? If he was forced to marry Rose, he could not be accused of benefiting from any heir they might then have. He was doing the honorable thing, not simply begetting an heir.

If he did have to marry her he'd simply have to ensure she did not get with child. That should not be too difficult; they had managed it for two years now.

His muscles loosened as he finally saw a way in which he could marry Rose and protect her while maintaining his vow not to have children. Now all he had to do was convince her that doing the honorable thing was the only way to keep her safe.

It wasn't until he was watching Drake run across the ballroom toward him that he remembered her reason for any remarriage was to have children.

How could he deny her the child she wanted simply to keep his vow?

As Drake hugged him, Philip felt a longing so deep it shook his inner core until he swore his bones rattled.

He wanted a child, too. With Rose.

Chapter Sixteen

It only took Maitland three days to discover Kirkwood's true financial situation. What he learned was enough to have him braving the snow and cold to report to Philip in person.

"It is as you suspected," he told Philip as he stretched out his long legs in front of the fire in the room Rose had set aside for Philip—the late Duke of Roxborough's study. "Kirkwood's son, Francis Gowan, has not only made some bad investments but he's also raked up huge gambling debts."

Maitland took a swallow of his brandy and shook his head. "The young fool has almost brought the marquess to his knees. I suspect Kirkwood has not yet used his position as Drake's guardian and stolen from her because he knows I'm Rose's investment adviser and therefore watch her—and Drake's—finances closely."

"Damn the man. And his son." Philip almost wished Kirkwood had stolen money. Then, at least, there would be a case they could take to the chancery and leverage they could use to have him removed as Drake's guardian. "So what now? We now know he has a motive. At the house party he certainly had means to harm the boy. But we have no proof. Without proof, the chancery will see no reason to remove him."

Maitland's brow furrowed as he watched the flames in the grate. "I'm not sure having him removed as Drake's guardian would keep Rose safe anyway. What is to prevent him from arranging her marriage to his son, and then getting rid of Drake? Once Rose is part of his family, he can take his time staging an accident to kill the boy. And her."

The very thought had Philip's blood boiling in his veins. How dared Kirkwood try to harm those he loved? And yes, he could admit that he loved Rose. As for Drake, he thought of the boy as his own son. However, all that did was fill him with guilt as he was stuck between honoring his vow or living a wonderful life his brother never got to have. "Then what are we to do? We cannot simply sit by and let it happen."

"Of course not." Maitland crossed one leg over the other, leaned his head back against the chair, and studied the ceiling as he considered. "We have to catch him committing a crime that will see him ruined. Something that cannot be hidden or explained away. Only then will we be able to expose his true intentions to the *ton,* and ensure protection for Rose and young Roxborough."

"Do you have a plan?" Because he certainly didn't. "How do we catch him without putting Drake in danger?"

Maitland grimaced. "No, I don't. And the child's already in danger. The problem for us now is that Kirkwood will not harm the boy himself. He'll hire people to do his dirty work. That makes it devilishly difficult to prove he was the mastermind behind the deed. We'd need more than the word of a damned hired thug to make an accusation of murder-for-hire stick to a marquess."

Philip didn't like it, but Maitland was right. "Then we need to call a meeting of the Libertine Scholars. Grayson is one of the best strategists I've ever known. He might be able to come up with a plan." Suddenly, emotion ripped through him like a hurricane. "God, I wish I had agreed to marry her now. Then Kirkwood would have nothing to gain from their deaths, and she and Drake would be safe."

"You could still marry her." Maitland hadn't taken his attention from the ceiling. "Quietly, and by Special License. It's not too late."

Yes, it was. And that could be laid at his door, too. "Rose won't marry me now. Not if she thinks I'm doing so out of duty."

Maitland snorted. "Rubbish. She'll marry you fast enough if it's the only way to save her son."

Philip said nothing. Wouldn't that be worse? How ironic that two people who loved each other could be forced into marriage in such a way that they'd always doubt the other's love.

What would Robert have done? If he'd loved Rose he'd have married her without a second's hesitation. What would he say about Philip's reluctance? About his vow? Philip tossed back the last of his brandy and knew there wasn't enough spirit in the world to dull the ache inside him. The choice between honor or love was one no gentleman should have to face.

It had been the longest three days of Rose's life. For the first time since the snow fell she was grateful for the inclement weather. Otherwise she had no idea how she would have kept Drake inside. He was bored. And when little boys got bored the entire household knew about it.

Philip had been wonderful and had done his best to keep him entertained. But even he was running out of games to play and things to do. As a last resort, he'd suggested an outing and he and Maitland had swept Drake off to a meeting of the Libertine Scholars at Sebastian's house. The prospect of an afternoon's fun with Henry had done the trick.

Now Rose was exhausted. And oddly nervous. That unease wasn't helped by her knowing that Philip was sleeping only down the hall. Or that she could put an end to all this by telling him about his child.

It was wearing, and emotionally draining.

Drake was so excited to have Philip staying, and Philip—well, he could not hide his feelings for her son. Each morning they would sit as a family and eat. Each night she tried to ignore the longing, need, and desire in his eyes as she said a cool good night.

The only reason she had not succumbed to her desire and crept into his bed was because she did not want him to discover her thickening waistline, or for her to have to explain away her nausea in the mornings—although it was lessening.

She hoped the men came up with something soon, and quickly. If they did not, she'd have no choice but to confess her condition and agree to a marriage. If only she knew a marriage was his choice, not his duty.

At least the snow had stopped and people once more ventured out into the street. With Philip and Drake out of the house, Rose could at last see her modiste—in private. She desperately needed new gowns to accommodate her changing figure.

Madam Durand was due at three. Rose sent Elaine off to the attic to find some of the gowns she'd worn when she was carrying Drake so they could discuss design and other ideas with Madam Durand.

In her room, dressed only in her shift and robe, Rose could not settle.

She still had not written to Lord Kirkwood with an explanation of her sudden departure from the house party. It must be done. Whether it would lull him into believing she was innocent of his plans, she did not know. She doubted it. But she could play this game, too.

She was so engrossed in her thoughts that she did not pay attention when her door opened, thinking it was Elaine returning with the gowns.

Only as the footsteps got closer did she realize the person was wearing boots.

She looked up, but it was too late to scream. An arm wrapped around her neck and a cloth of sickly smelling ether pressed into her face.

The last thing she saw as she fought for consciousness was Francis's cold, hard eyes above her. Funny the thoughts that drift into your mind. Francis had his father's eyes. Kirkwood had made his move.

Chapter Seventeen

The sound of men, their voices raised in argument, brought Rose back to her senses. She had no idea how long she had been unconscious. Or where she was now. She only knew her head pounded, her body felt like rock, and her mouth tasted of sand. What was more, she could not lift her eyelids no matter how hard she willed them to obey her.

"I won't let you marry her." It was Kirkwood's voice. "For God's sake, she is with child. No, no, I have made an arrangement with Tremain. He's signed a document giving me most of Roxborough's assets upon Drake's death."

"A document?" Francis almost shouted the words. "What kind of fool are you? We cannot trust Tremain. That document is evidence, and he'll use it against you. When he exposes this plan, *he* will not be the one to hang."

Kirkwood growled low in his throat. "I'm not the fool here. He will do exactly as I say. I hold proof that he killed that young girl, Claire, all those years ago. After all these years Tremain thought he'd got away with it. Why do you think he agreed to my two-thirds cut? Because he has no choice. Besides, if I know him, he's already plotting how to rid himself of Rose as soon as possible to enable him to take another rich wife."

The clink of glass on glass and the gurgle of liquid told Rose one of the men was pouring himself a drink.

"It's still risky," Francis said. "Better to keep the business within the family."

"What if her child is a boy?" Kirkwood said. "The bloodline —*my* bloodline—must remain pure. I'll not have Cumberland's bastard take my title. The babe ruins everything. I only let the affair with Cumberland go on for so long because I knew he would never marry her, and I had thought he'd be more careful about getting her with child. However, it did give me time to build my reputation as the fair and patient guardian, so that no one will suspect me—us—in this matter."

Francis laughed. "It won't come to that. The child might be a girl. But even if it is a boy, the problem is not insurmountable. Many children die in infancy. Either way, we'll have the money."

"Money." More liquid gurgled. "All you think about is money. We would not be in this situation had you not been so greedy. I tried my best, but you are your mother's son. Weak. Rash. Without honor."

"Honor!" Francis almost howled the word and then snorted with laughter. "You're prepared to kill a child to save a title, and *I'm* the one without honor."

There was a *crack* as flesh met flesh, and Rose hoped Kirkwood had loosened several of his son's teeth.

"You'll pay for that, old man," Francis said thickly, all humor gone. "You have nothing to say about what I do. As soon as she wakes I'm marrying her and then we set sail for the Americas. By the time we return—and with her big with child—no annulment will ever be granted."

"There is more to this business than your marrying the woman." Kirkwood sounded frustrated, and not only with Francis. "We'll have access to her jointure immediately, and that will stave off the creditors for now. But to get our hands on the real money, young Roxborough has to die."

"I'm sure you'll think of something, Father." There was something mocking now in Francis's tone. "After all, it won't be the first time you've evaded a murder charge. But killing Mother all those years ago was different. She had no one to protect her." Francis paused before adding, "They'll guard the boy once they know what I have done."

Kirkwood had killed his *wife*? Rose's fear almost sent her back into unconsciousness.

"I'm his guardian," Kirkwood said. "That gives me certain rights. He will stay with me while you are on your extended honeymoon. They have no grounds to make a case to the chancery. But we must be patient. He can't die immediately or Cumberland will raise hell."

Philip. Rose's heart lifted in a savage joy. Oh, yes, Philip would most certainly raise hell.

Francis's next words stopped her breath.

"No. Cumberland has to die, too. I'm not coming home only to be challenged to a duel—and he will want to kill someone for this."

Philip wasn't the only one. Rose would do her best to kill both men if they touched a hair on her son's head.

"Christ," Kirkwood snapped. "We can't kill everyone. I still say that to throw in our lot with Tremain is less risky. I need my money. Let Cumberland kill Tremain."

Fury raced through Rose's blood so violently that it made her fingers tingle. *His* money! It was hers. It was Drake's. It was not Kirkwood's.

Warily, she slitted one eye open.

Francis paced back and forth in front of the fireplace, obviously considering the idea. "That would work. We could pin everything on Tremain. Let him marry her. We kill the brat and get our share of the money. Then we frame Tremain for Drake's death, and watch Cumberland challenge him to a duel and kill him."

Kirkwood smiled, full of ice and teeth. "Now *that* is a plan I like. We get the money without having another man's bastard in our bloodline. Very well. Now, until I can get word to Tremain, we just have to keep her hidden."

On those words they both turned to where she lay.

Rose kept her breathing steady and shallow, pretending unconsciousness. They must have thought her still insensible because they turned away again and continued their conversation.

"Tremain left to travel north to Mr. Hemllison's house near Yorkshire." There was the sound of a drawer opening, the scratch of quill on parchment. "We need to get word to him immediately."

"What about Cumberland?" Francis sounded concerned. "Would he or his friends know about this house? Should we move her somewhere else?"

"It's unlikely," his father said. "Besides, this is the safest place to keep her. The priest's hole has kept its secrets for hundreds of years. Even if Cumberland finds the house, he will never find her."

Rose risked another peek in time to see Kirkwood scatter sand on the note to dry it. Then he folded it and added his seal. He strode to the door of the room and threw it wide.

A man appeared in the doorway. "My lord?"

Kirkwood shoved the note at him. "I want this taken to Lord Tremain. He's traveling north to Yorkshire on the main road. Stop at all the coaching inns along the road until you find him."

"Yes, my lord," the man said and left.

Kirkwood closed the door with a sharp click and glanced over to where Rose lay, still feigning unconsciousness. "Quickly now. Move her before she wakes."

Francis hurried to do his father's bidding. He heaved her over his shoulder, thumping her in the breast as he did so. She bit her tongue to silence the moan of pain. Then, to her horror, he walked toward the large inglenook fireplace.

For one awful moment she thought he was about to throw her in. Instead, Kirkwood moved in front of them and ran his hand over the stones on the right. There was a grating sound, and the stone pillar itself moved back slowly to reveal a low doorway.

In the light from the room behind her Rose could see Kirkwood had obviously planned her imprisonment for some time. A narrow bed had been pushed up hard against one wall. Its mattress was thick enough, but there were no sheets, only a stack of blankets piled at the foot, and a single pillow at the head. A chamber pot was shoved carelessly under the bed. A pitcher—which she hoped contained something to drink—sat on a rickety-looking table next to the pillow, a slop bucket beside it.

Francis stooped down to enter the room, strode across to the bed, and dropped her unceremoniously onto the mattress. Then, without a word or a second look at her he turned and strode back out.

As the secret doorway started to close, the light began to dim. Only then did Rose realize she'd seen no candles on the table, no lantern. They were leaving her alone. In the dark.

But she didn't dare make a sound to show she was conscious. The light dimmed. Dimmed further. Vanished.

She curled up on the piled blankets, shaking, and sick to her soul. No one knew where she was. What if something happened to Kirkwood and Francis? No one would ever think to look here. She and Philip's child would die together in the dark. And Drake. What would happen to her son?

Exhausted and terrified, she pressed both hands over the gentle swell of her belly. "It's all right," she whispered to the little life within her. "You're safe. I won't let them hurt you. Sleep. Your father will come for us."

But for all her brave words, a tear trickled, warm and wet, along her cheek. "He will come," she said again, and there in the silent dark, she prayed with all her might for Philip to find and save them all.

Chapter Eighteen

It was dark when Philip arrived back at Rose's townhouse no further ahead on how to catch and discredit Kirkwood than when he left. He carried a sleeping Drake into the house and handed him over to a footman.

"His Grace has eaten like a hungry bear all afternoon," he told the man. "Take him to his nanny. He'll probably sleep till morning." He turned to Booth. "Where's Her Grace?"

"Still in her rooms, my lord," Booth said. "I have not seen her since the modiste left."

Philip nodded and started up the stairs. "I'll see her before I change for dinner."

He took the stairs two at a time, his body humming with excitement.

It had become clear during the men's discussion that the safest option for all concerned would be for him to marry Rose, and as soon as possible. Tomorrow he would seek a special license. But tonight he would do everything possible to convince her that his heart belonged—and would always belong—to her, and that the very practical reason for their marriage did not alter that fact.

He reached her bedchamber and tapped briskly on the wood. No one came to answer the door. He knocked again. Still no answer. With growing trepidation, he turned the door handle and entered.

The room was dark and cold. What the hell? "Rose?"

There was no reply.

She had not been well. She might be unconscious on the floor. He could step on her in the dark. Where the devil was her woman?

He backed out of the room, shouted down the stairs for the butler, and seized a lit candle from the hallway sconce. Then, holding the candle aloft, he stepped back into the room.

The first thing he noticed was the gown tossed carelessly across the bed. But Rose herself was not in the bed. He moved toward the chairs set before the dead fire. But they, too, were empty.

Then he saw the chair from her writing desk. It lay on its side on the floor. But Rose wasn't lying beside it. Where was she?

Fear took his breath like a fist to the throat. He wanted to call out for her but he couldn't form the words. On shaky legs he moved to the bathing chamber. It, too, was empty.

He was coming back into the bedchamber when Booth came in in a flood of light and questions, a gaggle of servants at his heels.

"My lord?" The butler took in the state of the room, the open curtains, the dead fire in the grate. "Where is Her Grace?"

Philip finally managed to fill his lungs with air. "That's what I want to know. Where's her maid?"

"I haven't seen her, my lord." Booth swung around on the other servants crowding behind him. "Find Elaine, and bring her here immediately."

Two footmen disappeared.

Philip's heart told him what his brain refused to accept. Neither woman would be found in the house. "What visitors did Her Grace have this afternoon?"

Booth's face went blank. "Only the modiste, my lord."

"Very well." Philip couldn't stand still. Rose was in danger.

Afraid. Alone. But *he* wasn't alone. He stopped in midpace. "Booth. Send a lad to each of the Libertine Scholars. Tell them it is an emergency, and ask them to meet me here as soon as possible."

"At once, my lord." Booth rattled off instructions to another footman, who bowed and left the room. "I don't understand, my lord. What has happened to Her Grace?"

"I don't know for certain yet." But he could make an excellent guess. Philip gestured to the man to draw aside. "Was the modiste the one Her Grace usually patronizes?"

Booth's eyes widened. "Now that you mention it, my lord, no. She was dressed in the height of fashion but was taller than Madame Durand."

Philip's gut did a long, slow roll. "How long did she stay?"

"Not long, my lord." Booth's hands, normally so controlled, were clenching and unclenching into fists. "And when she left she took"—his eyes popped wide and his face turned sheet-white—"oh, my lord, she took a large trunk with her. The footmen brought it down. Elaine said Her Grace was donating some of her old gowns to charity."

"Which footmen?"

"I was one, my lord."

Philip glanced to the door. One of the two footmen Booth had sent to find Elaine had returned. "Was the trunk heavy or light?"

"Heavier than one that held only a few gowns, my lord," the man said. "But Elaine said Her Grace had added a few other things, as well."

"Where is Elaine now?" But he already knew the answer. Elaine was working with Kirkwood and had disappeared.

"Not in the house, my lord," the footman said. "But her things are still in her room."

"Show me."

It didn't take Philip long to search Elaine's room. It was small and scrupulously tidy. There was nothing incriminating in her dresser or in the trunk.

Frustrated, Philip stood in the middle of the room and forced himself to calm down. If he were Elaine, and living in this tiny space, where would he hide any personal correspondence?—assuming she had not simply burned it.

The idea came quickly. During the war there was only one place he'd been able to keep private correspondence. He moved to the bed and flipped the mattress off it. A letter lay on the board of her bed frame.

Yes! He reached down and plucked up the note. But it was not what he expected. The letter was addressed to *him*.

Lord Cumberland,

I have done something unforgivable but could not find any way out of the mess I have caused.

Lord Francis Gowan, Lord Kirkwood's son, has taken Her Grace to Chatsworth Manor. You know where that is, I hope, as it's in Devon.

I could not leave this note anywhere obvious as His Lordship is watching me.

He is not the man I thought he was. Please hurry. He means to marry Her Grace, but even though you have forsaken her, I know you will not let a man like him bring up your child....

Your child... Rose was carrying his child.

The room around him seemed to tilt. Philip staggered, and the note fluttered to the floor.

No wonder Elaine had been so frosty to him in the garden; she honestly thought he'd walked away from his child.

His *child*.

His heart clenched so hard in his chest he thought he was having a heart attack. This was a dream—a dream he thought he'd never have. Now he knew it was all he'd ever wanted.

And Rose had not told him.

How could he blame her?

He could not. He would not. But he wasn't about to let

anyone take his chance at love and happiness away. Lord Francis Gowan was a dead man.

He crushed the note in his fist.

"My lord." It was the footman. "The gentlemen are arriving."

"Thank you."

If Francis had already married Rose, she'd be lost to him forever. Philip pushed the anger, hurt, sorrow, and roiling fear away. No, by God, she would not. Not even if he had to make her a widow for a second time.

Philip had just reached the foyer when first Sebastian and then Grayson were admitted to the house.

"What's wrong?" Grayson asked.

"Lord Kirkwood has Rose," Philip said. "We head for Devon."

Rose kept her eyes closed. Behind closed eyes she could pretend she was not surrounded by pitch-black. That those scurrying noises were not vermin.

She curled tightly into one corner of her mattress, rubbing her abdomen gently while she whispered to her unborn baby that Philip would save them.

But as the hours passed, and no one came, her assurances changed. Rescue didn't have to come from Philip. It just had to come.

She had not long fallen into a light doze when the grating sound of the stone entrance opening brought her awake. She tensed, praying it was not Tremain. That he was far up north near Yorkshire, and it would take him a few days to travel back.

But when she saw who came in, carrying the flickering candle, raw anger blew her fatigue away, and she surged off the bed. She'd landed one hard slap on Elaine's cheek before the woman's words penetrated her mist of rage.

"My lady, please." Elaine sounded frantic. "We don't have time. Lord Francis's men will be back soon. We have to flee now."

With that, Elaine gripped her arm and started dragging her back through the hidden entrance.

Even the small amount of light coming from the fire as Rose stumbled into the room made her blink, and her eyes started to water. Half-blind, she allowed Elaine to guide her through the house to the back stairs of the silent manor.

When Elaine opened the door to the outside, though, she cursed. "It's snowing."

Rose looked down at her feet. She wore only the dainty slippers she'd been wearing when Francis had spirited her away. She was also still clad only in her shift and robe. "I'll freeze to death out there if they don't catch us first."

Elaine pulled off her own shawl and wrapped it around Rose's shoulders. "I wish we could find you something more, my lady, but I've looked through the house and there is nothing there, not even blankets. I'm sorry. I should have brought one from the room where they kept you. But I dare not go back and we dare not stay longer. The snow will cover our trail, so it's the perfect time to leave. There is a cottage about a mile to the left."

A mile. "Where are we?" Rose asked, her teeth already chattering.

Elaine eyed her cautiously. "Devon. Near the coaching inn where we stayed on our way to Lord Kirkwood's house party. I'm not sure precisely where. But we must leave. Then we must find shelter. Perhaps at the cottage we'll find some clothes."

Rose cast a glance back over her shoulder and then out at the gentle snow. Already she could feel her limbs starting to tremble. One mile. She could do that. She placed a hand over the child curled up in her womb. Of course she could. She had no choice.

"Then let us go before the snow really starts to fall. We will have to move fast."

And wrapping the shawl more tightly around her, she stepped out into the cold and moved off in the direction of the cottage.

Even though the ground was not yet covered by the white flakes, it still took them far too long stumbling in the dark before they smelled the smoke from the little cottage's chimney.

By the time they opened the gate Rose knew she was in

trouble. She could no longer feel her feet, and her hands—which she had tucked into her armpits for warmth—were like blocks of ice.

When she stumbled on the path, Elaine ran ahead and pounded on the door. It opened a fraction of an inch and a woman's face appeared. "Who's there?"

"Can you help us please?" Elaine sounded frantic. "Her Grace is almost frozen to death."

"Her Grace?" The door opened wider. "Lord have mercy!"

Rose, having reached the house, almost collapsed on the doorstep, but the young woman threw the door open wide, grasped her under the arms, and helped Elaine half drag her into the house. The door slammed behind them with a comforting *thud*.

"Put her near the fire and I'll bring blankets." The young woman glanced down at Rose's feet. "And thick stockings, too."

Only a few minutes later Rose had been stripped to the skin and was swaddled in blankets before a blazing fire, with only her face showing. Elaine had removed her sodden slippers and replaced them with thick stockings.

She let the warmth return to her frozen bones. Soon she wanted to scream from the pain of her thawing hands and feet.

When Rose's hands stopped trembling, the young woman pressed a mug of hot tea into them. As the heat of the liquid warmed her fingers they began to tingle again, and her insides began to thaw.

"Elaine," she said to the woman she had thought her friend. "You will tell me everything later. But first you will get out of those soaked garments and into something warm yourself."

Elaine stopped rubbing warmth into Rose's legs and bowed her head. "Yes, Your Grace."

Rose closed her eyes and drank her tea, letting the tingle of returning warmth nip and bite. She wasn't safe, but she was safer than she had been. And her child? Yes, the child was safe. And Drake, too, would be safe because he was with Philip.

Elaine returned, dried and in a thick winter gown, and took up her gentle massage once more.

Rose took another sip of tea. "I want to thank you for saving me tonight," she said quietly, "but I cannot for the world understand why you betrayed me in the first place."

Elaine's eyes filled with tears. "I thought that since Lord Cumberland had denied your child was his, that you'd be disgraced. I could not bear that."

At the sound of Philip's title, the woman, who had been stoking the fire, turned their way, eyebrows lifted.

"We will discuss this later," Rose said. It was all she was prepared to say with someone else listening.

For the first time Rose actually took note of the woman who was helping them. It was obvious she was with child. It was also likely they were putting her in terrible danger by their presence. If Lord Francis or his men called here—as was possible given the cottage was so close to the manor—they might kill this innocent witness to their wicked deed.

"Thank you for helping me," Rose said. "You are most kind. What is your name?"

The young woman made a curtsey. "Faith, Your Grace."

"You're *Philip's* Faith?" The words slipped out before Rose had time to think.

A frown crossed her face. "Do you mean Lord Cumberland?" Rose nodded.

"Aye," Faith said. "Lord Cumberland and his younger brother saved me from—from a terrible life."

Now it was more than the pain in her hands and feet that made her want to weep. "When is your child due?"

Faith smiled and patted her belly. "In three months."

That meant Philip had been with Faith while in a relationship with Rose. No wonder he did not want to marry her. He did not love her as she loved him.

"His Lordship has been most kind." Faith sounded almost tender.

"I'm sure he has. He's a kind man." Rose meant the words.

"Yes, he gave me a job at the big house and even found me a husband." Her hand rubbed over the large swell under her apron. "My child won't be born out of wedlock as I'd feared."

Unlike the child Rose carried. Could she force Philip's hand by telling him of the child? The past few hours had made her sure of one thing: she would sacrifice anything, her life, her happiness, for the innocent little life she carried. She would even marry a man who did not really love her, to protect it.

If she survived this kidnapping.

Rose glanced toward the door. "Is your husband at home? There are some very bad men looking for me."

Faith shook her head and her face softened. "But he should be back soon. He went to the market. He doesn't like leaving me on my own, but we wanted to sell our cheese before the snow sets in."

"Your arranged marriage is to your liking, I take it?" Rose said, hardly aware of what she was saying.

Faith nodded. "Yes, Your Grace. David is a fine man. I think I fell in love the moment we met. He took my hand, and smiled, and bowed over my hand as if I were a proper lady." She looked down at her bump. "He loves me and is prepared to raise another man's child. I did not know men as kind existed in this world."

Rose bit her lip against a tart reply. Of course the man would be happy to bring up an earl's bastard. Philip would, no doubt, provide a large regular payment for the child's keep.

Suddenly, the door handle rattled. All three women froze.

Then, as the handle began to turn, Elaine jumped in front of her mistress, and Faith rose to her feet.

The door opened and a man blew in on a swirl of chilled air and snow.

"Oh!" Faith's face lit up as she rushed toward him, hands outstretched. "Thank goodness you are home, love. We must send word to Flagstaff Castle. Lord Cumberland needs to know where to find Her Grace."

Chapter Nineteen

It had taken two days for Philip and the others to reach Devon. Now, less than half an hour after his arrival, Philip paced his study at Flagstaff Castle like a caged beast.

"Where the hell is Chatsworth Manor?" He swung around and started to pace in the opposite direction. "Damn it all. If we don't find her soon it will be too late."

"Calm down," Sebastian said. "You're not thinking. Francis can't have arrived in Devon more than four to six hours ahead of us. We rode on horseback. He would have had to take Rose in a carriage. What do you know of Chatsworth Manor?"

"Nothing." Philip shoved restless fingers through his hair. "That's what worries me. This is my county"—he thumped the desk with his fist and dropped into a seat—"so how could I not have heard of the place?"

"Perhaps," Arend said slowly, "it's a recent sale, and was previously known by another name. Which houses in the area have been sold in the past six months?"

At Arend's suggestion, something niggled at the back of his mind. Wasn't there an old manor house on the far-flung east side of the Flagstaff estate that had been sitting empty for years? Yes. As he recalled, there had been a dispute over ownership. Robert had tried to buy it a few years ago, but ownership had still been in question then.

He had no idea whatever happened to the rundown house and land, but he was certain the house had not been called Chatsworth Manor.

Before he could say so, there was a knock on the study door. Almost immediately, it opened and Philip's mother, Lady Cumberland, walked in.

All the men rose to greet her.

Smiling, she waved them back. "Oh, do sit down, gentlemen. I just heard that you were here, and that Her Grace is missing. Is there anything I can do to help?"

Nothing happened in this house without his mother knowing. There wasn't much in the county that escaped her notice, either. "Actually, Mother, there might be. Please do sit down."

Christian quickly stood and offered Lady Cumberland his chair. Once she was comfortable, Philip explained the situation and showed her Elaine's note. "That old manor near the eastern corner. Could that be the place Elaine is referring to as Chatsworth Manor?"

Lady Cumberland's brow furrowed. "I can't tell you what the house is called now, dear boy. It used to be Dashington Hall, but I do know it was sold not long ago. Old Fred will be able to tell you more. He knows everything that goes on here."

Fred was their head groom—or had been. He still pottered around the stables but was getting too old to work a full day. His son was now head groom. But Fred had extended family all over the estate and in various positions. In fact, his brother's boy, David, had become smitten with the lass Philip had rescued for Maxwell and married her. A happy ending all around.

Please, God, let this be another happy ending.

Philip stood and moved to his mother's chair, bending down to place a kiss on her cheek. "Thank you, Mother. If you will excuse us, we will be off to talk to Fred."

She merely patted his cheek. "Of course, my dear. And make sure you bring Rose safely home."

It was already dark when the men arrived at Fred's cottage, a mile from the castle. The night was cold and snow was beginning to fall.

Fred was both surprised and pleased when Philip rode up with the six Libertine Scholars, Sebastian, Christian, Arend, Maitland, Grayson and Hadley. He'd also brought along many of his men. When Philip was asked about Dashington Hall he nodded sagely. Yes, her ladyship was right. Although he didn't know who had bought it, he thought it might now be called Chatsworth Manor.

"Although it queers me what be wrong with *Dashington Hall*," the old man grumbled. "It's been Dashington Hall dunno how many years."

Philip tried to keep the conversation away from the past. "What about strangers, Fred? Any strangers about recently?"

"No. No strangers." Fred kicked at a flurry of snow. "Well, Lord Kirkwood, as is now. Still as cow-handed as he were as a lad. Still slumps like a sack in the saddle. But he's too high in the instep to even nod to the likes of me, so I suppose I could call him a stranger."

Philip's spine stiffened. "Kirkwood? Where did you see him?"

Suddenly finding himself the center of everyone's focused attention, Fred took a step back. "It were over by the property you be asking about. Dashington Hall as it was."

That was all Philip needed to hear. "Thank you, Fred. I'm grateful," he said and then strode down the path, and vaulted onto his mount's back.

As the men rode for Chatsworth Manor, Philip fought to control his anger, to keep his fury and frustration from communicating to his mount. But he couldn't control his imagination. If Francis or Kirkwood had harmed Rose, there was nothing he wouldn't do to avenge her.

He refused to consider he could be too late. He finally understood Grayson's words. *When you find a love like no other you will fight to the death to keep hold of that love.*

He also finally understood Robert's actions. His brother had loved him, loved him more than his own life. If the roles had been reversed, Philip would have gladly given his life for Robert's. *Gladly.*

While he was still to blame for dragging Robert into the war, he finally saw that—by living this joyless half-life he had chosen—he was actually denigrating the sacrifice Robert had made. Robert had died to give Philip a chance at a full life—and to his eternal shame he'd almost mucked this up, too.

He couldn't lose Rose.

Philip leaned over his horse's neck, urging him to go even faster. It was only when he saw a light bobbing along the road that he slowed. Even so, he was almost on top of the person before he realized the staggering lantern-holder was Elaine.

He pulled his horse to a skidding halt, slid out of the saddle, and landed lightly on the road, ready to confront the treacherous woman.

He made no effort to try to look less threatening. "Where is she?"

The lady's maid was already breathless, but the snarl in his voice made her clap a hand to her heart.

"Cumberland." It was Grayson, voice cool, yet with a warning edge. "Let her catch her breath."

Philip wanted to shake her, but he stood stomping his Hessians on the snow-covered road, his horse's reins in one hand, until Elaine had managed to find enough breath to speak.

"Thank God you are here," she gasped out. "I helped Her Grace escape from Lord Kirkwood, but I'm sure he and Lord Francis Gowan won't be far behind us. I took Her Grace to one of your estate cottages, my lord. The couple's names are Faith and David."

Philip almost collapsed with relief. But he had to ask. "Has he"—he closed his eyes briefly—"has he married her?"

"No, my lord." Elaine shook her head while stamping her feet to keep warm. "Not yet."

Philip's breath left his chest in a rush, and he groped blindly for the support of his horse's neck. *Thank you, God.* Rose was still free. Still his.

Gathering his stormy emotions, Philip turned to the men. But before he could issue any instructions to send them off into the night, Grayson gripped his shoulder.

"This is our chance," he said, urgent and low. "If the seven of us can catch Kirkwood and Gowan in the act of kidnapping Rose, our affirmations, together with Rose's word, will be enough to bring them to trial and make a case to the chancery to remove Kirkwood as Drake's guardian."

Philip cursed into the stormy night. Grayson's words made sense, but any restriction on his desire to race to Rose's side and kill Lord Francis made his skin crawl.

He gestured one of his men over. "Take Her Grace's maid back to the castle." He helped Elaine up onto the man's horse. "We shall talk later. Thank you for helping Her Grace."

The man didn't wait for Elaine's response, but wheeled the horse around and set off in the direction of the castle.

Philip swung back into his saddle. Then he and the others started off at a gallop to David Horton's cottage.

Rose wished she could ask to lie down. After her third cup of tea—liberally laced with David's whisky—she was no longer cold. Now, however, the room was behaving oddly, and she was starting to feel very hungry indeed.

When her stomach finally decided to protest its lack of sustenance and growled like a savage dog, Faith gave a horrified gasp and jumped to her feet.

"Oh, Your Grace," she said, her face flaming. "I'm so sorry. What must you think of me?"

A few moments later Rose found herself being served fresh, warm bread, along with delicious homemade cheese.

"Fresh baked this morning, Your Grace." Faith was still crimson. "I should have known that you'd be hungry. I don't know what I was thinking."

Rose swallowed another bite of the crusty bread and smiled at the young woman, feeling better already. "You've no need to apologize for anything, Faith. You've done more than I could hope for, and I'm so grateful. You've put yourselves in danger for me." She looked over at David, who stood guard by the window. "I won't forget it."

"Movement," David snapped out. "In the trees. Faith, into the other room. Quickly."

The floor swayed as Rose stumbled to her feet, still holding her bread and cheese. Then Faith was beside her, pulling her in the direction of the other room, which was their bedchamber. Faith pushed her gently onto the bed and then whisked back and closed the door.

And just in time. David must have opened to the visitors because Rose could hear the low murmur of voices. It went on for quite some time.

Then the bedroom door opened.

For a moment she thought she was seeing the imaginings of a fevered brain. Then she was in Philip's arms, cradled tight and secure against his rock-hard chest.

Still disbelieving, she breathed him in. It was his scent. It was Philip. He had come for her. He was here, and she was safe.

"Rose, my darling Rose." He pressed kisses all over her face and throat. "Thank God. Are you all right?"

How could she be anything else now that he was here? "Yes. I'm just tired and"—she lifted the forgotten bread and cheese in one hand—"starving."

"Are you sure?" He gazed down into her face, his eyes never leaving hers. "I'm sorry," he said quietly.

She nestled her cheek into his coat. "You're here now, and that is all that matters."

It was only then that Rose considered Faith, and her feelings. She had seen Philip catch Rose up, witnessed his embrace, heard his endearments. How it must hurt to see the father of your child welcome another woman in such a way.

But Faith did not seem at all hurt. She was watching them with a dreamy look on her face and a secret smile.

But before Rose could think too much more about it, David called from the other room. "Someone else is coming."

Philip carefully lowered Rose back down to the bed and turned to Faith. "Stay here and stay quiet," he said. "My friends have the cottage surrounded. We want to catch Francis and Kirkwood in the act."

He turned back to Rose, his eyes full of regret. "I'm sorry, my love. It's dangerous, but it's the only way we can prove their villainous scheme and stop them."

Did he think she would object? "Good. I want that wicked man and his son as far away from me and Drake as possible."

She'd hardly finished speaking when the front door slammed open.

"Drop the pistol, my man"—it was Lord Francis—"and tell me where Her Grace is. Quickly, or I'll put a bullet through your heart."

Faith's face drained of color, and only Philip's quick movement of warning made her stifle a cry.

"There's no need for that." Kirkwood sounded his usual urbane self. "Her Grace, the Duchess of Roxborough, is ill and not in her right mind. She ran away from us, believing she was being kidnapped, when Lord Francis and I were merely escorting her home to Cornwall."

Rose had wondered why Kirkwood had chosen to hide her in a house in Devon. Now the reason became clear. If they were stopped or caught, all the men had to say was that they were escorting her home.

It would be her word against Kirkwood's. The word of the scandalous Wicked Widow against that of a powerful and well-regarded marquess—a man with whom she had always been friendly. She would never win Drake's freedom that way. They had to compel Francis and Kirkwood to admit their crime—and there was only one way to do that.

She struggled to her feet, forcing herself to stand tall. When Philip put out his hand to stop her, she shook her head.

She moved closer. Whispered in his ear. "I have to make them admit what they have done and what they intend to do. We need proof before you and the other Libertine Scholars can bear witness and arrest them."

Indecision, fear, and finally resignation flickered over his handsome face. When he nodded, she pressed a kiss to his lips and then slipped past him, and through the door into the main room.

"Come, Lord Kirkwood," she said as if chiding a child Drake's age. "I believe David here is well aware that you have no intention of escorting me home. You plan to force me into marriage either with Viscount Tremain or with Lord Francis in order to control my financial assets. And we both know your unholy alliance doesn't end there. Your plans go a great deal further."

Kirkwood stepped toward her and it took an effort for her not to step back. "Rose, my dear," he said. "You are overwrought and tired from your pregnancy. You are speaking absolute nonsense."

"I am not speaking nonsense. Neither am I overwrought—no thanks to your idiot son. I suppose I should be grateful, Lord Kirkwood, that you suggested Tremain marry me rather than Lord Francis." She cast Lord Francis a withering look. "Being married to this imbecile would have been hell."

Her taunt had the desired effect. Lord Francis's lip drew back in a sneer. "You haughty bitch. Yes, my father's idea was to marry you off to Tremain. He definitely doesn't want a Cumberland cuckoo in the Kirkwood nest. But I disagree."

"Shut up, you fool," Kirkwood growled.

But Francis was too enraged by her taunt and her escape from his clutches. He prowled toward her, a vein throbbing at his temple.

Rose refused to cower or move back. She knew her defiance would anger him more. "Really? You disagree?"

His eyes flashed fury. "Yes. I do. Now I think I would very much enjoy schooling you to be a respectful, obedient wife. A pity that our romantic runaway match will have such a tragic end. The *ton* will be overcome with pity for me when both you and your son have a terrible accident. But I shall be more than adequately consoled by Roxborough's money."

"Francis!" Kirkwood's voice cracked like a pistol shot. "That is enough. The woman is baiting you."

But Lord Francis was past reason. He swung around on his father. "I am not a child to be told what to do. Tremain can go to hell, and so can you. I'll marry the bitch, and if I marry her then I get the money."

"The money." Kirkwood was almost as furious as his son. "The only reason we need the damned money in the first place is because you have brought the Kirkwood title to near bankruptcy."

"And for money," Rose said, sickened and disgusted, "you'd kill an innocent child."

"Yes." Kirkwood turned his pistol on her. "I'd kill anyone to save the Kirkwood name and estate. In fact, it would be easier if I kill you now, and blame it on David here. Of course, I'll have to kill him, too. What else could I have done when I found that he'd kidnapped you and then raped and killed you?"

His teeth glinted in the firelight and the light in his eyes made him look crazed. "With you dead, I'll have ample time to set up an accident for young Roxborough. In the meantime, as his guardian, I'll have access to his funds. No one will ever know that, of course, because the poor boy will die before he comes of age. Perhaps riding that pony Cumberland gave him for Christmas."

A red haze seemed to drop down over Rose's eyes, over her mind. She was not even aware that she moved. But the sound of her palm meeting flesh brought her back to herself, and Kirkwood's howl of pain was almost as satisfying as the feel of her nails scoring his face, tearing bloody trails down his cheek. "Coward. Murderer. Touch my son and I will tear out your eyes."

"My God!" Lord Francis doubled over, whooping with laughter. "Little hellcat!" he gasped. "Worthy of the Kirkwood name."

"Bitch!" Kirkwood shoved Rose away and raised his pistol.

Rose staggered back, arms protectively around her belly. The muzzle of the pistol seemed to yawn like a cavern before her. *Oh, Philip. I'm sorry.*

"Stop!"

Maitland's thunderous roar echoed through the room.

Kirkwood swung around, pistol leveled at this new threat.

Maitland stood in the doorway with a pistol in each hand, one aimed at Kirkwood, the other at Lord Francis. "Lower your weapon, or I swear to God I'll shoot you both."

Rose's heart thundered in her chest, almost drowning out the sound of Kirkwood's curses. She couldn't pull her gaze away from the door where Maitland stood, and behind him, Hadley. Two dukes had witnessed Kirkland's treachery. Kirkwood was done for.

David slipped behind the men to go to Faith in the other room as Rose staggered over to her chair by the fire once more. The nightmare was finally over.

"Cumberland!" Maitland raised his voice. "Do you want to do the honors?"

Philip strode out of the bedroom, face grim. "It will be my pleasure." He went first to Kirkwood and took his gun. Then he moved over to Francis and did the same. Then he handed both guns to Hadley, who had come to stand behind him, and stared at Lord Francis.

"Normally," he said coldly, "I would ask you to name your seconds. But I don't cross steel with common cowards. This is how I deal with cowards." His fist shot out and slammed into Lord Francis's jaw. "And kidnappers." A second punch. "And murderers." A third. "You come near the Duke or Duchess of Roxborough again and I will kill you."

"Not necessary." Maitland sounded confident. "I think we have enough evidence to get a conviction."

"I concur," said Hadley. "I heard his diabolical plan—and saw him aim to shoot Her Grace."

The room was suddenly crowded as the rest of the Libertine Scholars pushed into the small cottage. The air felt too close, but the chill had seeped back into Rose's bones. She let her eyelids close.

"What do you want to do with them?"

It sounded like Sebastian. She opened her eyes. What would Philip do with her now? Send her away? She swallowed down tears.

"Take them back to Flagstaff Castle." Philip gave Kirkwood a very unfriendly look. "Old castles have their advantages. I have the perfect dungeon for you until the magistrate organizes your arrest and trial."

Relief rushed through her. It wasn't her he was sending away. She needed to tell him about their child. She blinked, trying to get rid of the black spots before her eyes. "Philip?"

A moment later Philip knelt at her feet, gripping her forearms in trembling fingers. "My God, Rose. When I agreed to bear witness, it was not to your death. What the devil did you think you were doing? He could have killed you."

Intended to. Would have. "But he didn't." Why was everything so far away? "And Drake is safe." And Philip was safe. And their child was safe. "I'm so c-cold, Philip. Why am I so cold?"

Philip swore and surged to his feet. A moment later she was cocooned in a blanket, wrapped like a mummy. Still, she couldn't stop her limbs from shaking. Even the blanket and heat from the flames seemed to make no difference.

Somewhere, a long way off, she thought she heard a man's warning shout as she began to slip from the chair. And then Rose heard nothing at all.

Chapter Twenty

A warm, soft mouth touched Rose's forehead. The scrape of whiskers tickled her nose, familiar lips nibbled over her face, and then pressed more insistently against her lips.

She knew it was Philip. She recognized the way he always used to cradle her when he stayed the night, as if she was the most important person in the world to him.

Like it used to be.

She did not know where to go from here. So much had happened to them over the past four months. She knew what she wanted. She wanted to marry this man, but she also wanted him to love her. His dalliance with Faith she would forgive, but could she forgive other dalliances that might come? What if he could never fully give her his heart?

She already knew the answer. This time, she would not let pride stand in her way.

Her ordeal at Francis's and Kirkwood's hands had brought it home to her that life was full of risks. She wanted Philip in her life, in their child's life. She would risk everything if, by the slightest chance, Philip could come to love her the way she deserved to be loved.

"I know you're awake," Philip teased in her ear. "And I know you're hungry. Your stomach has been growling for the last hour."

She stretched and yawned. "How long have I slept?" She opened her eyes—and got a shock. They were in Philip's bed at Flagstaff Castle.

On previous visits, when she'd been invited to stay, she'd crept in here in the dark of night many times. However, this was not nighttime. Sunlight danced across the cheval mirror in the corner of the room, and in its reflection she saw the two of them lying in his bed. Well, she was in the bed; he was fully dressed lying on the bedspread.

"Why am I here?"

"Because you've been asleep for more than ten hours, my love." He patted her on the bottom. "Come. You need to eat."

She'd meant, why was she in his bed? And then the smell of toast and other foods hit her nostrils and made her mouth water. "You know the way to my heart, my lord. Food is just what I need."

"Anything for you, my love. Anything," he added softly.

He sounded so serious she rolled over so she could see his eyes. "Anything?"

"Absolutely anything you desire." He stopped talking and gazed down at her with such sadness in his eyes she wanted to cry. "I've got such a lot to apologize for. I let my own guilt and insecurities almost destroy what we share. I hope I haven't destroyed us already. Have I?"

She would not get a better opportunity. She might have to marry him but she did not want there to be any more confusion or lies between them.

"When I was eighteen," she said slowly, "I was a timid mouse. I let my father sell me into a marriage that would benefit my family. But even as I stood at the altar I knew I'd never be happy. My legs shook so badly I could barely walk, and when I promised to love, honor, and obey, I knew that I'd do none of those things."

She stopped, fighting back tears and memories. "When

Roxborough took my hand in his and pressed a kiss to my cheek—because we were now man and wife—I shuddered with revulsion."

"I'm so sorry," Philip said quietly. "It should never have happened to you."

She waved his sympathy away. "I'm not asking for your pity. I'm trying to say that my marriage changed me. I learned I wasn't a timid mouse. I learned I was capable, that I could pursue what made me happy, and that it wasn't wrong for me to want joy and love. Marriage to Roxborough made me believe that I did not want to ever remarry—but it also gave me Drake, the most precious gift of all. What I feel for him is a love truly consuming."

She reached out and cupped Philip's cheek, hoping he understood. "Life's trials and tribulations affect us, mold, or twist us into the people we become. We react to the circumstances we face. And I understand why you feel you must put Robert first, before me."

He stiffened. "I need to explain. I don't—"

"*Shhh.*" She pressed a finger to his lips. "*Shhh,* let me finish."

She needed to, before she lost her nerve. "As a young girl I used to be infatuated with you. The closer my marriage to Roxborough came, the more I thought I loved you. But it wasn't love. I was a scared and lonely child who didn't know what love was."

It embarrassed her now to know it was true. "When we started our affair I had no thoughts to the future—except I was sure I never wanted to remarry. And if I hadn't met you I would probably still feel that way. But then I got to know the man you'd become."

"Rose," he said more urgently. "If you would just let me—"

"Not yet." She couldn't let him distract her. "It was so easy to fall in love with you, Philip. And when I fell in love with you, my desire for a future filled with marriage, children, and love, grew strong. I wanted that future with you, but I did not know how to tell you. You never spoke of the future, and you made it quite clear that marriage was not for you. It hurt to learn you did not love me enough to leave the ghost of Robert behind. But this—being kidnapped, the threat on Drake's life—has taught me life is fleeting."

A tear slipped down her face. Best she get it over with quickly. "I have something I need to tell you. Something that might make you angry. But it's something I will never regret—even if it means I am forced to marry you . . . another man who does not love me." She paused before looking him in the eye and said, "I am carrying your child."

She waited for an explosion of disbelief, of anger. But the expression she saw on Philip's face was joy. He pulled her into his arms and kissed her soundly.

When he finally let her up for air, his words were the ones she once dreamed he might say. "I don't think I've ever been this happy. Our babe, our child. How did I get so lucky?"

"Lucky?" She pushed at his chest and eyed him suspiciously. "You are not angry?"

"Do I look angry?" He kissed her again, smiling like a cat that'd discovered a pail of cream. "No, I'm not angry." Then his smile faded. "But I will regret until the day I die the fact that you were afraid to tell me such wonderful news. I will grovel for as long as you want me to. It should have been the happiest moment in our relationship, and I took that joy from you. Will you forgive me?"

Didn't he understand? "But you will have to marry me now, unless—" Her smile died and she shoved out of his arms. "Or do you think you can treat me as you have Faith? That I'll conveniently marry another, so as not to shame you?"

"What?" His look of confusion irritated her more. "What has Faith got to do with anything? And no, by God, you will not be marrying anyone but me."

Now she was incensed on Faith's behalf as well as her own. "How can you ask what Faith has to do with it? She's the other woman carrying your child."

For a breath, Philip looked completely blank. Then he burst out laughing. When he laughed so hard he nearly rolled off the bed, her temper got the better of her. She shoved him hard, sending him tumbling to the floor with a crash.

And still the wretched man laughed.

She crawled to the edge and glared down at him. "I don't think it is at all funny."

"Oh, Rose." Philip rolled onto his knees. "My darling, Faith is not carrying my child. I have no idea who the father of her child is—probably one of the customers at the brothel Maxwell saved her from."

Brothel? Oh, no! Rose sat back, torn between joy and embarrassment. She'd been right when she'd told Faith that Philip was a kind man. She'd been wrong when she'd thought he had betrayed her.

Philip crawled back onto the bed and knelt before her, all laughter silenced. "How could you possibly think I needed any other woman when I had you?" He reached out and cradled her face in his palm. "You. My bright, courageous, flirtatious, warm, sensual, *beautiful* Rose."

He thought she was courageous. "Probably because you did not wish to marry me," she said, trying to sound haughty.

"I was a fool." He gave her that smile, the one that turned her inside out. "An imbecile. A chump." His smile died. "Once again I've made a muck of everything. I was arrogant enough to think that I was solely responsible for Robert's death. And you were correct that day when you challenged me about Robert. I did not believe I deserved to be happy. I thought that I was benefiting from my brother's death—a death to which I had in some way contributed. But now I realize I need to find a way to live with that guilt. Being a martyr changes nothing."

That sounded hopeful. "So what will you do?"

He moved until there was barely an inch separating them. Rose was sure she could hear the steady beating of his heart. "And now I realize *why* Robert did what he did. He died for the love of another. He died because he loved me. It made me realize that, without those we love, life is not worth living. I will serve, protect, and cherish those I love. That is how I can best honor my brother.

"I'm ashamed it took almost losing you to make me understand the truth—that love is all that matters, and the greatest part of ourselves that we can give to another. Even were you not carrying my child, I would beg for your hand in marriage, because I love you more than anything or anyone in this world."

Then he kissed her.

It started out gentle, but soon turned to want, need, and passion. She tasted his desperation, his regret, but most of all, his love. It was his way of showing her he meant every word.

She put everything she had into the kiss. She hoped it would never end.

And then her stomach growled.

They broke apart laughing.

"I think we should eat," Philip said. "You'll need your strength for tonight when I show you just how much I love you."

She giggled like an excited young girl. "I shall look forward to wearing *you* out first."

He winked and moved off the bed. "Either way I win."

It was as though they had never been apart. Love flowed between them as comfortable as the silky robe he lifted onto her shoulders. As warm as his smile.

He led her to the small table Wilson had set up in the bedchamber. It was covered with her favorite dishes.

Philip held out a chair for her, waited until she was seated, and then took the one opposite her. "As soon as the snow clears we will head to London. Drake needs to hear the news from us, and we want him with us when we marry by special license." He smiled across at her—and, to her surprise, proceeded to pour her a cup of tea. "I want my family together."

Tears pricked behind her eyes. "Thank you. That's perfect. Drake already loves you as much as I do."

"I love the boy, too. I shall take a petition to the chancery to have Kirkwood removed as Drake's legal guardian, and—with your permission—I'd be honored to take on the role."

"I would like that very much." She pinched herself. "This seems like a dream. I'm so happy. I love you so much."

He reached for her hand. "We will make our life more than a dream. It will be real, full of desire, respect, friendship, and lots of love."

"Yes, please. That's a dream I want to live every day."

"With you by my side, my beautiful Rose, I know our love will only grow stronger. Now, eat your breakfast. Mother wants to see you and to welcome you to the family."

Family.

The very word used to revolt her. But now it thrilled her, made her heart sing. And this time she would have a family based on love.

Love. The strongest foundation of all.

Epilogue

Christmas, Flagstaff Castle, one year later

Rose looked anxiously out the window, her gaze sweeping the long drive, and then up at the sky for the hundredth time. Did the clouds look darker and more ominous than ever?

"Do come away from the window, Rose," her mother-in-law said. "And stop hovering. The men will be back soon. You worry too much."

She gave Dowager Lady Cumberland a weak smile. Did a mother ever stop worrying about her child? "It's not the men who concern me."

The Coldhursts and Blackwoods had arrived two days ago to share Christmas with them. Maxwell was arriving tomorrow, and hopefully Douglas, too. Thomas remained in India much to Dowager Lady Cumberland's sorrow.

Her husband had planned a full week of celebrations. He was enjoying his new life as husband and father.

Poor Philip had a little shadow now. Drake hero-worshipped her husband and followed him whenever he could. Philip adored her son, thinking of him as his own and she would be forever grateful for that. But Philip did not let that stop him from being a good father and disciplining her boy when he needed it. Drake would need a strong guiding hand as the Duke of Roxborough. She prayed he never turned out like Lord Francis Gowan. She knew Philip would ensure her son turned into a fine young man, and he was a wonderful role model.

The men of their little party—Philip, Sebastian, and Grayson—had decided to go for a ride over two hours ago and, while it had not yet snowed, it was still cold outside as the sun began to set low on the horizon. Drake and Henry had been allowed to go to the inn as a Christmas treat. Drake had been more excited about being allowed into an inn with the men than about being allowed to accompany them on the ride.

Beatrice came to stand at the window beside her. "Our husbands would never let anything happen to the boys, and you know it."

"I do," Rose said. But her heart and head rarely agreed on anything these days.

Portia joined them, standing on Rose's other side. "Let's go and get the rest of the children before the others get back. They love the Christmas tree. I thought we could let them open one gift each before they go to bed tonight. We will all need an early night as I suspect the children will be up at the crack of dawn tomorrow to open the rest of their presents."

Portia's son, Jackson, was almost eighteen months old, while Claire, Beatrice's daughter, was two. Claire's nanny had her hands full with the little girl who already bossed Jackson about.

Rose didn't need any encouragement. Early that July she'd presented Philip with a son, and it would be his first Christmas. Little Drury—meaning *loved one*—was a strong, healthy boy. She'd worried initially about Drake's reaction to his half brother. Drake—although not enamored enough to spend time with a baby who did nothing but eat and sleep—spoke proudly of him, and she hoped one day he would be Drury's fearless protector and companion.

Once back in the drawing room with the children, Rose handed Drury to his proud grandmother and took her seat next to them.

Claire and Jackson, meanwhile, ran around the room, stealing sweetmeats off the table when they thought no one was looking. Finally, the attraction of the Christmas presents got to be too much for Claire, and soon she had ordered Jackson to sit beside her while she picked up each gift and shook it, trying to guess what was in it.

"Don't you dare open any of them," Beatrice scolded. "Or there will be no Christmas for you, young lady."

"I'm just looking," her daughter shot back.

The door opened at that moment, and in walked the males of their party, all freshly bathed and dressed. Drake—wearing the same breeches, stockings, waistcoat, and jacket as Philip—walked in proudly, hand in hand with Philip, the man he called Father.

Rose blinked back a tear, even as she smiled.

She had one thing to thank Kirkwood for. If he had not kidnapped her, Philip might not have ever declared his heart. Now he told her he loved her at least once a day. And she could never hear it enough.

The two of them walked to stand before her. Drake looked up at Philip. Philip winked down at Drake.

Drake cleared his throat, and then bowed to his mother. "Mother, you look exceptionally pretty tonight."

Rose's heart swelled and filled. "Why, thank you, Drake. You, too, look very handsome."

Her son preened like a little peacock. "I know. I am dressed the same as Father, and he said you only have eyes for him because he is the handsomest man in the world."

Everyone in the room roared with laughter.

Philip's face went red. "You weren't supposed to tell her that."

The boy frowned up at him. "But you did say it."

"That I did, son. But sometimes things we talk about are best left between us men."

Drake's little chest puffed out with pride at being seen to be a *man*, and one who was able to share secrets with his father. "May I go and play with Henry now, please?"

Philip ruffled his hair and nodded, and Drake raced off to the far corner of the room where the boys had set up a battlefield with toy soldiers. Henry was busy trying to pry a cannon out of Jackson's pudgy hand.

Philip bent down and kissed Rose's cheek, and then his mother's, as he stroked Drury's head. She loved the light of happiness in his eyes and knew she'd never been so content.

Soon it was time to open presents, and the room was filled with the excited cries of the children and the more subdued conversation of the adults.

Philip, knowing that Drake's gift would create mayhem, kept its presentation till last. Just when Drake was on tenterhooks wondering if perhaps there was no gift for him that night, Philip carried in a box. A box that made scratching sounds and small whimpers under its lid.

Drake's eyes grew big and round and he rushed to take off the lid. He reached in with an excited squeal and lifted out a little puppy.

"What is his name?" After his first squeal of excitement Drake handled the little animal with awe and cuddled him close, obviously sensing the puppy was scared by all the noise.

Philip crouched down beside him. "He is waiting for you to give him a name. What do you think it should be?"

The puppy was an English Pointer and all white except for a large brown patch around his stomach. Drake studied him for a moment. "Xury, Robinson Crusoe's loyal friend."

Philip nodded. "That is an excellent name. If you treat Xury well he will be your best friend forever. Xury will grow quickly and he will need lots of exercise each day. You will have to run him through the fields, and you'll let Timmins help you train him."

Timmins was the keeper of the hounds.

Drake flung his arms around Philip's neck. "Thank you, Father. I'll take special care of him."

"That's good," Philip said. "Because he will need lots of care."

The little boy nodded. "May he sleep in my room tonight?"

Rose was about to protest, but the question had been directed at Philip. "If your mother agrees."

She saw the look of hope on Drake's face and couldn't bear to watch it die. "Very well."

He beamed from ear to ear. "Thank you, Mother," he said in the grown-up voice he was starting to assume around adults. But then he dissolved into a child again, thrilled and excited by the puppy and the future joy of play. Soon he and Henry were rolling around with the puppy—and ignoring anyone else.

None of the other presents given out that evening could match the excitement of Drake's.

Except that Rose had a secret.

Later that night as they walked up the stairs to bed, Rose knew of only one thing that would make her life even more perfect. A little girl. Or perhaps another little boy. She really didn't care.

As soon as the door to their bedchamber closed behind them, Philip pulled her to him. "If I'm the handsomest man in the world, you—my gorgeous wife—are the most beautiful. I swear you grow more radiant every time I look at you."

She didn't want to spoil the mood, but since her thought downstairs she had to ask. "Do you know, I was actually grateful to Kirkwood tonight."

Kirkwood and Francis had been found guilty of attempted murder—hers and Drake's—and been sentenced to death. Rose, however, had requested leniency. Instead, Kirkwood was stripped of his title and lands, and both men were sent as convicts to Australia. Philip told her it would have been kinder to let them hang.

"Do you think," she said slowly, "that you would have asked

to marry me of your own free will if Kirkwood had not kidnapped me?"

A haunted look flashed across Philip's eyes, the one she used to see in them when he thought of Robert. "I'd like to think that I would have, but I will never know. I can tell you this—that you own my heart now. I love you more than the air I breathe, and I thank God each day for bringing you to me. Can you live with that?"

"Yes, yes, I think I can." Her response was to kiss him, long and with lingering tenderness. "I thank Robert for bringing you into my life, not God. I'm sure he was looking down that day at his graveside, and giving you a kick in the arse. He sent me to make sure you didn't wallow in guilt for the rest of your life. What a waste that would have been. I see you with our children—how good you are with them. Robert would be proud."

The smile that sent her pulse soaring spread over his handsome face. "And while we're speaking of children," he purred, "I would like to spend tonight making another one."

This time it was her turn to give him a special smile. "No point," she said, and patted her belly gently.

"You are with child?" Joy filled Philip to the brim as he placed his hand reverently on her stomach.

She nodded, and her eyes danced and shone. "Merry Christmas, Philip. I hope you're pleased with your gift."

"I am." He lifted her up, strode to the bed, placed her on the sheets, and then followed her down to lie carefully beside her. "It's the most wonderful gift in the world. A gift made in love, by love."

As he began to remove her gown, he showered kisses over every inch of the skin he bared. "But that does not mean we should not practice making more."

She gurgled with laughter. "They do say practice makes perfect."

"Perfect." He halted his perusal of her near-naked curves and whispered, "We *have* perfect. We have a perfect love, and a perfect family, and a perfect life."

He used to call Robert the perfect earl, and Robert would always reply in the negative. Tonight he could almost hear Robert reminding him that no one was perfect.

His brother had been right.

People weren't perfect. Life wasn't perfect.

But love made everything seem perfect.

Tonight with Rose, the love of his life in his arms, and another child in her womb, life was more than perfect.

And so he set about showing the woman who had given him the greatest gift of all—her heart—how much he loved her back.

Want to see who captures Helen's heart?

Read on for an excerpt from
A Dream of Redemption
by Bronwen Evans

A forbidden love and a chilling mystery tease the senses in this sensuous historical romance from the USA Today bestselling author of A Kiss of Lies and A Love to Remember.

Bookish and independent Lady Helen Hawkestone is expected to marry well. But, having grown up with warring parents, the institution holds little appeal. The trick, she realizes, is to marry for love—a task that's easier said than done. Only while Helen is raising funds for her do-gooder sister's orphanage does she meet a man who arouses her curiosity. Lowborn and yet so dignified that Helen can't help but try to elicit a response, Clary Homeward is an enigma—a heart-stopping, body-stirring, forget-her-social-upbringing enigma.

A single offense against a noblewoman such as Lady Helen would ruin a man like Clary. Her sister, Marisa, rescued him from hellish poverty and employs him with her charity work. Try as he might to push her away, Helen tempts him to want things he could never have. But when girls from the orphanage start disappearing, destined for a grim fate Clary knows all too well, Helen insists on helping. And soon Clary wonders whether something more were not just possible but inevitable—even right.

Excerpt - Prologue

London, England, 1815

Helen barely waited for the door to the Duke of Lyttleton's London residence to open before racing inside and up the stairs to her sister's bedchamber. It had been over six weeks since Marisa had been wounded up north, resulting in a life saving operation. Finally, to Helen's relief, her sister had been well enough to come home. But Helen needed to see that Marisa was recovered for herself and her heart pounded in her chest as she hurried up the stairs, sick with guilt at being unable to be there when Marisa needed her.

At her sisters bedchamber she slowed, her rollicking stomach easing when she heard voices and laughter from within. She leaned her head upon the door and said softly to herself, "Thank goodness."

It was only as she made to open the door latch that she noticed a young man sitting on the floor a few paces down the corridor with his head in his hands. She moved slowly toward him and when he looked her way all she saw was silver gray eyes filled with fear and sorrow.

She did not know the gentleman. His garments were made

from quality fabric but looked a little out of place in this house. The clothes were made with lots of lace and finery all quite feminine in nature. He had very curly hair, ringlets almost, and from a distance he might be mistaken for a very young boy, but when he looked her way his face was all man. Chiseled cheeks, refined nose, proud chin.

Her pulse leapt at the sight of him. Handsome to the extreme, as if a young Adonis statue had come back life. For one fleeting moment his beauty made her forget her injured sister lying in the bedchamber behind her. She blinked a few times.

"Are you all right?" she asked.

"I will be fine if Her Grace is well. Is she...will she be all right?" he asked his voice soft but deep with emotion.

"I shall go and see, but I hear laughter from within her room so I suspect she is well on the road to recovery. May say were asking after her?"

He shook his head as he levered himself up off the floor. "I am of no importance. Do not trouble her."

How odd. No importance, but he kept vigil outside her room. "Are you a relative of His Grace?" she asked. "How rude of me. I'm Lady Helen, Marisa's sister," and she offered the young man her hand.

He stood looking at her as if she had two heads. Finally he stepped forward and hesitantly took her gloved hand, bowing low, still not giving her his name before he quickly let go and stepped back.

"I should not be here. If you could let me know Her Grace's condition on your way out I would be forever grateful."

"I cannot"-

-"Of course you can't, how improper of me to ask."

As he made to turn away she grabbed his arm on instinct and they both jumped at the contact. She quickly removed her hand as bolts of tingles shot through her. He too looked shocked. "I merely meant I don't know your name so I do not know whom to ask for, in order to update you on Her Grace's condition."

He drew himself up to his full height and she had to crane her neck to meet his gaze. It was only then that she noticed his age, he looked to be around her age, ten and eight, yet his manner and worldly wise eyes had originally made her think he was much older than she.

"Clarence, my lady. If you give the message to Brunton he will see that I receive it."

She nodded. She would find the butler and give him news. He took one final look at her as if studying a painting and turned and walked toward the back stairs.

She watched until he was out of sight and only then did she notice how fast her heart was racing. How odd. Not even Lord Hadley Fullerton made her as unsettled as this young man did, and she'd been hopelessly in love with her brother's best friend since she'd been a young girl.

Who was this young Adonis? Why was he sitting outside her sister's door?

Clarence was probably another young man fallen under Marisa's spell, but her sister had recently married the Duke of Lyttleton. He was a man unlikely to take kindly to those who would be overfamiliar with his wife.

She could understand why Clarence had fallen. Everyone loved Marisa. She had a personality that lit up any room and a face that could rival Helen of Troy. How ironic that she was the one her parents had named Helen. The quiet little bookworm was very different from her vivacious sister.

Brunton, Maitland's butler would know who this young man was. He must be someone of importance to be staying in the house.

She pushed her unsettling feelings aside as she entered Marisa's room. A wave of relief turned to waves of joy as she saw Marisa was up and sitting in a chair by the fire.

She raced to her sister's side and embraced her. "You had we so worried."

"I'm fully recovered, only Maitland is being overprotective and insists I stay in my room for a few days."

She glanced across at her brother-in-law. Maitland looked as if he'd aged ten years. She'd worried her sisters marriage might have been a mistake but the love in Maitland's eyes was not in doubt.

She did not visit long as she could see Marisa was tiring. As she rose to leave she suddenly remembered Clarence. "By the way. There was a young man, Clarence, sitting in the corridor outside your room quite distraught at the idea you were unwell. Who is he?"

She saw her sister share a glance with her husband before saying, "He is a young man who helped us with Victoria." She turned to Maitland, "Are they both in the house?"

Her husband nodded.

"Clarence has a younger brother, Simon. I can't explain everything now, as I'm tired. But do let them know I'm well, and thank him for his thoughts."

Helen said her goodbyes and when she opened the bedchamber door to take her leave she bumped straight into a boy.

"Is Her Grace better now?"

She smiled down at him as she pulled the door closed behind her. "You must be Simon." The boy nodded. "You can tell your brother that my sister is recovering and will be right as rain in a few days."

"Thank you, my lady. You must be Lady Helen. Clarence told me you were as beautiful as an angle."

She could feel her face heat as Simon beamed a smile. She almost said that Clarence was the most beautiful man she'd ever seen but managed to bite her tongue.

"Why don't you go and put Clarence out of his misery. Tell him Her Grace is well."

She watched him race off toward the backstairs as she made her way downstairs to talk with Brunton. Clarence and Simon perked her interest. There was a story here, one her sister did not wish her to know. Perhaps Brunton would explain why these two were now living in the Duke of Lyttleton's house, and why they were so obviously devoted to Marisa.

Excerpt - Chapter 1

"Lord Portman has a large estate in Sussex, not so far from ours."

On a long drawn-out sigh, Helen carefully placed her cup of tea back on its saucer and set it on the edge of her sister Marisa's desk.

"Please stop. I am not interested in Lord Gerald Portman and therefore there is no need for you to sing his praises."

Although Lord Portman was a nice enough chap, when she chose a husband she wanted the first word she thought of to describe him, not to be *nice*.

Virile. Handsome. Masculine...

Marisa sat back in her chair and rubbed a hand over her eyes.

"I know you mean well Marisa, but I've decided to stop looking for a husband."

"You're giving up?" her sister all but yelled. "You're two and twenty, Helen. Time is marching on." Marisa eyed her suspiciously. "You're not still in love with Hadley?"

"Don't be silly. It was youthful infatuation. I'm pleased for Hadley and Evangeline." And she was. She had once thought that Hadley was her Prince Charming, but he had never shown an ounce of interest in her other than as the younger sister of his best friend, her brother Sebastian.

"Then what is stopping you from looking for a husband?"

Helen let her sister rant for a few more minutes before calmly saying, "I did not say I was giving up. I'm merely stepping back and allowing fate the chance to play a hand."

Slumped over her desk, Marisa asked, "Why?"

"Because all the women I know found the love of their lives through fate. All of them married amazing, handsome men who did not primp and line up at balls to dance with them. I won't find what I'm looking for in the middle of a waltz."

Marisa stayed silent. There was nothing she could say. Helen's logic was irrefutable.

"I understand what you are saying but what if fate does not throw a man in your path?"

"I'm sure fate has some plan for me. Or else I would have given in to everyone's meddling. Sebastian is worse than you. He keeps inviting young men to dinner, only he picks the most sedate and boring men in London."

"He's our brother. He's hardly likely to bring a rake home to meet you."

They both giggled. "I don't want a rake, either."

Marisa raised an eyebrow.

"Only an honorable rake then," Helen conceded. "Sometimes I think the Libertine Scholars were the only handsome, rakish, honorable rogues left, and I missed out."

Marisa preened. "It's our fifth wedding anniversary in three weeks, and I'm still giddy with love."

Helen smiled and hugged her secret to herself. Marisa's husband, Maitland, had secretly asked Helen to come and stay to watch over the children and nanny while he whisked Marisa off to a secret location for a few days. He told Helen he wanted his beautiful wife all to himself for a few days, and he knew Marisa would not leave their children with only the nanny.

Helen wished she could find a man as romantic as the Duke of Lyttleton.

Marisa added, "I must admit I would not have looked twice at the young men around the *ton* at the moment. Perhaps your idea of letting fate take a hand is the right one. You usually find something when you least expect to."

"It would help if I knew what I was looking for."

Just then there was a knock on the door and the children's nanny entered. "I'm sorry, Your Grace, but little Stephen is crying and won't settle. He wants his mother."

Marisa rose to see to her son. "Please wait, Helen. I want to discuss a trip to the modiste with you. I want the perfect dress to wear on my wedding anniversary."

Helen nodded as Marisa left the room. Helen loved her nieces and nephews. They were orphans that Marisa had collected from her various orphanages. She owned and controlled several. A carriage accident had left Marisa unable to have children and Helen once thought her sister's world had ended. But as she expected, Marisa fought back, and with the love of Maitland set about building her lovely, if somewhat unconventional, family.

Helen rose and moved to the wall to look at the portraits of Marisa and Maitland's children, and the young men and women of the orphanages that Marisa had helped over the last five years.

Marisa really was an amazing woman. Helen tried to help when she could, but being unmarried meant she did not have the same freedom that Marisa had. She wished she could do more. If she married she probably could.

Just then there was another soft knock at the door. She stayed silent thinking that if there was no reply the person on the other side would believe that no one was here. Instead, the door opened and in walked Mr. Homeward, her sister's private secretary and overseer of the orphanages.

As always Helen's eyes appreciated the man. She was not in his line of sight so for once she could stare to her heart's content, and her body was *very* content.

Over the last five years he'd grown from a young and unsure lad into a cannot-help-but-notice-him man. He'd filled out. He was big, tall, and all lean, hard muscle. He still had his ringlet ebony hair but his chiseled cheekbones and strong jaw didn't let his hair make him look feminine. His virility and beauty knocked the breath from her lungs every time she saw him.

The housemaids twittered around him, hanging on his every smile, hence why he was given his own bachelor quarters on the edge of Mayfair. He'd disrupted the household too much when he originally lived under this roof. The other reason was his younger brother Simon. They wanted to be together in their own home. Helen respected that.

She watched Mr. Homeward walk to Marisa's desk and begin to go through her diary. He began muttering as he flipped through the pages and Helen wondered if Marisa let him go through her private appointments.

"Good morning, Mr. Homeward."

His hand paused on a page as he looked in her direction, his eyes showing no embarrassment at being caught with his hand in Marisa's diary. "Forgive me, Lady Helen, I did not realize you were still here." Then he calmly returned to flipping the pages over.

She pushed off the wall and began to walk back to her chair by the desk. The woman in her irked a tad that he could dismiss her presence so easily. Most men drank her in. She was known as a *ton* diamond, a title she usually hated. It made men most insincere.

"Is there something I can help you with, Mr. Homeward? You can't seem to find what you need in my sister's private papers." She emphasized the word *private*.

He didn't even look up or stop his searching. "Her Grace allows me access to her diary because she prioritizes the orphanages' issues above everything else."

The way he said it without even looking at her implied everything else was superfluous. As if her life of social calls, shopping, and balls was a waste. He was probably right but she didn't know what else she could do. An unmarried lady of her standing was not free to gallivant around the city pursuing good causes. Not if she wanted to make a good match. For an unmarried lady her reputation was the only thing that was her own.

Her mouth dried and for the first time in a long while a man made her feel insignificant. Usually men flattered and preened around her. He must have noted her silence for he finally stopped his page shuffling and looked up at her.

"Do you know where Her Grace is?"

"She is with her son."

More muttering. "Will she be long?"

"I have no idea." She sat back down and decided to see if she could stare him out and make him as uncomfortable as he was trying to make her. She had no idea why he acted like this around her. His disapproval of her existence was obvious, and unfair. Mr. Homeward was polite to her if she did see him, and always kept in the background, but his manner around her bordered on indifference and that's what bothered her.

She knew Mr. Homeward and Simon came into Marisa's life when she had just married and was the target of her husband's enemy. However, she did not know why or how Mr. Homeward had become Marisa's man of business. She was sure there was some terrible story behind it all because her sister would brush off any attempt by Helen to learn more. Curiosity was a terrible thing, but Mr. Homeward was an enigma. An attractive enigma that for some reason she wanted to know more about.

"Is there something urgent you need her for? I can always send a servant to fetch her."

He stood up straight and made to leave the room. "No. It can wait."

"What can wait?" Marisa asked as she breezed back into the room.

Mr. Homeward's demeanor changed in a flash. A look of reverence entered his gaze as he looked at Marisa. "Your Grace, I need to find a suitable time for you and me to pay a visit to the orphanage you have just acquired in Dulwich. I think it should be sooner rather than later."

As Marisa took her seat, she asked, "Did you look in my diary?"

Mr. Homeward flashed a look at Helen as if to say *I told you so*.

"Yes, but the only date free is the sixteenth."

Helen sat up straight. Marisa would be away that day. That was during the few days that Maitland wanted to surprise his wife with a romantic liaison. She couldn't let her sister agree to a trip on that day. But how could she stop her without giving the surprise away?

She cleared her throat. "Marisa, would you mind if I got more involved in your charity work? Perhaps I could take the lead on this new orphanage. With Mr. Homeward's help, that is."

"I don't think that's a good idea." Mr. Homeward's tone was quite emphatic.

She leaned forward and ignored the virile man glowering at her and spoke to Marisa. "Since I am putting my other plans on hold, I need something to do with my time. I'd really like to help, you are getting too busy."

Marisa looked at Mr. Homeward before looking at Helen. "I'm not sure that's a good idea. It's a new orphanage and we have not really taken stock of how it is operating. You may—your sensibilities—may be shocked at what we find."

She wracked her brain to think of another reason for why Marisa could not agree to that date. If she could shoot daggers at Mr. Homeward she would. "Mr. Homeward was just implying how superfluous my life is. I really do want to help. Please let me do this," she asked softly.

"Clarence!" Marisa scolded.

"I'm sorry, Your Grace, but I did not imply any such thing. I merely said you put the orphanages first."

Marisa nodded and Helen could see her chewing her bottom lip, which meant she was thinking. "Do you know you are right,

Clary. I *have* been putting them first and Maitland keeps reminding me I also have a family. I give a lot of my time to the orphanages, and it's very rewarding, but my husband and children need me, too." She turned to Helen. "Are you sure about this? If you want to take charge of the Dulwich orphanage it will be a lot of hard, and often painful, emotional work. You'll lose your heart to the children and it will become a lifelong commitment."

Was she ready? Mr. Homeward's eyes bored into her as if daring her to say yes. He was usually Mr. Calm, so totally collected, quiet and emotionless, blending into the background, but right now his eyes blazed. She wanted to say yes just to see his reaction. However, she did not want to accept for the wrong reasons. The children deserved a total commitment.

Helen thought about the children Marisa helped and she'd seen the joy her sister took from it. At the moment Helen's life was empty. She lived in her brother's home with his wife and children and felt like an imposer. Her sister and her brother both wanted her married off. Oh, she understood they wanted her happy, too, but if she said yes to helping with the Dulwich orphanage, her life would have some purpose. Then she could keep busy and let fate take a hand in sending her prince charming.

Besides, she grinned to herself, it would annoy Mr. Homeward.

"I would be honored if you'd let me become more involved, and I vow I will not let you down."

She could almost swear that she saw steam coming from Mr. Homeward's ears but for a second she also thought she saw fear. When she looked again all she saw was anger. She sat up straighter.

Marisa clapped her hands together. "Perfect! Maitland will be pleased. Clary, arrange for a trip to Dulwich on the sixteenth. You may have to meet with Helen a few days beforehand to go over how our orphanage reviews are conducted."

Mr. Homeward's face was a mask of calm once more. He simply nodded at Marisa and said to Helen, "If you could send me a note when it would be suitable to meet?"

"Certainly. If it's all right with Marisa, I'll have a small desk moved in here, too. Then I shall be close by should you need me." And she smiled sweetly at Mr. Homeward, wanting to needle him more.

"That's a wonderful idea, Helen." Marisa smiled. "Now, Clary, if there is nothing more, Helen and I have a shopping trip to plan."

Clary's teeth were grinding as he calmly took his leave of the ladies. He didn't even slam his office door, but closed it quietly behind him, and then he cursed. And cursed. And cursed.

His day had started out badly and just gotten a whole lot worse. His latest lover, a young opera singer, had decided she wanted more than he was prepared to give, more than they had agreed on when they started their affair, and on her way out of his bed this morning she'd almost unmanned him when he politely declined her offer and then ended their liaison.

But this, this having to work with Lady Helen was far worse.

Lady Helen was his angel. She was the purest, most innocent, kind, and beautiful person he'd ever had the privilege to meet.

She'd been so kind to a young man, a stranger, sitting on the floor in the corridor when Her Grace had been injured. Taking the time to reassure him. But he'd been too wracked with pain to think much about her.

He could still remember the day he'd fallen under her spell. He had arrived for his first day in his new role and he came out of his office to see a vision of purity and beauty standing in the foyer.

The front door was open and the sun was shining in behind her, giving her an ethereal glow. Her fair hair was piled on top of her head and was laced with pearls that glinted in the sunlight. She was dressed in a gown of emerald and it made the green of her eyes stand out in her clear, creamy complexion.

When she saw him she smiled. He barely heard her say hello as she walked toward him. Her face was exquisite. Her eyes were filled with warmth, and her luscious lips looked completely void of sin. It was obvious that she had no idea just how stunningly gorgeous she was.

He could barely breathe.

So pure. So innocent. So perfect...

He fell in love instantly.

Then he'd remembered that he was not good enough to lick the dirt on her dainty slippers. He always kept his distance because he was too scared to be near her in case his sordid past tainted her in some way. He ran his hand through his hair and chased those memories away.

She already haunted his nights. Now he would see her every day.

He would have to spend much of his time in her company.

It would be heaven.

It would be torture.

He could hardly wait.

FREE Novella - A Lady Never Concedes

I've a FREE short novella to introduce my SISTERHOOD OF SCANDAL series - A LADY NEVER CONCEDES.

I hope you enjoy meeting the ladies of the Sisterhood of Scandal.

Lord Julian Montague, the second son of the Marquess of Lorne has been Miss Serena Fancot's best friend since childhood. When Julian starts talking about taking a wife, Serena is very aware they are no longer children.

Why does she suddenly notice just how lovely his dimples are and how tall and handsome he is? His clothes fit him like a tight glove and he has a body to rival Apollo. Suddenly, she can't help but notice how the women in society's ballrooms drool over him.

Worse still, he's not once tried to kiss her, or hold her hand, or whispered words of love in her ear. Does he not see her as the love of his life? Has she left it too late to make Julian realize he is the only man she'd ever wish to marry? Has she left it too late to show him he's the love of her life? That won't do. But how do you make your best friend fall in love with you?

Grab your FREE copy

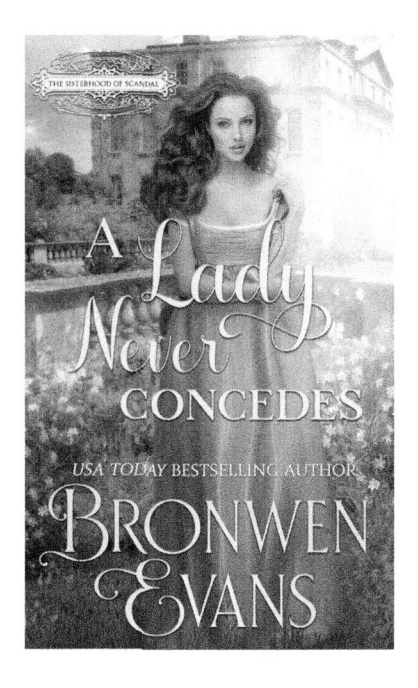

Dedication

I dedicate this book to Ray Collins, my critique partner, editor and good friend, who has persistently helped me in my writing career. Always ready with words of wisdom, endless patience, and a kind heart. I will be forever grateful.

Acknowledgments

I'd like to acknowledge my long list of dedicated beta readers who kindly gave me feedback on Rose and Philip's story. Most of you are members of Bron's Bold Belles and have been so encouraging of every book I write. Thank you for being honest with me. The book is stronger because of it.

About the Author

USA Today Bestselling author Bronwen Evans is a proud romance writer. She has always indulged her love of storytelling and is constantly gobbling up movies, books, and theatre. Is it any wonder she's a proud romance writer? Evans is a three-time winner of the RomCon Readers' Crown and has been nominated for a RT Reviewers' Choice Award. She lives in the Hawke's Bay, New Zealand with her two Cavoodles, Brandy and Duke.

www.bronwenevans.com

Thank you so much for coming along on this journey. If

you'd like to keep up with my other releases, specials or news, feel free to join my newsletter and receive a FREE book too.

Also by bronwen evans

Bron's Book List

Historical Romances

Wicked Wagers
To Dare the Duke of Dangerfield – book #1
To Wager the Marquis of Wolverstone – book #2
To Challenge the Earl of Cravenswood - book #3
Wicked Wagers, The Complete Trilogy Boxed Set

The Disgraced Lords
A Kiss of Lies – Jan 2014
A Promise of More – April 2014
A Touch of Passion – April 2015
A Whisper of Desire – Dec 2015
A Taste of Seduction – August 2016
A Night of Forever – October 2016
A Love To Remember – August 2017
A Dream Of Redemption – February 2018

Imperfect Lords Series
Addicted to the Duke – March 2018
Drawn To the Marquess – September 2018
Attracted To The Earl – February 2019

Taming A Rogue Series

Lord of Wicked (also in a German Translation)

Lord of Danger (also in a German Translation)

Lord of Passion

Lord of Pleasure (Christmas Novella)

The Lady Bachelorette Series

The Awakening of Lady Flora – Novella

The Seduction of Lord Sin

The Allure of Lord Devlin

Sisterhood of Scandal Series

A Lady Never Concedes - FREE short story

A Lady Never Surrenders

Invitation To Series Audio Only (now called Taming A Rogue series)

Invitation to Ruin

(Winner of RomCon Best Historical 2012, RT Best First Historical 2012 Nominee)

Invitation to Scandal

(TRR Best Historical Nominee 2012)

Invitation to Passion

July 2014

(Winner of RomCon Best Historical 2015)

Invitation To Pleasure

Novella February 2020

Contemporaries

The Reluctant Wife

(Winner of RomCon Best Short Contemporary 2014)

Drive Me Wild

Reckless Curves – book #1

Purr For Me – book #2

Slow Ride – book #3

Fast track To Love (This Christmas) Novella - book #4

Coopers Creek

Love Me – book #1

Heal Me – Book #2

Want Me – book #3

Need Me – book #4

Other Books

A Scot For Christmas - Novella

Regency Delights Boxed Set

To Tempt A Highland Duke – Novella

Highland Wishes and Dreams - Novella

The Duke's Christmas List - Novella

Printed in Great Britain
by Amazon